NOT THAT IMPOSSIBLE

ISABEL MURRAY

NOT THAT IMPOSSIBLE

If this was your classic Cotswolds murder mystery (it's not) and Jasper Connolly was a proper journalist (he isn't) then when a dead body is discovered in a local man's house, Jasper would write an award-winning front-page article, and his journalism career would finally be up and running.

Instead, he gets scooped by his ex-English teacher, gets yelled at by his editor, and is starting to think that he'd be better off sticking to his actual career of being a personal trainer.

Meanwhile, Detective Chief Inspector Liam Nash, the straight, married man who has never shown even a tiny bit of interest in Jasper?

Turns out Liam is not straight, he's not married anymore, he is *definitely* not a fan of Jasper showing up at his crime scenes...and he can*not* seem to stop kissing Jasper.

After years of thinking that his dreams of love and happily ever after were impossible, it's starting to look like maybe, just maybe, Jasper was wrong.

Wouldn't be the first time.

~

Not That Impossible is a 75k-word romantic comedy about a wannabe journalist who might not wannabe anymore, and a grump of a detective who is finally getting over himself and going after what he really wants (it's Jasper).

There *are* also a couple of dead guys somewhere in the mix, but not all mysteries get solved. Besides, who even cares about that with all the kissing and stuff going on? This is a romance!

1

It was raining hard. I slammed my car door and jogged from The Lion's tiny carpark to the porch, head down and shoulders up. It was mid-February, and it was *miserable*.

Grey skies. Wet roads. Chill wind. All the Christmas lights in town had been taken down and packed away weeks ago. Even all the sales had finished, and with the sparkle of Christmas in the rearview and the promise of spring a good few weeks ahead, people were hunkered in to wait out the between times.

It was lunchtime, but the day was dark enough, with a thick, soggy mass of grey clouds pressing down on the moss-tufted roofs of Chipping Fairford, that it made me want to climb into my comfiest sweatpants, make a cup of tea, and curl up on my sofa.

Preferably with my soulmate and the love of my life, Detective Chief Inspector Liam Nash.

Since Liam was married to a woman and had zero interest in being my soulmate, the love of my life, or snuggling up on my sofa, I'd take a good book in second place.

Or Netflix.

I hadn't bothered to put my coat on for the short run to the pub, and I regretted it immediately. The warmth of my car was stripped away and the wind gusted cold rain straight into my face. I sped up, splashing through puddles and getting my socks wet. I didn't even notice the couple rushing in from the side, until we all ended up trying to get through the door at the same time.

I was taller than either of them by a good few inches, so I stretched an arm over their heads, pushed the door open, and scooted them in ahead of me.

The man blinked up at me in surprise. The woman flashed a killer grin.

I smiled back. I didn't recognise her, but I recognised the man she was with—well enough to know they weren't a couple.

Unless Ray Underwood, the man of my best friend's dreams, had made some big life changes, and I felt like Adam would have known about it if he had.

Adam was about as obsessed with Ray as I was with Liam. He also had way more of a chance of a happily ever after, despite their uncomfortable history, as Adam and Ray were both gay, and neither of them were married.

I paused on the mat by the door to wipe my trainers dry. One, because it's polite. And two, because I knew from bitter experience that wet trainers and wooden floors don't mix.

Only the fact I can actually do a full split—although I prefer to warm up first and *not* have it happen as a surprise —has saved me from serious groin injury on more than one occasion.

I brushed a hand over my wet hair, shook out the rain, and headed over to the bar. Ray and his friend had gone through to the restaurant area and I watched through the open archway as he fussily picked one table, then changed his mind and picked another, before going back to the first table. His friend seemed to find it all highly amusing.

I ordered a sparkling mineral water from Zoe behind the bar.

"Ice?" Zoe said. "Slice of lemon for you?"

"Just ice, please," I said.

I took my drink over to a small table in the corner, one with a great view of the restaurant area. Ray's table was in my direct line of sight. I personally didn't care about it one way or the other, but Adam would when he got here.

He had a sixth sense for Ray Underwood. A sixth sense, and a hell of a hard-on. He'd walk into the room and he'd *know* Ray was there. I'd seen it happen. He'd go still, as if someone had called his name, then he'd swivel to face wherever Ray was.

It was eerie.

I thought it was perhaps a family trait. Liam was Adam's cousin, and he had the same kind of talent when it came to me. He always seemed to spot me before I could spot him, and when I did see him? He was leaving.

I slumped in my seat and moodily sipped at my water, the ice clinking against my teeth. I sucked a cube into my mouth and crunched it noisily as I gazed around. The pub wasn't what you'd call crowded, but it was slowly filling up.

I didn't usually eat lunch here—I didn't usually *eat* lunch at all. Most days, I poured a protein shake or two down my throat between classes at the gym, as early afternoon was one of our busiest times.

We were both working hard at the moment. Adam was taking as many shifts as they'd give him at the Premier Lodge, a local chain hotel, saving up to pay for his master's degree which he wanted to start in September. I was doing my best at the gym while writing on the side and praying for the big break that would kickstart my journalism career.

I checked my watch. I hoped he wouldn't cancel. I'd missed him a lot over the last couple of years.

My parents had moved to Chipping Fairford when I was thirteen. Although Adam and I hadn't got on at first, we'd bonded through a spot of teenage delinquency, and after that we were inseparable. We grew apart after leaving school. He went off to Cambridge to study architecture, and did some modelling on the side. I failed to get into university, and stayed here to disappoint my parents by becoming a personal trainer. He came back when his mum had her pacemaker operation, and he decided to stick around. Even if his mum hadn't needed him, I was pretty sure he'd have come back for Ray.

The door opened and Adam strode in. He looked like a complete snack, all tall and lean with bright copper-blond hair and dark hazel eyes. Despite what people liked to think, it had been a very long time since we'd fooled around.

I could still appreciate his hotness, though.

Ray had left his friend at their table and was at the bar, ordering drinks.

Adam saw me and headed over. I'm going to make his day, I thought, grinned, and pointed at the bar.

Adam glanced in the direction I was pointing, stopped dead, then turned on his heel and all but ran over there, sending me a distracted thumbs-up.

I crossed my arms over my chest and settled in to enjoy the show.

Ray wasn't the most observant guy in the world. Adam had to damn near mount him before Ray even noticed him standing there. He turned crossly to Adam, who was doing a great job of crowding him, his head tipped back as he gazed up wonderingly into Adam's beautiful face, and—

Liam Nash was staring at me.

I felt his attention like a punch to the sternum. Unfortunately for me, I'd just taken a sip of water, and I choked on it.

When had Liam...?

So much for Ray being unobservant. Liam was here, and I hadn't noticed?

He was sitting in the restaurant area, a few tables behind Ray's. He'd positioned himself with his back to the wall, food was waiting on the table, and the chair opposite him was empty. I had a straight shot across the room, all the way into his stern, steely, beautiful blue-grey eyes.

I knew the colour well, even though the lighting in the pub was dim and made them look dark. I also knew the stern, steely, impatient expression well. That was his default expression when looking at me.

He watched me choke on my drink without any visible emotion, but I felt the disapproval wash over me nonetheless. Holding his gaze, refusing to be cowed, I wiped the back of my wrist over my wet chin and mouth, and—wait.

What was that?

His expression flickered. Just for a split second, but...it flickered. No one else would notice. I'm an expert on Liam Nash. *I* noticed. His gaze had dropped, and bounced back up.

I straightened.

Liam scowled.

I blinked at him.

He looked like he really, really wanted to break eye contact.

Liam Nash would try to stare down a bear, though, let alone me.

Well. I wasn't going to look away first. I loved looking at Liam and I rarely got the chance. We didn't exactly run in the same social circles, and he'd moved away from Chipping Fairford a couple of years ago to one of the smaller villages.

I slouched down on the padded bench seat, stretched out my legs, and admired the view.

Liam Nash was a solid man. He was big, six feet one or two inches tall, making him about an inch shorter than my six-three. He'd played rugby up until his mid-twenties, and it showed.

You could really wrestle a man like that.

Just...throw yourself on him and not worry about hurting him or crushing him. You could get him on the ground and roll around a bit. You'd both be thrashing. Panting and heaving against each other's straining bodies. Fighting for dominance. Limbs entwining. Thrusting. And...

Okay, I had to stop turning myself on. I could hear my own breathing.

Liam's cheeks had turned red and his scowl had turned murderous. He looked like maybe he'd come over here and tell me off in a minute.

I wouldn't *hate* it.

I mean, I'd rather he came over here and did something else entirely, but I'd take a telling off. Happily.

I'd sit there and nod my head, and let him rant a bit like he usually did.

Then I'd say, "Sorry, Detective Chief Inspector Nash," go home, and probably manage to get about three steps into my hall before I came in my sweatpants.

I sighed, and glanced away.

There was no point in torturing myself. Liam was off the

menu, and he had been for years. I'd attended his wedding, for god's sake. Worst day of my life. He was out of bounds. Not an option. Never to be mine.

He was taken, off the market, a one-woman man.

He was—

Huh.

Apparently, he was having lunch with a woman who was definitely *not* his wife.

My eyes widened as the tall, willowy woman—wow, she was *gorgeous*—strode from the passageway that led to the ladies' room at the back, trailed a flirtatious hand over Liam's shoulder as she passed, and slipped gracefully into the chair across from him.

I looked from his face, to the back of her shining blonde head, then to his face again.

Oh my god.

The woman said something and laughed.

Liam dragged his fuming glare away from me and gave her a tight smile in response. She leaned over the table to touch his cheek fleetingly before catching up her glass of white wine and reclining back. Confidence oozed from her slender body.

Something was oozing from Liam's body, too. It wasn't confidence.

I knew very well what a confident Liam looked like, and this wasn't it. He looked...uncomfortable.

I should fucking well hope he *was* uncomfortable!

I was ninety percent sure this was a date.

The balls of him, honestly. In the pub at lunchtime! He was a *detective*! He was supposed to know the mind of a criminal!

You'd think he'd at least have the smarts to do it in a small, out-of-the-way kind of country pub where all the other adulterers took their lunch dates, rather than blatantly breaking his marriage vows in front of the whole town!

I didn't know what to do. I did *not* know what to *do*.

...did I have to do something?

I stared at Liam as he ploughed through what looked from here like The Lion's best steak-and-ale pie.

Every now and then, Liam's gaze lasered my way. He had resting bitch face at the best of times. Something was pissing him off, because right now, he had active murder face.

I didn't know why he was aiming it at me, though.

Feeling daring, I raised an eyebrow at him.

His fork halted halfway to his mouth.

I narrowed my eyes. Yeah, I thought. I'm judging you. You cheating bastard.

His nostrils flared.

Oh, flare them all you want, Detective Chief Inspector Cheaty Pants Liam Nash.

His cheeks turned a dull red. The contrast really made the blue of his eyes pop.

Holding my gaze, he very jerkily and very deliberately sawed into his food, stabbed at a hunk of pie, and shoved it in his mouth.

He chewed and glared, glared and chewed. He was so busy chewing and glaring that he didn't seem to notice that his date was miffed at losing his attention.

She subtly played with her hair, she shifted in her seat, she leaned forward. He continued to look straight past her, cutting across the room and into my wide, disapproving eyes.

He jumped when she ran her foot up the inside of his leg.

That tore his attention away from me.

Not for long, though.

He smiled at her and said something that made her shrug and lean back, picking up her glass of white wine. He dabbed his mouth with a napkin, set it beside his plate, and got to his feet.

Uh-oh.

The first tickle of doom skated up my spine.

I really hoped he was getting up because it was his turn to go to the toilet.

Nope.

He was definitely heading my way. At a fair clip, too.

His stride was forceful, determined, and he was closing in on me.

For an astonished second, I thought he wasn't going to stop. I thought he was going to come over here and crush me into the wall.

Sounded *amazing*.

He just kept coming. To anyone else he probably looked brisk and purposeful. To me? I had an advanced degree in annoying Liam Nash. No, a doctorate. I was a professor of pissing him off.

And he looked at his limit.

He came all the way up to where I was slouching on the bench seat and, since I'd been sitting with my legs comfortably spread, he went right between them. One hand went over my shoulder and gripped the back of the seat. The other went palm flat against the wall.

Liam dropped his head to stare directly down into my wide eyes as I tipped my head back to look up at him looming over me. "What," he said tightly, "is your problem?"

2

_____

*M*y problem was that the man of my dreams had all but pinned me to my seat and I was only wearing sweatpants, meaning that the effect his proximity had on me would very soon become embarrassingly obvious.

My problem was that Liam was in shirtsleeves. His plain white dress shirt was tucked into a pair of businesslike charcoal trousers, showing his solid and (mostly) flat abdomen. I could smell his body wash (it was divine), and his body heat was already mingling with mine. He'd rolled his sleeves up his strong forearms, and if I turned my head, my cheek would brush against the soft skin of his inner wrist.

My problem was that with Liam this close to me, the whole world fell away, and it took the majority of my higher cognitive abilities with it. Which is why my genius response was to grunt, "Huh?"

"I said," he forced through gritted teeth, "What is your problem?" He ducked down a fraction lower, and I couldn't help it.

My gaze dropped to his lips.

"Jasper," he growled.

Right. "My problem is that you are an arsehole," I said.

"Yeah? And?"

I gasped in outrage. "My god, the *nerve* of you."

"For fuck's sake, Jasper."

"You just...I can't believe you'd...right here in front of everyone. You *dick*."

His eyebrows lifted slowly.

I leaned up and said, "Come on, man. Have some class. Your poor wife. How is she going to feel? How could you do this?"

He tilted his head. "Do what?"

The noise that came out of me was *not* a squeak. It was a high-pitched pressure release, that was all, and he probably didn't even notice as I scrambled to say, "Blatantly date another woman in front of the whole of Chipping Fairford!"

Liam's lips twitched. "It's not that busy today. I don't think the whole town is here."

"That's not the point! You're *on a date*! And don't you dare try to tell me that isn't a date. She was playing with her hair. She was *touching* you."

"I can see that upsets you, Jasper, but my love life is not your business." He kept his gaze steady on my face. "Never has been, never will be."

"Oh my god." I went to shove him. It was a stupid thing to do, but I was so disappointed in him. I laid both hands flat on his chest, and regretted it instantly. I was basically cupping his pecs. Horrified, I gave him a feeble push and snatched my hands away. He swayed gently back then forward. "You cheating cheater!"

He made a sound at the back of his throat, a cross between an *mm* and an *ah*.

I squirmed subtly.

I hated myself for being turned on by such a bastard.

"I'm not cheating on anyone, Jasper," he said calmly. "I'm not married."

"Wow," I said. "*Wow*. I mean...just wow. I was *at* your *wedding*, Liam."

He sighed. "I'm divorced."

That cut my indignation off at the knees. "What?" I wheezed. "What?"

"Divorced," he said, slowly enough to be insulting.

He tightened his grip on the seat by my shoulder and leaned forward. I caught my breath, thinking for a wild second that he was going to kiss me or, I don't know, bite me. All he did was push off the wall and bring his left hand between us.

"No ring," he said.

I grabbed his wrist and tugged his hand closer, holding it in both of mine as I got a better look.

No ring.

Very carefully, I traced the base of his ring finger. His hand flexed but he didn't pull away as I turned it over. There wasn't even a dent left to show one had ever been there. No strip of paler flesh. Just Liam.

I smiled brightly up at him and he gave me a startled smile in return.

Then Adam ruined it by saying grumpily, "Liam, why are you straddling Jasper? And Jasper, why are you holding his hand?"

Liam's smile vanished. He tugged his hand away and straightened. "Adam," he said in a clipped tone.

"Liam." Adam muscled him out of the way, and threw himself into the seat beside me. "Well? What are you doing to Jasper?"

"Trying to get him to stop ogling me."

I sputtered angrily. "Ogling you? I wasn't! I—"

Adam sighed. "Oh, Jasper."

"Oh my god, don't *oh Jasper* me! I wasn't ogling him, I thought that the arsehole was here on a date! I was disapproving of him."

"Ah," Adam said, looking sheepish.

Because he hadn't told me that Liam was divorced.

Information that Adam knew very well I would have been interested in having.

"Can I assume that you'll leave me in peace to enjoy the rest of my lunch now?" Liam asked.

Adam snorted. "Live in hope."

I scowled at him, and then I turned my scowl on Liam. "Listen, you're the one who came over to be all confrontational. I was sitting here minding my own business."

"You were sitting there eye-fucking me," Liam said.

I scoffed. "You wish."

"I do not wish, Jasper."

"If I were eye-fucking you, trust me, you'd know about it."

"I know. I did know. Because you were doing it, and you're spoiling my date."

"I think you're managing that perfectly well on your own," Adam said.

"What?" Liam said crossly, tearing his glare away from me to aim it at Adam.

Adam lifted his chin at the table. We all looked over.

Liam's date had turned on her chair, and was staring across the room at us.

She was not happy.

"Shit," Liam muttered under his breath.

"Is that Harriet Landon?" Adam said.

"Yeah."

Adam waved. "I haven't seen her in years."

The woman rolled her eyes and waved back exaggerat-edly. Then she turned her hand and made an an effortlessly cool beckoning gesture at Liam.

I noticed the micro-reaction as he stiffened.

Liam did *not* like being told what to do.

He turned on his heel without even glancing at me again, and strode back to his table.

"Harriet Landon?" I said as Liam sat down, picked up his knife and fork, and the date continued as if he'd never been over to drop a bombshell on my poor unsuspecting head.

"One of his ex-uni friends. They used to be a thing way back."

"Catching up with old mates, then?" I said hopefully.

"Sure," Adam said after a beat of silence.

"Speaking of mates..."

Adam's shoulders hunched.

"Why didn't you tell me he was divorced?"

He sighed. "Because I knew what it would do to you."

"What would it do to me?" I said.

"It would fire up your obsession with him again. Jasper, my arsehole cousin is not the man for you."

"Okay, one? It can't possibly *fire up* my obsession again because that fire is eternal and unwavering and will be burning bright when the sun devours Earth. And two, can we not call it an obsession? That makes it sound weird. He's my soulmate."

Adam groaned.

"Shut up," I said. "I don't tell you to get over your obses-sion with Ray."

"Because it's not an obsession," Adam said. "He's my soul—oh for fuck's sake you've got me saying it now. He's the love of my life. And he'll realise that one day, if I can get him to stop hating me long enough to give me a chance."

Adam's attention cut over to where Ray and his friend were having drinks. I felt his focus like a heat shimmer in the air beside me. I was surprised Ray couldn't. He was chattering away to his friend, blithely unconcerned that Adam was there.

"Yeah, and Liam's the love of my life," I said to Adam. "If I can get *him* to stop hating *me*." And be into dicks.

He grunted and we sat there like a pair of losers, drinking our drinks and staring hungrily at men we could never have, pretty much as we'd been doing for the last few years.

I'd been fascinated with Liam from the day we met when I was fourteen and he'd arrested me and Adam for tagging the millennium monument in the town square with pink spray paint (we were innocent). The more I saw him, the more I liked him. Like became a teenage crush, my teenage crush became love, and here I was.

Turned twenty-four, and hopelessly infatuated with a man who would never give me a second look, even if he was divorced, because he was straight, and he only saw me as his little cousin's best friend.

The thing between Adam and Ray was newer.

Ray moved to Chipping Fairford a few years ago. Adam took one look at him and that was it. Game over. He used to hang out after his shift at the Co-op, pretending to work so he could bump into Ray, or take on extra hours stocking the shelves, in case Ray came in and Adam got the chance to talk to him.

Of course, back then Adam was eighteen and Ray, who was Liam's age, never even gave him a second look.

Not until last year, when Adam came back from

Cambridge university and slept with Ray's boyfriend, Fraser. That got him a second look all right.

He'd had no idea that Fraser was in a relationship, let alone in a relationship with Ray.

Despite that, I had no doubts as to Adam's eventual happy ending. He was a force of nature. Sexy, tousled, determined nature who had set his sights on Ray and would get what he wanted, because that's how Adam rolled.

As for my happy ending...

I met Liam's gaze across the room again. He held it for a moment before deliberately turning back to his date.

"I'm pissed off with you," I told Adam. "You should have told me he's divorced."

"He's not the right man for you, Jasper."

"Obviously, I know that. What with him being, you know." I waved a hand in his direction. "Into tall and beautiful women and whatnot."

Adam grimaced down at his beer.

"You still should have told me," I said. "I'd like to have known."

"Sorry," he said. "Actually, no. I'm not sorry. It was on purpose. I don't want you with someone like Liam. He wouldn't treat you right." He slung an arm around my shoulders, tugging me in to his side, and dropped a quick kiss on the top of my head. "You need someone kind. You deserve a man who appreciates you for all your weirdness."

"Uh—"

"Someone who will stand up and point at you and say, this guy. This is *my* guy. The one for me. My little freak. Fight me."

That was sweet. "Am I weird, though?"

"Jasper," he said fondly. "You're perfect."

"Awww."

"And you are the kind of gentle, loving sweetheart that Liam would bulldoze into the ground. I'm not having it."

"Right. It's not your decision one way or the other. You're not my dad, this isn't the 1800s, and I'm not some sort of precious *Bridgerton* lady." Adam could be so domineering sometimes. "Also, I'd like to state for the record that having Liam bulldoze me into the ground sounds totally amazing."

"Gross," Adam said.

"Like, I'd love it if he'd just throw me down and jump on top—"

"Stop it."

Not a chance. "Tear my clothes off. I'd tear his off. There'd be clothes everywhere. It would be like a clothes tornado. And then we'd both be hot and panting and naked, sliding around all over each other—"

"Jasper," Adam was laughing so hard now he could barely get it out. "You have to stop."

"No. I'm getting to the good part where I triumph, and I mercilessly take Liam like a mighty warlord takes his eager war prize and—oh no. Oh, fuck. He heard that, didn't he?"

Adam was in stitches. He had both hands over his mouth to hold in his laughter.

Liam looked back over his shoulder at me with another of those simmering glares. He stalked ahead to open the door for his date. She'd also heard, going on the gentle shake of her Burberry trench-coated shoulders, and the muffled yet ladylike snort.

"Goddammit." Liam's face had been red. Mine felt like it was absolutely purple, I was blushing so hard. "You are the *shittest* friend ever, I'm not even kidding. Adam! Why didn't you stop me!"

"I tried!"

"Not hard enough!"

He was still laughing, his bright hazel eyes glittering.

I slumped in my seat, running a hand over my hair. "Crap. Wow, that's embarrassing."

"Don't worry about it. You've done worse."

"That's not as comforting as you seem to think."

It was true, I had done much, much worse. Adam didn't know the half of it.

Adam probably thought that little scenario was off the cuff. It wasn't.

One of my very darkest secrets: I wrote Liam Nash fanfiction.

And, not exactly a *dark* secret, but a secret nonetheless: in all my erotic stories, I was never the warlord.

"Come on," Adam said with a friendly jostle. "I can name five worse things off the top of my head without even thinking."

"I'd rather you didn't."

He held up a finger. "The day you met."

I slapped his hand down.

He lifted it again, this time holding up two fingers. "His wedding day."

It wasn't my finest moment, that was for sure.

Adam held up another finger. "That time you—"

"Are we having lunch or not?" I said to cut him off. "Because some of us have work this afternoon."

"Lunch," he said. "I'm starving."

I had nothing scheduled at the gym until step class at five, but I had an afternoon date with my MacBook. I was going to write another article for the *Chipping Fairford Inquirer*, submit it by Friday, and the editor, Ralph Gardiner, would *definitely* publish it.

The whole time we ate our lunch, Adam watched Ray.

"I'm going for it," he said suddenly. "I'm done waiting."

"For what?" I said around a mouthful of chicken salad. I swallowed, and looked from him to Ray and back. "For Ray?"

"Yes."

I looked at Ray doubtfully. "I mean, maybe you could have had a shot, now you're a sexy ex-model architect and stuff—"

Adam grinned at me.

"Rather than being the creepy little checkout boy at the Co-op—"

"I've been taller than Ray as long as I've known him. I was *never* the creepy little checkout boy at the Co-op—"

"—who keeps staring at him. But I'm not sure you'll ever be able to get over the issue of sleeping with his boyfriend."

Adam scowled. "Fucking Fraser," he said. He straightened up. "I'm not going to let that wanker get between me and Ray, and our eventual happily ever after. Ray needs someone who appreciates him, and looks after him. That someone is me. We are meant to be, and Ray will just...have to see that at some point."

It wasn't much of a plan. But, "I believe in you," I told him. "You'll get Ray, I'll get over Liam, and our years of pining over unattainable men will be at an end."

"I'll drink to that." Adam held up his beer.

I clinked it with my water, which was now lukewarm and flat with melted ice.

I didn't think I was ever going to get over Liam.

It was probably time for me to at least try.

3

*I*t was still raining when we left the pub. We hovered in the protection of The Lion's small porch, gearing up to brave the dismal afternoon. In late spring, the porch was covered with cascades of purple wisteria that drove the tourists wild. Today, it was providing some much-needed shelter from rain that had stepped it up to a determined soaker.

Adam shrugged on his sexy leather motorcycle jacket and I pulled up the hood of my sweatshirt.

"Do you want a lift home?" I said, staring out at the road.

Traffic whooshed by, the tyres sounding extra loud on the wet tarmac. Leaves clogged a drain in the gutter a few feet away and water frothed out merrily. Some bubbles escaped to slide down the hill, only to coast into the road and be brutally popped by passing cars.

"Nah, I'm good. I'm on my bike."

"It's no trouble. Come on." I tipped my head in the direction of the carpark. "I'll drive you home, and we can come back and pick up your bike later."

Later, when it had stopped raining and the roads weren't like a waterslide.

Not to be his mother or anything, but I hated Adam riding that death trap disguised as a motorcycle on the best of days, let alone in shitty conditions with low visibility.

Adam turned to me and snagged the dangling strings of my hoodie. He pulled them tighter until the hood cinched up around my face and only a small circle was left to see out of. "I'll be fine," he said. "I'm very competent."

"I know *you* are. It's all the other idiots on the road I worry about." I yanked the strings out of his chilly hand and fussed with the hood, loosening it.

"Mm-hmm." He nudged me. "I'm careful. And I really am sorry for not telling you about Liam."

I gave him a level stare.

"Okay," he said with a grin. "I'm still not sorry about Liam because I'd definitely do it again. I'm sorry you're upset?"

"You know what? That's a non-apology and I do not accept." I shoved him out from under the porch. "Enjoy the rain."

Adam gasped and ducked his head against a brisk gust of wind. He crammed his helmet on with deft, practiced movements and flipped the visor up. "We're cool, though, right?"

"Of course."

He strode off to his bike and I sprinted for my car.

I drove home through the rain, my wipers going at full speed. I, on the other hand, went ten miles below the speed limit the whole way. I parked, grabbed my gym bag from the passenger seat, took a deep breath to brace myself, and dashed up the drive to the front door.

Unlike The Lion, my little terraced house didn't have a

dinky and picturesque porch to shelter under. By the time I'd fumbled the wet keys with my cold fingers and got the door open, I was all but soaked through.

"*Brrrrrrr,*" I said dramatically as I burst in and slammed the door behind me. I dropped my bag, stripped off the hoodie and kicked off my trainers. I decided I may as well get rid of my sweatpants while I was at it, and ran upstairs in just a t-shirt.

I jumped into the shower and sighed happily as the hot, hot water pounded down. My house was tiny, my mortgage was crippling me and giving me way too many sleepless nights, but my water pressure was to die for. I'd stay in my shower for an hour, given the chance.

Unfortunately, I worried about things like climate change as well as mortgages and Adam sliding under a bus on his stupid bike, so I kept it to a respectable ten minutes.

I wrapped a towel around my waist and scrubbed another over my hair, drying it roughly. I got out my large pump bottle of Aveeno lotion and slapped a handful on my chest and arms.

As a personal trainer and gym instructor, I was in and out of the shower multiple times a day. It was terrible for your skin. If I didn't moisturise, I'd be an itchy, flaky mess.

I finished rubbing in the lotion and headed for the bedroom, detouring when the doorbell rang. And really, I should have known who was standing on the other side of the door, simply by how irritable he managed to make it sound.

But I didn't.

I went downstairs with my bath towel around my hips and my hair towel still slung around my neck, and opened the door.

Liam Nash stood on my doorstep.

We stared at each other.

"Hi?" I said after a ridiculously long silence.

Liam was bundled up in a puffy yet manly North Face jacket. It was the kind of jacket that would keep you alive at the top of Ben Nevis in a blizzard just as well as it would keep you dry and toasty on a rainy Tuesday afternoon in the Cotswolds.

Also, it was an eye-watering highlighter orange. So if he *was* in a blizzard at the top of Ben Nevis, Search and Rescue wouldn't have any trouble spotting him from a helicopter.

Or space.

His hand, still raised from ringing the bell, was hanging in the air. Rain streamed down his arm and off the point of his elbow.

"Do you want to come in?" I said, when he didn't respond.

Liam's hand dropped. He opened his mouth. No sound came out.

All the lovely warmth from my shower and the brisk lotion massage was rapidly being sucked away by the cold dark day beyond my cosy hall. I was getting goosebumps here. My nipples were hard.

And Liam would notice that, since they were right in front of his face.

His eyes were slightly wider than usual, locked on mine with fierce determination. As I watched, they slowly, slowly drifted down. He looked like he was fighting it, but he lost. The moment he did, he gave me a full body scan.

It was quick, laser sharp, and over in a second.

It gave me more goosebumps than the cold air. I shifted awkwardly.

I wasn't shy about my body. I didn't give being half naked in front of other people a second thought. I couldn't, given my job. But unfamiliar self-consciousness began to rise, along with my pulse rate, as he went back for a second scan.

I couldn't quite put my finger on this one. Along with all the usual impatience and irritation I was used to seeing from him, there was something else that I really, really wasn't used to seeing from him.

If it was from anyone other than Liam, I'd say it was...sexual?

Of course, that made me preen. Subtly. But, yeah. I preened for him.

Only for him.

I cocked a hip, smiled, and rolled my shoulders back. When he didn't even blink, I took hold of the ends of the hair towel around my neck, and let my biceps do their thing.

Liam's jaw tightened. His eyes snapped back to my face and narrowed.

I laughed nervously, letting go of the towel. "Okay," I said. "What?"

"Nothing," he barked.

"Huh?"

He looked confused for a second, then said, "No."

Whaaaat was happening? "No? No what?"

"Just...no."

"Right."

We stared at each other for another thirty uncomfortable seconds. Rain pattered down.

"Okay," I said, an odd sense of disappointment descending. "So...um. I should probably go and get dressed?" I clenched the towel where it was knotted at my waist.

Liam glared at the towel. He glared at my abs, which tensed under the attention. He glared back at the towel. Then he said, "Fuck it."

"Wha—*oh my god.*"

He stepped in, muscling me backward into my hall, slammed the door shut behind him, and grabbed the back of my neck, yanking me forward. My body collided with his. His coat was cold and wet against me, and I didn't even care.

"I am kissing you," he announced.

I waited eagerly, but... "No, you're not," I said.

He puffed air through his nose like an angry bull, and leaned in so close I felt it against my face. He still didn't kiss me. "Do you want it?"

"What? Are you kidding me?" Was he *kidding* me? "Are you seriously asking me that? Obviously I want you to kiss me. Obvious—*mmph.*"

Oh my god.

He did it.

He was doing it.

Liam Nash was kissing me.

And I have to say, he wasn't being gentle about it. Thank god.

He walked me backward, his lips firm and demanding on mine.

I gasped when my back hit the door. He opened my mouth with his, and his tongue glided against mine with a sinuous twist that dragged a whimper out of me.

My hands flew up and I unzipped his wet coat, shoving it open and grabbing his sides, dragging his warm body against me. I pushed at his shoulders, trying to get the coat the rest of the way off, seeking more contact. He shrugged impatiently and the coat hit the floor. I threaded my hands into his damp hair, gripping and pulling him closer.

He angled his head, licking slow and deep. If he hadn't already wedged a thigh between my legs, my knees would have given out and I'd have hit the floor as sensation streaked through me and turned me into an overcooked noodle.

He was pressed against me from ankle to mouth. I had the door at my back, Liam at my front, and I was comprehensively pinned.

I loved it.

Oh, god, I loved it so much.

He had an arm around my waist. He gave me a yank forward, enough to shove his hand down behind me to palm my butt, and he groaned into my mouth. I moaned helplessly in response.

I had never been wrangled like this in my life.

I shuddered with the thrill of it. I'd studied a number of martial arts as I built my personal trainer skills portfolio. I was pretty hot shit at jiu jitsu and Muay Thai. I wasn't unused to being close to another man, let alone another man trying to immobilise me.

But this was *Liam*.

And it wasn't competitiveness driving him, or me. It was desire.

My body went soft and pliant in a dizzying rush. He kissed me and kissed me. A hand at my hip encouraged me to tilt my pelvis into his. Yes! I thought happily. Let's rub off on each other!

Liam had something else in mind.

He pushed the towel up my thighs, and pulled back from my eager mouth to stare into my eyes as he did it.

I shivered from the overwhelming sexiness of the moment.

I was the first to admit that I wasn't all that sophisticated when it came to sex. Mostly my experience centred around handjobs, blowjobs, and the occasional penetration when I could talk myself into it. I wanted to be the one on the bottom, but I'd only managed it a couple of times. In general, guys seemed to want me to fuck them rather than the other way around.

So having Liam's stormy blue-grey eyes simmering mere inches from mine as he dragged the towel up, having him cataloging my response, seeing his kiss-swollen lips hitch at one side in a pleased, lopsided smile, was over-whelming.

And that is why a terrible, needy little whine came out of my throat.

It horrified me, but Liam seemed to like it.

His hard hands gently stroked up to cup my bare buttocks, one in each palm. His smile grew as he leaned in and kissed me again.

With his hold on my arse, he pulled me rhythmically into him over, and over, and over.

It was too much.

I broke away and my head fell back with a soft thud against the door as I gasped up at the ceiling unseeingly. Liam went for my neck, pressing open-mouthed kisses into my heated skin, grazing with his teeth.

"Liam," I said. "*Liam.*"

He murmured something I couldn't hear against my throat. The neck kisses became softer, lighter. *No.* Was he stopping? I couldn't bear for him to stop. I wasn't even thinking about orgasms, I just wasn't ready to not be in his arms anymore.

I yanked off my towel.

He stilled against me, breathing hard.

I bumped my hips into him, slid my hands along his jaw to hold his face, and kissed him as sweetly as I'd always dreamed of kissing a man.

He braced his hands against the door either side of my

head, arms tucked close and pressing against me. I felt the fine tremor of tension in his body.

"Liam," I whispered against his mouth.

He grabbed me.

He literally hauled me away from the door, locking one arm around my waist and the other around my shoulders. There was more of the dizzying manhandling that was now my absolute favourite thing in the world, other than his mouth on mine, and then we were in my tiny sitting room and falling to the sofa.

I hitched my legs up and wrapped them tight around his hips. I held his face again, pulling our mouths back together. He braced over me, squashing me into the cushions.

I was in heaven.

I'd dreamed of this sort of encounter with Liam more times than was remotely healthy, I'd written stories about it, and the reality was a thousand times better than anything I had imagined.

Liam was right here, hot and heavy, surrounding me. He wanted me—wanted me a *lot*, going on the erection I felt against my abs—and he was greedily taking everything I'd ever yearned to give him.

He coasted a hand the length of my body, from shoulder to hip then down my thigh before reversing. Long, drugging touches that made me relax more and more until I became nothing but sensation beneath him.

"Soft," he said, his voice rough and deep. He gazed down into my face, his expression unreadable.

Well, he for sure wasn't talking about my dick.

"M-my skin?" I said, arching into his touch as he stroked me again. "I moisturise."

He hummed and pushed up, rearranging us until he was straddling me. I reached for him. He caught my hands and held them together at my chest in one of his. With his other hand, he continued to explore my body.

I bit my lip, eyes fixed on his face, trying to work out what he was thinking. I couldn't. Not a damn clue.

He did another of those full sweeps, like he was trying to make sure he'd touched me everywhere he could reach.

He drifted a hand up the side of my waist, and squeezed. I don't know why that felt like the sexiest hold ever, especially when he was restraining my hands, which was objectively sexier, but it was.

He *held* me.

He gripped the side of my ribs and I breathed into his hold, expanding into it, cupped in his palm. He slid his hand in and dragged it over the cobbled abs I work so hard for.

"Goddamn," he muttered. He stroked my stomach a few times as it heaved under his touch. He circled his thumb around the rim of my bellybutton once, then again, then his explorations went in the opposite direction I'd been hoping for.

He brushed light fingers up my chest, even as he slowly lifted my restrained hands over my head to press them into the sofa cushion.

I choked and arched beneath him in one long, involuntary ripple.

His eyes flared with heat and he gripped my wrists even more firmly. He kept his other hand teasingly light as he brushed over my pecs, and then startled me by flicking a nipple.

I caught my breath and smiled up at him.

Maybe I shouldn't have done that. Maybe he didn't want me to smile, I don't know. For some reason, that smile seemed to break the spell.

"Jasper," he said. It didn't sound great.

One day, I thought fiercely. *One* day, I'd hear him say my name the way I wanted him to say it. Hell, this had happened. Anything was possible, right?

One day, he'd say it and he'd sound happy to be saying it. Not exasperated, or angry, or—like now—sorry.

I pulled my hands free easily and reached for him. He caught them before I could get them back to where they belonged, which was holding his stupid face. He squeezed my wrists gently and gave his head a half-shake.

It was over. I knew that. "One more," I said stubbornly and broke out of his hold again. He blinked with surprise. "One more." I pulled him down.

He stared at my mouth, then my eyes, then back at my mouth. I didn't pout, exactly, but I definitely licked my lips and did something that was pouting-adjacent and hopefully irresistible, and—

He kissed me again. This one was like the first kiss, startling in comparison to how soft and tender they'd become without me noticing.

This was hard, desperate, demanding.

Over.

He pushed up and off me. I didn't even try to hold him back. I did have some pride.

Zero fucking shame, though. I lay there and let him look at me.

Yeah, I thought. Get a good look.

I took a deep, deep breath, and sighed it out as I dragged a hand down my chest and gripped my cock. I was so hard at this point, I nearly came at my own touch.

I met his gaze with a challenging glare that made him, for some infuriating reason, smile.

"No," he said, and shook his head.

"Yes," I bounced back.

He firmed his jaw. Ducking down, he cupped my cheek and said with absolute conviction, "This was wrong. I apologise. It won't happen again." He kissed me, and left.

I watched him walk out of the sitting room. I heard the quiet swish of fabric as he collected his coat. My front door closed with a gentle click.

"We'll see," I said, with just as much conviction.

4

_____

It didn't take long for all the heat Liam had fired up in me to drain away in the cool air of the sitting room. My breathing was already back to normal. Out of habit, I checked my pulse. It had snapped back to its steady resting rate of 50 bpm.

I was sprawled out like a hussy on the sofa. One leg had slipped off and I had a foot on the chilly carpet. One arm was flung over my head. I still had a hand on my cock.

I squeezed gently, and sighed.

I did _not_ see that coming.

I eased my hand up and down my painfully hard cock. It wouldn't take much to bring myself off.

Liam had...holy _crap_. He'd wrangled me, and pushed me about the way I'd longed for. He'd squashed me and held me down—I could break free but he didn't know that—and for that brief moment, I'd felt consumed by him.

It was glorious.

My hand sped up, the sound of it loud and deliciously obscene in the cold and silent room.

I rolled off the sofa and onto my feet, and bolted up the stairs.

I wasn't going to waste a genuine real-life Liam-Nash-induced-*on-purpose* erection with a half-hearted orgasm as I lay there feeling sad and also regretting not turning the heating on when I came in.

I flung myself facedown on my bed and made a thorough disgrace of myself as I humped my hand and pretended it was Liam's.

Pretended that it hadn't ended downstairs after all.

That I was here because Liam had coaxed me tenderly from the sofa and escorted me up the stairs. That he had laughingly asked which way to the bedroom, and then taken over and guided me, stopping en route to press more kisses to my eager mouth.

He'd lowered me to the mattress, whispered that he wanted me—*on your stomach, baby*—and then...and then...

I moaned into the duvet.

And then he slipped a hand between me and the mattress and told me to work for it, that he loved my beautiful arse and wanted to see it as I pumped into his grip, and—

I shuddered and came all over my duvet.

I lay there panting, face hot with a mix of delighted embarrassment and good old-fashioned physical exertion.

Groaning, I flipped to my back.

Damn it. I'd changed the duvet just this morning. I hadn't been a teenager for years. I really didn't have any excuse for losing control that badly.

I hopped into the shower, cleaned up in record time, and got dressed in a clean pair of sweatpants and a compression shirt. Normally on a writing afternoon I'd snuggle in old plaid flannel pj bottoms and a cosy jumper but I was running out of time. I had to leave for the gym in an hour and a half, and I hadn't even turned my MacBook on today.

I stripped the bed, grabbed a clean duvet cover from my linen closet and changed it. Laundry on, I made a cup of tea and carried it to my desk.

It wasn't until I'd opened up my daily notes app and taken a sip of tea that the deeper ramifications of what had happened in my sitting room percolated.

"Huh," I said blankly to my blinking cursor.

Liam wasn't straight.

Or at the very least, Liam had a heretofore unsuspected flexibility when it came to men.

I'd pined after him for years, and I hadn't kept it to myself. I'd been obvious and vocal in my admiration of him.

A highlight real of my many youthful and extremely unsubtle attempts to get his attention played through my mind, and I cringed.

No wonder Liam was always irritable with me. He must have been absolutely appalled.

No man wanted a gawky, romantic teenager mooning around after him, like something was ever going to happen if I put myself in the way often enough.

I slunk lower in my seat and hunched my shoulders. I'd been a nightmare.

It hadn't really sunk in until the day I saw him standing in church beside his radiant, glorious bride, that I was missing some key assets to attract the likes of Liam Nash.

I'm not even talking about her boobs.

His wife, Verity, was tall, athletic, had a mane of gleaming mahogany hair, a First from Oxford University, a stellar career as a barrister in London, a trust fund, a fucking *horse*, and worst of all?

She was nice.

I'd blundered along, filled with optimism and the kind of self-centred bullheadedness of youth that convinces you that if you just *want* something hard enough, you'll get it. Until that day, I'd managed to ignore the fact that I was the wrong gender. It didn't seem relevant.

Forget being the wrong gender: how could I possibly compete with the vision of beauty, confidence and success that was Verity?

I couldn't.

And that was the despairing conclusion I had reached six years ago when I woke up hungover the morning after Liam's wedding, tangled up with Adam in his too-small bed.

I'd cracked my eyes open, moaned when cruel sunlight immediately seared my sensitive eyeballs, and attempted to retreat under the covers, where it was dark and safe.

Adam wheezed as I jammed an elbow in his side in the midst of my half-hearted flailing. He attempted to shove me off, but we'd been sleeping in the same bed since we were fourteen. I knew all his tricks. I didn't even have to think about it. I locked my legs around his and flopped about until I was on top.

"Jesus, Jasper," he'd croaked. "Stop crushing me or I'm gonna throw up."

"If you throw up, I'll throw up," I muttered, and slithered off him back to the mattress. "We'll be stuck in a loop. It'll be disgusting. Your mum will hear us and come in, and she'll be so mad."

"Shhhh," he said, patting at me clumsily.

"Mmf." I pulled a pillow over my head and sought sweet oblivion.

No go.

I couldn't stop thinking about yesterday and last night. I really hoped that the worst of the images flashing through my mind were the ragged shreds of lingering nightmares. I had a horrible feeling that was wishful thinking.

"Stop puffing so loudly," Adam said a few minutes later. The mattress shifted as he rolled out of bed. He snatched the duvet off me and slapped my arse. "Wow. Someone's been doing their squats."

I clenched and released my buttocks in a half-hearted twerk, and he laughed.

I hadn't slept with Adam like this for a while. Everyone thought we were friends with benefits, but other than a brief period when we were each other's training wheels for hand-jobs and blowjobs, things weren't sexual between us.

Since then, I'd shot up from a weedy little five-foot-some-thing kid to a six-foot-one, two-hundred-pound eighteen-year-old, and I wasn't done growing yet. Adam was keeping height with me, even if he was lankier. I had no idea how we'd both managed to get in the damn bed in the first place.

I had no idea...

"Adam?" I said.

He snatched the pillow off my head and I groaned again at the light. "What?" he said.

"I don't remember getting here."

There was the wedding, the reception, beer, something fuzzy that my brain was trying to shut down, and then...here.

"If I were you, I wouldn't try," Adam said. His voice faded as he went into the en suite bathroom. I heard him peeing. It went on and on and on. My bladder twinged in sympathy.

"Your poor mum didn't have to get us up here, did she?" I said when he wandered back in. Mrs Blake was tiny. Strong, but tiny.

"She had help."

I rolled over and Adam grinned at me. I raised a brow, and glanced down. Oh. I was naked. "Ew, I wasn't naked in front of your mum, was I?"

"No, no. The clothes came off once she was gone."

"Phew."

Adam was still smiling.

"What?" I said suspiciously.

"Not a single thing, buddy."

I managed to get myself into a sitting position, swayed a bit, then got up to standing and crept to the bathroom.

Adam wandered back in when I was still standing at the toilet.

"Do you mind?" I grumbled.

"You're taking too long." He reached into the shower and turned it on.

I eyed it with interest. Still peeing.

"I'm first," Adam said. "Don't even try getting in here with me."

"We can't both fit anymore," I said with an eye-roll. I regretted it instantly. "Ow."

Adam's shower was a minuscule cubicle that was barely big enough for one person, let alone two.

"We can't both fit in my bed anymore, either, but that didn't stop you," Adam said.

I grunted, finished up peeing—finally—and went to wash my hands and brush my teeth. Adam got in the shower and he moaned decadently as the hot water hit him. If there had been even an inch more room, I'd have been in there with him like a shot.

I settled for squeezing some toothpaste onto a shaky finger, and poking it half-heartedly around my teeth.

It was all a bit much in the effort department. I squeezed

from the tube directly into my mouth, stuck my head under the tap to top up with water, and swished.

"I do have mouthwash," Adam said from the shower, scrubbing shampoo through his mop of red-blond curls, flinging suds everywhere. "It's right in front of you on the shelf."

I gargled, and spat. "No more alcohol," I said, clutching the taps to stay upright when the act of bending over and straightening up threatened to take me to my knees. "Ever, Adam."

He snorted.

"I am turning over a new leaf," I said.

Adam shut off the water and stuck an arm out, opening and closing his hand demandingly. I passed him his towel.

He gave me a skeptical look as he tied the towel around his waist.

I pondered my statement. "I'm going back to my old leaf," I said. "No alcohol at all. I've decided I don't like it."

I'd been eighteen for about three months, which was the only reason Liam was unsuccessful in his attempt to arrest me for underage drinking. I had a vague memory of him giving it a go, and of Adam laughing when I fumbled out my wallet and driving license to prove my age.

This was the first time I'd got drunk. I vowed that it would be last.

I vowed a lot of things that day, feeling like death in Adam's bathroom. He shuffled me into the shower and when I couldn't help myself from sniffling, he pulled me back out and wrapped me up in a tight hug.

To my embarrassment, I'd given up and full-on cried. Sobs. Snot. The works.

Adam knew that I'd had a thing for Liam. I wasn't subtle. The whole town probably knew.

But until he was holding me on the bathroom floor as I fucking lost it like only a teenager in love can, even Adam hadn't known that my thing was real.

He hadn't known, as I'd sat in church that day as his plus-one and watched Liam stand up with a gorgeous, *nice* woman, as I'd sat in the marquee at the reception that night and watched them dance in each others arms...Adam hadn't known that my heart was breaking.

You broke my heart, Liam. You broke *it.*

I remembered sobbing those words into my pillow night after night.

In fact, I did it so often that my memories shifted and got muddled, to the point that I began to remember saying it to Liam's stern face. He'd gripped my shoulders, holding me back, and he'd whispered, *I'm sorry, Jasper. I never asked for it. I don't think of you that way. And you shouldn't ever let yourself get hurt over someone like me.*

Which of course couldn't ever have happened, because my memory of that touching nightmare was in Adam's bedroom while Adam was busy throwing up in the bathroom, and by then, Liam would have already been driving into the sunset with his wife.

Liam was, and always had been, an impossible dream.

Over the years, I grew up. I tried not to love him. When I found myself weakening—which was every time I saw him, and every time we interacted— all I had to do was look in the mirror and superimpose an image of beautiful, poised Verity Nash over my plain, wistful, very-much-a-man's face. It was one hell of a dose of reality. Probably not awesome for my self-esteem. But it worked.

Until today.

Because now, not only was Liam a) divorced and b)

dating, he was c) apparently into men and even, dare I say it, d) into me.

I didn't know what to do about it.

But I felt myself smiling.

Then my vision swung back into focus and that fucking cursor was blinking at me like it always did.

I checked the clock.

Okay.

I had an hour before I had to suck down a protein shake, drag myself back out into the dark and the rain, and go and be peppy at the gym. I could come up with a few article ideas that Ralph was going to *love* in that time, I was sure.

Or, I'd try.

Not that anything remotely exciting ever happened in Chipping Fairford.

5

"You're all doing so well!" I bellowed over the music. "Especially you, Brenda! Keep pedalling. Doesn't matter how fast you go. So long as you're moving, you're winning. Woo!"

I wasn't a fan of yelling *woo* at people, but a certain level of enthusiasm was expected from a personal trainer/gym instructor. My senior spin class expected it more than most. If I didn't toss out a few *woos*, I had concerned pensioners cornering me after class and asking what was wrong, why was I sad, did I want a cookie?

I was up at the front on the instructor's bike and I'd clipped my phone to the handlebars where it was shielded by the bike's console. I poked at the screen to wake it up and see if Adam had replied to my WhatsApp yet.

Nope.

Scowling, I looked up and inadvertently made eye contact with Ed at the back of the room. He valiantly tried to speed up. I could hear his knees crackling from here.

Feeling bad, I called out, "Ed, great job! You're doing

great, remember to stay at a speed where you're having fun. Because that's why we're all here, am I right?"

I surveyed the room. They were giving it their best, but not many of them looked like they were having fun. I glanced at the speedometer. While I'd been distracted thinking about Adam, I'd crept up to a brisk twenty miles per hour.

Time to take it down before I killed someone.

"Okay, that is more than enough of the fast stuff," I yelled. "Let's wind it down to a gentle cycle along a country lane! The birds are singing! There's honeysuckle and shit in the hedgerows! Can you feel that lovely warm summer sun? Is this Chipping Fairford in February? No! It's June and we are in Italy! We are in Tuscany! Great!"

Everyone looked relieved as we slowed to a gentle ten miles per hour. And then more relieved when I told them all to take the incline down to zero.

I changed the music to Enya, which was very popular for cooldowns with this crowd, and looked at my phone again.

Still nothing from Adam.

For the rest of the session, I gave the room my full attention. Most of the class was back to smiling by the time we'd finished. I got a couple of frosty side-eyes as the group dispersed and a full-on glare from Ed as he limped dramatically past me, but on the whole, it was fine.

In the break room, I threw myself onto the sofa and got back on my phone. I skimmed through the conversation with Adam.

It wasn't much of a conversation. It was a string of messages, all from me.

Adam had left me on read.

ME

Hey! I need Liam's number!

Hellooooo

Okay, you're probably busy at work. Lemme have it when you have a sec, k?

Adam, I know you're reading these. Gimme Liam's number!

Still nothing.

I was trying hard not to be upset about being ignored.

I kind of had a problem with it.

In general, and in particular with Adam.

The thing was, my life hadn't gone exactly to plan. More precisely, my life hadn't aligned with my parents' plan.

My dad was an accountant and my mum was a big deal in an investment bank in London. Their plan was that I should follow in their footsteps: be incredibly intelligent, get the highest possible grades in my A-Levels, get into Oxford or Cambridge, and spend the rest of my days working as an accountant or a hedge fund manager.

If I couldn't manage that, they'd settle for me being a neurosurgeon.

I still get the cold sweats when I remember the day we learned my A-Level results. It's not like I'd had a stellar academic career up to that point, and had fallen at the last hurdle. I was a solid C-student and always had been—and *that* was when I could sit still long enough to concentrate. How I was supposed to suddenly pull some A's out of my arse, I don't know.

With my unimpressive exam scores I couldn't get into any university, let alone Oxford.

My parents were disappointed, they sat me down and

told me all about it in uncomfortable detail, and then they washed their hands of it and left me to my own devices.

Mrs Blake had pushed and shoved me into signing up at the local college in Witney, and my P.E. teacher had always said that I'd make a great personal trainer. Since they were the only two adults who'd ever had anything positive to say about my abilities, I ended up studying fitness and nutrition, and became a personal trainer.

Meanwhile, Adam went off to enjoy his glamorous life in Cambridge as a student and part-time model, and he didn't have time for me. He came back to Chipping Fairford to visit his mum. I went over to Cambridge once or twice. It wasn't the same.

Even though he'd come home for good now and things were like they used to be, apparently I could still get insecure.

I texted him again.

ME

You're a dick

"Jas, you're gonna be late for your Legs, Bums and Tums class," Melanie said as she skipped into the break room, high blond ponytail swinging.

"Crap." I'd wasted my whole break sitting around and brooding. "Thanks, Mel." I leapt up, stuffed my phone in my shorts pocket, and rushed off to the studio.

"YOU'RE A DICK," I SAID TO ADAM THREE HOURS LATER WHEN he finally deigned to answer the phone. "You know I hate being left on read, Adam."

He sighed. "Shit, I forgot. I don't mean I forgot you hate

it, I know you do. I meant I forgot you texted. It's been a crazy day. Two people quit, the new guy decided that working in a hotel isn't his true calling or whatever and never even bothered to show up, someone broke the wifi, and my boss cried on me."

"Oh. Sounds like a shitty day."

"Yeah. Still, I'm sorry. I wasn't deliberately ignoring you."

"Cool," I said. "Okay, lemme grab a pen." I cut across my sitting room and into the kitchen to snag the pen and notepad I kept by the kettle. I tended to have *ideas* while waiting for it to boil. "Go," I said.

"Go where?"

"Gimme Liam's number!"

Adam hummed.

I straightened. "Are you serious?"

"I just don't think it's a good idea."

"You made your opinion on the matter clear enough at the pub, thanks."

"Why do you need his number, anyway?" Adam said.

"I want to send him a dick pic, why do you think?" I snapped.

"Oh my god, *don't.*"

"Oh my god, I was *joking.*"

Although....?

Maybe Liam would be into that?

I palmed myself thoughtfully, and filed that one away for later.

"Adam, give me his number, for fuck's sake."

"Promise you won't send him a dick pic."

"No."

Adam sighed. "Okay. Please don't get hurt, Jasper. Just because he's divorced and living back in Chipping Fairford, it doesn't mean anything's changed."

Boy was he wrong about that. Everything had changed. *Everything* had—wait. "He lives here?"

"What?"

"He *lives* here now?"

There was a tense silence.

"I cannot believe you," I said. "First you didn't tell me he was divorced, then you didn't tell me he lives here now, and you sure as shit never told me he is into m—" I cut myself off with a choke before I outed Liam in my indignation.

"Into what?" Adam said suspiciously.

You know what? *No.*

If I thought Liam was straight, right up until I had his tongue in my mouth and his whole body on mine, then presumably everyone else thought he was straight.

Also, that was *it*. It was cute and all that Adam was trying to protect me but I didn't ask him to. I was used to being rejected. I was a *writer*.

I was rejected *professionally*.

"He's into m-Marvel," I said.

"What?"

"He is into Marvel movies."

"Marvel movies."

"Yes."

"What the hell does Marvel movies have to do with anything?"

"Don't change the subject," I said.

Adam sighed. "You've spent long enough wanting a man you can never have," he said softly. "What kind of a friend would I be if I encouraged you?"

"It's a phone number, Adam."

"Okay. Write it down. And if he's mean to you—"

I laughed. "If?"

"*When* he's mean to you, let me know. I'll kick his arse."

"Thanks," I said with a grin. "That won't be necessary. Should his arse need kicking, we both know I could do it with one hand tied behind my back. And a leg."

"I don't know what you expect is going to go differently," Adam said, "but here's the number."

I jotted it down, read it back to make sure I got it right, and ended the call.

"Everything," I said into the silence of the kitchen.

I expected *everything* to go differently.

6

"Okay," I said. "This is it. You can do this. You can *do* this. Jasper? You *can* do this."

...and yet I was not doing it.

After the call with Adam, I'd added Liam's number to my contacts, and proceeded to spend ten whole ridiculous minutes staring at the phone screen. It went dark and I had to re-enter my passcode to wake it back up three times.

I kind of couldn't believe I even had it. The holy grail of phone numbers.

"Okay," I said again, and wandered into the sitting room. I perched on the edge of the sofa, stared at the phone some more, then gingerly opened up a text conversation.

How would a very mature and sexually confident man who wanted to say, *Oh, hi! So, you had your tongue in my mouth earlier and I was wondering if you'd like to give that another go some time,* kick off a conversation?

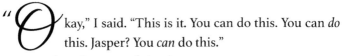

ME

What's up?

No, not that.

Ummm…

Good evening.

That was stupid. It sounded like I was welcoming him to a restaurant.

Bro!

Hell, no.

Right. This wasn't getting me anywhere.

Before I could second-guess myself, I went old-school and pressed the call button.

It rang and rang, long enough for my mouth to dry out completely while my hands started to sweat, before Liam answered.

"Nash," he said.

I dropped the phone.

Grunting, I bent over and swiped it up from the floor, blushing like a fool even though there was no-one there to see me. I jammed it against my ear. "Hi!" I said, way too loud.

"Hello."

"This is Jasper."

There was a brief pause. "Jasper?"

"Um. Connolly. Jasper Connolly?"

"I know who you are, Jasper." He sounded amused. Warm, almost.

It was throwing me off.

"Great!" I said. "Good. Okay, so Adam gave me your number." Whoops. I didn't mean to start by dropping Adam in it. Never mind. Liam would probably blame him anyway. "Don't worry," I scrambled to add. "I didn't tell him why I wanted it. I mean, he thinks he knows and he's not wrong, but he doesn't know *all* of it." He didn't know that Liam had wanted me back.

"Why did you want it?" Liam said.

"Well...is this a good time to talk? Sorry, I should have asked that first. Are you at work? I don't know your shifts. Are you alone?"

There was another pause. This one was longer. I squirmed uncomfortably on the sofa. Eventually, he said, "Do I need to be alone?"

"What?"

"Is this the kind of conversation I'm going to want privacy for?"

It was unfair what a lovely voice Liam had, honestly. It was always deep and a little gruff, but usually it was sharp, too. Impatient. Right now, it was deep and had a mellow tone to it that I wasn't used to.

"I think so. Possibly?" It was private. I was going to bring up his sexuality. I didn't want to blindside him with it if he was at work. "Where are you?"

"I'm at home," he said. "In bed."

I immediately imagined Liam in bed.

He was wearing nothing but an artfully placed duvet and a come-hither smile.

I mentally removed the duvet, and—

"Jasper?"

"Yes! Sorry. Um. It has come to my attention that you might be into men."

"What makes you think that?"

I squinted at the phone. "You *kissed* me."

"Yes?"

"I mean...that's not all you did. You kissed me. You lay on top of me and you held me down. You touched my arse, Liam. You touched it a lot."

"Right. I—"

"A *lot*," I said. "You cupped it." Cupped it, and squeezed it, and used his hold on it to drag me over him. "And you touched the rest of me. All over. Apart from my cock, which was disappointing because I'd really have loved it if you'd...*oh*. Oh, Liam." Things began to make sense.

"What?"

"Was that your first time with a man?" I said gently. "Were you shy?"

"No," he snapped.

"There's nothing to be ashamed of!" I rushed to reassure him. "There really isn't, it's perfectly natural to be nervous or hesitant when exploring another man's body for the first time."

He made an odd sound.

"It's probably overwhelming and exciting, too, isn't it? Please don't be embarrassed. It's been a while since I was a virgin, but I think I recall being a bit weirded out?"

I absolutely wasn't even remotely weirded out. I was enthusiastic, all the way. Adam pretty much grabbed my dick one day, I grabbed his, and we were off.

"What you're feeling is normal, Liam."

"What I'm feeling is annoyed, Jasper."

"I can understand that. Maybe this isn't a part of yourself you're ready to accept. Or even try again. Which is *fine*, although also I hope isn't true, because I'd very much like to offer myself up for any gay exploring you'd like to do. I think I'd be great at it. I'd get naked and lie there spread out for you, and you could do whatever, no pressure."

I had an instant boner at the thought of it.

"We could put on some soothing music." Wincing, I said bravely, "Like Enya. And have the lights really low. Or candles. I promise I'd be quiet, and you could see what you liked. You could stroke whatever caught your interest, or... or..." He'd said my skin was soft and seemed fascinated by it. "Or put some lotion on me. Whatever you want. We could see where it went. If orgasms happened—I won't lie, I'd have trouble not orgasming under those circumstances, so if you didn't want that, if that would be a bit frightening for you, then I could go online and order myself a cock ring or something, let me know—then no pressure. Also if erections were lost or didn't show up, also no pressure. No judgment. How does that sound?"

"Okay," Liam said. "Let me recap. You're offering to buy yourself a cock ring, which you will then wear, while letting me massage you by candlelight, with Enya playing in the background. Because you think I'm a virgin."

"Gay virgin. I'm pretty sure you've had a sex with a woman. Not assuming, though!"

Liam was quiet for a long moment.

"Hello?" I said after the silence dragged on.

"Yeah."

"Oh. Good, you're still there. I thought you'd hung up on me."

"I'm tempted."

"Are you getting shy again?"

"No."

"If you are, though, it's fine."

"I'm not shy." He snorted an irritated breath. "Did it really seem to you like I didn't know what I was doing?"

"You're a natural," I said encouragingly. "When you've gained some experience and you're more relaxed about things, you won't be afraid of penises."

"Right. Jasper?"

"Yes?"

"I am not afraid of dicks."

"Okay. It would be normal if you were, being a formerly heterosexual man in his thirties encountering them for the first time. But okay."

"I am not afraid of dicks," he said, biting the words out.

"I hear what you are saying."

"Do you *understand* what I am saying, is what I want to know."

I thought about how he had run his hands hungrily all over my willing naked body, except my dick. "Yes," I said kindly.

"Jasper," he said, "the reason I didn't touch your dick is not because I'm afraid of dicks, what the fuck."

"Okay."

"You want to know why I didn't touch your dick?"

"If you want to tell me, then yes, but Liam? No judgment."

He said furiously, "It's because I wanted to take your perfect, beautiful cock in my hand, and jerk you off until you were writhing and begging for me to let you come."

My cheeks scorched with heat. "What?" I said faintly.

"Yeah. I wanted you sobbing beneath me. Shaking with need. I wanted to pin you down and hold you on the edge until you cried, and only then would I let you go over. I'd watch you come apart under me, and then if you asked very, very nicely, I'd let you watch while I jerked off on you."

The blood was pounding in my ears. "So...not a gay virgin?"

"No."

"Well. Um." I had no idea what to say. "Offer still stands?"

"The generous offer to let me give you a candlelight massage to Enya?"

I scowled. "You don't have to say it like that. I was being supportive and understanding, Liam. I was trying to create a safe and unthreatening encounter for someone who might freak out at the thought of a dick."

"*Enya*, though?"

"Oh, all my seniors at the gym love her music."

He hung up.

"Hello?" I said. "Liam?"

I had to dial three more times, but he eventually answered.

"What now?" He was definitely no longer sounding warm or mellow.

"Uh, same, actually?" He didn't say anything. I ploughed on, "So. You're gay. How about that?"

"You want to try that one again? You know I was married to a woman. And it wasn't a platonic relationship."

"You're bisexual. How about that?"

"Jasper," he said. "I have to be up really, really early tomorrow for work."

"Okay, sorry. Me, too. I have a class at six. Ugh, they're the worst."

"Jasper."

"Um." Do it, I told myself. If you can offer to let him explore your nude and quivering body, you can ask him out. "Would you like to go and get a coffee sometime? With me?"

"No."

"Wow. You didn't take, like, even a second to think about it."

"I don't need a second to think about it."

"Have you given up caffeine or something? I'll buy you a herbal tea."

"I haven't given up caffeine," he said, his voice softening. "It's not a good idea."

"Two bros meeting up for a hot beverage? How could that possibly be a bad idea?"

"For a start, I'm not your bro—"

"Two dudes, hanging out in a coffee shop, getting their drinks on. I'll have an almond milk macchiato. You can have a camomile or whatever. I'll even spring for a doughnut."

"Hard no on the camomile. I take my coffee black, and I'm not exactly a hang out in the coffee shop kind of guy. I drink it on the go."

"Excellent. We'll meet for a walk in the park, with coffees."

"Jasper," he said. "We're not meeting for coffee."

I sighed. "Why not?"

"I don't think of you that way."

"Bullshit."

Liam laughed. "Yeah, okay. No point pretending I don't find you attractive. I should have said, I don't want to think of you that way."

My hand tightened on the phone. "Why not?" I was vaguely irritated at myself for sounding like a two-year-old with all the *why* questions. Mostly, I was grinning like a fool because he'd admitted it, out loud, in actual words.

Liam Nash found me attractive.

It was one thing to feel his heavy erection against me, his body against me, his mouth on me.

But *words*. I had the words!

"You're not my type," he said frankly. "And you're too young."

My excitement withered. Those words, I didn't want.

"I *am* your type," I tried, and didn't even sound convincing to myself. "I am, you—"

"Jasper, I'm sorry. I got carried away. I came over to... Okay. You were standing right there, looking like a fucking wet drea...Jesus. Looking like you do. Which is no excuse for my behaviour. I lost my head for a minute, and I apologise for that."

"No."

"Yes."

"Liam, no. Don't apologise for it, I—"

"I am apologising," he said relentlessly. "I'm sorry."

"I'm not." I sat down hard. "I'm not sorry. I wanted you to do it. I've wanted you to do it for years, and I want you to do it again."

"I won't," he said, and fuck him for sounding kind about it. "Listen, I've got to go."

"Wait." I scrambled for something, anything, to keep him on the phone. "Why did you even come over in the first place?"

He hesitated, then said wryly, "To tell you that just because I'm divorced, it doesn't mean I'm available, and you shouldn't go getting your hopes up."

My jaw dropped. "Holy shit," I said on a laugh. "I don't think I've ever heard anything so arrogant in my entire life. You actually took time out of your afternoon to get in your car, drive over to my house, knock on my door, and tell me that?"

"When you put it like that—"

"There's no other way to put it, Liam, you—"

"It's not that much of an assumption. Let's not forget that when I left the pub, you were talking about taking me like a mighty warlord takes his eager war prize."

I whined with embarrassment and pressed a hand to my hot cheek. "Oh my god. That was a private conversation!

About! Stuff that is not your business! It was a *fantasy* not a declaration of intent!"

"Uh-huh," he said.

This time, I hung up on him.

7

A few days after the embarrassing phone call, I was sitting in my writing 'studio,' searching for inspiration. One day, I planned on having a dedicated room for my studio. Currently, I was making do with the corner of my sitting room.

I'd set up my ageing MacBook on a small desk, and arranged the chair to face the wall. If I faced the window, it was too easy to get distracted.

My phone was on silent and safely tucked away in the kitchen. My giant water bottle was filled to the brim. I had some background music playing—a mix of nature sounds and gentle piano. Two of my clients had canceled due to a sore throat that was making its way around town, and I only had one class at the gym after supper.

The day was wide open for me to write.

The problem was, I didn't know what to write about.

It was a big problem. I had a personal goal to submit no less than four articles to Ralph at the *Inquirer* in February— more if possible—and here we were, over halfway through the month, and I hadn't even managed to produce one.

I glared balefully at the motivational banner I'd made and taped to the wall behind my MacBook.

It said, *Write! Write! Write!*

It had taken me three days to design the banner in Canva. I'd had to cycle into Oxford to buy some more ink for my old printer, some fancy paper to print it out on, and if I'd spent that time on writing, I wouldn't be in this situation in the first place.

It wasn't that the words wouldn't come. The problem was that the *right* words wouldn't come.

Because real life was boring. Or at least, not exactly story worthy.

I swung my desk chair from side to side. I picked up the biro from beside the bluetooth mechanical keyboard that I preferred to the the MacBook's keyboard, and clicked the top a few times. I drew my legs up until I was perched cross-legged on the seat, and dragged the keyboard onto my lap.

Some words were better than no words, right?

I shoved aside the nagging inner voice that was saying things like, *Jasper, don't you do it.*

And, *Jasper, I mean it. Don't you do it. You have an imagination! Use it for good. Come up with something the citizens of Chipping Fairford will find interesting, and read, and go oh, J.C. Connolly, yes. A classic of his. Very insightful.*

And, *Do not write something that will make them clutch their pearls and say, Detective Chief Inspector Liam Nash did* what? *He put what* where? *He was ruthless about it? Until J.C. Connolly begged for mercy and* cried, *but in a sexy happy way?*

I leaned forward, clicked the mouse, and my latest Liam Nash fanfic document opened.

My hands hovered over the keyboard as I scanned the last line.

"Bring him to me," the warlord boomed.

Cracking my knuckles, I glanced up at the clock at the top right of the screen. Ten minutes. I'd allow myself ten minutes, and then I would definitely get back to brainstorming. This would shake things loose.

"Bring him to me," the warlord boomed.

"Which one?" his second-in-command asked.

I was standing with the rest of the captives, the last of the defeated soldiers, those who had refused to throw down their arms and surrender.

We'd fought hard that day, for our families and our king, but the fearsome warlord Nash had swept across the land and crushed all resistance before him.

Now he sat on the throne of the deposed King Adam, who huddled in chains beside me. Nash's fierce army occupied the ancient and noble Hall of Blake.

The warlord's steely blue-grey eyes cut across the distance between us and penetrated mine.

"That one," he said with a sinister smile. "The tall one. The one who is built like a powerful warrior. Even from here and with one look I can see through his buff facade to the trembling fragile beauty he truly is deep inside. It is a beauty I would take for my own, and own it and possess it and devour it."

The second-in-command pushed King Adam forward.

"No!" The warlord barked. "That one is not a powerful warrior! And also, although many would find his leanly muscled form and fantastic hair wondrously beautiful, there is something about him that leaves me cold." Nash arose from the throne and prowled down the steps of the dais. He strode across the hall and came to a stop before me.

"This is the warrior I want." He gazed into my eyes. "This is my war prize, whom I shall take into my bed of silk and furs, and have pleasure me until the end of my days."

"This one?" the second-in-command said. "Are you sure?"

Nash shifted closer. "Of course."

"We've got some prettier ones in the back. Nearly all of them are prettier, actually."

Nash scowled over my shoulder at his doubtful-sounding minion. "I know what I want when I see it." He gripped my chin and lifted it, ensnaring my helpless gaze with his pitiless orbs. "And I take it."

"Oh no," I protested. "Please, think of my innocence! I am just a simple farm boy, conscripted by the cruel king—"

"Hey," said King Adam.

I clutched at Nash's strong wrist. "Allow me to serve you in other ways, mighty warlord."

He rubbed a thumb along my jaw. "What other ways do you suggest?"

I dropped my faltering plain brown gaze from his, but he raised my chin again and rested his palm over the front of my throat. "I want you to look at me, my beauty," he murmured, "while you tell me of all the ways in which you will serve."

Almost swooning at being called beauty, a thing I had secretly dreamed of in the long dark nights alone in my humble farmstead, I trembled like a helpless bird in his merciless grip. "I can cook a mean fry-up," I said. "Even though the cholesterol is super bad for you, and you should probably cut down on red meat. Especially if you're older and should be keeping an eye on your blood pressure."

The warlord's nostrils flared with displeasure. "Try again," he hissed evilly.

"Um. I can...brew coffee well. Chop wood all day long. And oh, sir, I will sweep your hearth and lay your fire, I will make your bed in the mornings and—"

"I have enough maidservants. Again."

There was only one more thing I could do. Shame singed my cheeks even as I whispered bravely, "I could dance for you!"

He made an interested noise.

Another secret I'd been protecting my long and lonely and under-appreciated life: I was trained in the art of sensual erotic dancing, despite being otherwise completely innocent of the ways of the flesh, untouched and saving myself for my soulmate. It wasn't weird or anything.

"Yes," the warlord said, visibly excited by the thought of me dancing for him. "You shall dance for me."

"But I shall never surrender my innocence!" I said, tossing my head.

"You will beg me to take it from you before we are done," he said with a confident laugh.

"Never!"

"Oh yes, you will."

"I loathe and despise you! You are the despoiler of the kingdom and I will never cease fighting."

"And yet you will still beg for my touch."

"I shall never betray my king or my country."

"We'll see."

"There is nothing you can do that would—oh!"

The warlord clasped me in his brawny arms and pressed his lips to mine. A strong, demanding hand cupped the manly bulge in my war breeches and rubbed knowingly. I shuddered and moaned in his grip, and—

"Really, Jasper?" King Adam broke in. "In the throne room? Gross."

He was standing right there beside me, with the other captured soldiers.

"Good point," I said.

I stopped typing and critically read over the story.

I sagged a bit. It was okay, and definitely about to get to

the good stuff, but things never quite read back the way I was expecting. When the words were flowing and I was in the zone, it was as if I was there, living every second.

When the words had stopped flowing and I read them back, I felt stupid.

It was fine. I could edit. I always edited hard, it was fine.

I glanced up at the clock. Oh, shit. Well, that took a lot longer than ten minutes.

Reluctantly, I exited the encrypted and password-protected notes app where I wrote all my sexy stories that no one but me would ever read, and opened up no-nonsense, businesslike Word.

I stared at my nemesis: the cursor.

Stop thinking about the warlord Nash and how he nearly rubbed one out of you in a crowded throne room, I told myself, and think about the *community*. Like a journalist. Like a *proper* writer.

What issues were important right now?

How did people in Chipping Fairford feel about...?

I racked my brains.

Ah! Ducks. Okay. People feeding bread to ducks. It was bad for them. I saw a woman and her kids doing that in the park yesterday during my morning run.

Was there a law against it? Should there be?

Would that make a good article? Stir up some debate?

Cut to the warlord's chamber. Crackling fire, fur blankets, me facedown and buttocks quivering, moaning as the warlord slides his—

No. *Ducks*, goddammit! Ducks, not dicks.

Why is bread bad for them? Did Chipping Fairford need a duck warden? A duck patrol? Community volunteers? Something?

"Shit," I said softly, and pushed away from the desk.

I stood up and decided to get the blood flowing. That always helped. Dropping to the floor, I did some pushups, some burpees, then rolled onto my back and worked my way through some sit-ups.

Physical stuff I could do without a problem. I was one of those insufferable people who liked feeling the burn, and being out of breath, and sweating. The kind of things my clients usually yelled at me for making them do.

Writing sensible non-fiction was a lot harder than I'd ever thought it would be when I announced to my parents that this was my *real* chosen career, since me being a personal trainer had left them unimpressed.

I ambled off to the kitchen to grab myself a cup of coffee. As I waited for the kettle to boil, I picked up my phone, and blinked when I saw the number of missed calls and voice-mail notifications.

Feeling lightheaded with panic—what? What had happened, what was wrong, was Adam okay? Were my parents? *What?*—I input the wrong code twice before I got it unlocked and went straight to the texts.

I nearly oozed to the floor with relief when a quick scan told me they were nearly all from Ralph.

And one from my dentist, reminding me about an overdue checkup. I guiltily ignored that one.

I decided to listen to the latest voicemail first. It was Ralph. "Jasper for fuck's sake you *said* you wanted a chance, and this is it, right? Get your arse over there. I want the scoop!"

What scoop?

I played the voicemail before that.

Ralph again. "Listen, a proper journo is available 24/7, not filming themselves playing computer games on TikTok or whatever the fuck you're doing. You're pissing me off. *Answer* your *fucking* phone!"

Wow. I stared at the phone. He screamed that last bit.

Clearly something big and newsworthy was going down.

My hands shook with adrenaline, both because I really didn't like being screamed at and because I was excited to finally be getting the chance to write a proper news article.

I fumbled the screen, accidentally started calling my dentist, hung up, and pulled up the first of the many voice-mails Ralph had sent. I put it on speaker as I darted out of the kitchen into the hall and dropped to the floor, yanking on my trainers.

"...first time a dead body's been found in Chipping Fairford the whole time I've been running the paper! Apart from, you know, the usual kind, people dying of old age and shit. I want you to get your arse over there, right now. This is it, Jasper. This is your chance. Get up in people's faces and don't take no for an answer. I want to know *everything*, d'you hear me? Call me as soon as you've got anything good."

Dead body? That was terrible. Who died?

"Address is number fifty-two, Sycamore Close." Ralph ended the message without saying goodbye.

I finished lacing up my trainers and snagged a hoodie from the coat pegs. I ran into the sitting room and over to my desk to grab my fancy Moleskine reporter's notebook and a pen before rushing out the house and down the drive. I pulled on the car door handle a couple of times and the alarm went off.

"Shit." I ran back up to the front door, got the keys in somehow—my hands were really shaking now—leaned in, and snagged the car keys from the hall table.

I ran back to the car, beeping off the alarm and unlocking it en route, and flung myself into the driver's seat.

"Okay, okay," I said. "Okay. Calm down. You're fine, you've got this."

I set my phone, notebook and pen on the passenger seat, and buckled myself in.

"Showtime." I giggled nervously, and backed out of the drive.

8

*S*ycamore Close was in one of the more humble, workaday areas of Chipping Fairford. You got the occasional tourist wandering through, looking vaguely disappointed by all the practical little houses on the developments that had sprung up between the 1920s and the 1950s, but not many.

I lived in a similar development on the other side of town. On any other day, Sycamore Close would look like my street. Most of the drives were empty at this time in the afternoon. Bins were neatly lined up and tucked against the house, waiting for collection day. Every now and then someone would stroll by, walking their dog or their toddler.

Today, I couldn't even turn down the street, let alone park on it.

I drove up to the junction, flipped on my indicator, and got briskly waved on by a policeman wearing a bulky high-visibility jacket. He stood squarely in the middle of the road, flanked by traffic cones, and his expression said he meant business.

I caught a brief glimpse of police cars and a couple of

vans clustered in front of a house midway down the road, then had to pay attention to my driving before I rubber-necked my way into the wrong lane.

I took the next left, parked up and grabbed my phone. While I wanted to leap out of the car and rush over to where the action was, I should probably take a moment to find out what the hell was going on. So far, all I knew was that someone had found a dead body at number fifty-two.

I also had a nagging suspicion that Sycamore Close should mean something to me.

I didn't *think* I knew anyone who lived here? I was a runner. I ran all over town, much preferring to be outside than on a treadmill. As a result, everywhere in Chipping Fairford was at least a little familiar.

It must have been that.

I listened to another two of Ralph's increasingly irate voicemails, but it wasn't until I went through his texts that the reason for my unease came clear.

Ray Underwood.

My stomach lurched when I saw his name.

Holy fucking *shit*balls, Adam was going to die.

He was going to go into a full decline.

Ray was dead?

Adam was going to mourn like—

Wait. I read more of the text. Okay. Ray wasn't dead. I slumped in my seat.

The dead body was at Ray's *house*. Ray had called it in.

Thank god. If Ray had been the body then Adam would have—

Oh, shit.

Was Ray a murderer? *Did he kill someone?*

I mean...

Adam was loyal. He'd visit Ray in prison. He'd be

faithful and wait for him to be released, and rehabilitate him and teach him the meaning of love and all about how killing is bad, but still.

He wasn't going to *like* it.

My thumb hovered over the call button. I moved it away before I followed through on my instinct to let Adam know that Ray was in trouble.

He'd find out soon enough.

And it would be more helpful if I got some actual information first. Otherwise Adam would come running, get fired from the Premier Lodge for leaving in the middle of his shift, and have to take up modelling again to finance his post-graduate studies. He'd *hated* being a model.

If ever there was a time for me to become the journalist I was born to be, it was now.

I grabbed my coat from the back, stuffed my notebook in the side pocket, and slipped my phone in my sweatpants pocket. I jogged down the road I'd parked in, turned onto the main road and kept jogging until I hit the turn into Sycamore Close and was yanked to a halt by the same policeman who'd waved me on in my car.

"Nope," he said. "Road's closed."

"I'm on the pavement, though."

"Closed. Move on."

"What if I live down here?"

"Do you live down here?"

"...yes?"

He gave me a flat stare.

"I'm pretty sure you can't stop people from walking along the pavement," I said.

"I can when there is a police operation in progress."

"Oh, is there?" I said. "Police operation? I hadn't noticed. What's going on, then?"

"Nice try, Jasper. I know you write for the paper. I read your blog piece on the bees."

"Yeah?" I brightened. It was the one and only thing Ralph had agreed to publish, and he'd only put it on the blog. Not even on the main site, let alone in the printed version of the paper. I didn't think anyone had read it. "What did you think?"

"You really like bees."

He wasn't wrong. I squinted at him, then snapped my fingers and pointed. "Mike," I said.

"Yep."

"My Wednesday Legs, Bums and Tums class."

"Yep." Mike waved on another car that was trying to turn in to the close.

"If you let me down the road, I'll let you off two sets on Wednesday."

He grinned. "No chance. Boss'll have my head."

"Ah. Yes. The detective in charge. Bit of a hard-arse, is he?"

Mike rolled his eyes, but didn't say anything.

"It's not Detective Chief Inspector Liam Nash, is it?" I said. "By any chance?"

"Yep."

"I know him!"

"My condolences," he said, then winced. "Don't quote me as saying that."

"You scratch my back—"

"I'm not letting you down there."

"Fine. But Wednesday is going to be pretty rough for you, Mike."

He shook his head at me, and waved another car on.

I trudged back the way I'd come.

There was more than one way to get to where the action was.

I leaned against my car and contemplated the houses in front of me, calculating roughly where they were in relation to where I'd seen the police cars and vans.

Hmm.

Ray's house was four, maybe five houses down from where I stood. If I were to do something sneaky like, oh, hop over someone's garden fence, cut across their lawn and down the side of their house, I'd pop out right opposite Ray's.

A risk-everything, story-hunting journalist would be halfway there by now.

Unfortunately, I was dithering somewhat at the idea of committing trespass in broad daylight and, if anyone happened to be looking when I emerged onto Sycamore Close, literally in front of the police.

My phone buzzed in my pocket, making me flinch. I pulled it out, saw Ralph's name, and grimaced as I answered.

"Hi," I said. "I'm on—"

"I don't care where you are, you're taking too long. I need something on the website within the hour. I sent Karen Strickland over there. I'll have to fucking pay her ten times as much as I'd pay you, but it's that or lose the story. It's already on Twitter and Facebook. The *Oxford Mail* will have it next. Be on fucking TikTok in a minute."

I sucked in a breath. Mrs Strickland. My fifty-something ex-English teacher, who'd retired a year after I left school, and was now my arch-rival at the *Inquirer*. "I am right here!" I said. "I'll write you something to post if you just give me a second!"

"You're too slow, Jasper. You don't have the killer instinct. You don't have the bloodlust. I need a terrier. I need a hunter. That's not you. I gave you a chance, but it's too late. She's on the job."

I clenched my jaw. "Ralph, I will get you that story. I am twenty feet away from the action."

"Yeah? So's Karen."

"She's lying. If she was here, I'd have seen her—"

I cut off as a small green VW Beetle with a pink flower decal drew up behind my car and parked an inch from my back bumper.

The door opened and Mrs Strickland got out.

"I'll call you when I've got the story," I said, and hung up. "Mrs Strickland."

"Jasper."

We glared at each other.

Okay, I glared at her as she cocked a brow at me, smirked, and strode across the road.

Goddammit. She was stealing my move.

Kind of. The house she'd chosen had a low stone wall with a small gate set in it. She let herself in though the gate, walked up to the back door, and banged on it briskly.

I didn't waste any time. I bolted over the road to the next house down and vaulted the tall, larch-lap fence.

I landed in a crouch on damp grass and straightened. The garden was mostly lawn, with tidy flowerbeds along the edges and a small patio by a French window at the back.

I ran over the lawn, down the side of the house, and came up against a tall wrought-iron gate.

I tried the handle. It was padlocked.

Well. Trespassing wasn't a hobby of mine or anything, but this wasn't my first time, either, so. Up and over it was.

Getting over the gate wasn't quite as easy as vaulting the fence, but I had the upper body strength of a Royal Marine commando. It wasn't hard.

Maybe I didn't quite have the skill of a Royal Marine commando, though.

I heard something rip as I swung over the top and my sweatpants got caught by one of the decorative knobs. My phone fell out my pocket and slammed onto the pavement.

I snagged it, stood up, and said, "Uh...hello," when I locked eyes with the woman two feet away, staring at me with mild surprise. "Oh. Hi, Mrs Hughes. You live here? I had no idea. Hi, Dougal." I crouched down and made kissy noises at the stout West Highland terrier who was standing beside her.

He stumped over and shoved his face into my waiting hands. I rubbed his ears gently. He groaned.

Mrs Hughes ran the bookshop in town. Dougal was a fixture in the shop. He was also a total fusspot. He dropped his butt to the ground and set his head on my thigh.

I glanced up at Mrs Hughes. "Bit of excitement today, hey?"

"Yes. It's not everyday a man randomly throws himself over my garden gate out of nowhere and nearly lands on my dog."

I grinned and ducked my head. "Sorry about that. Um. I meant the...you know. The whole dead body thing going on over there."

"It's all a bit unexpected, really. Poor Ray, you should have seen him."

I gave Dougal a couple more pats, and straightened. "Can I ask you—"

"Excuse me? Excuse me. Hello."

We both turned to look at Mrs Strickland.

She smiled. "I wonder if I could ask you a few questions?"

"...is *exactly* what I was about to say," I jumped in. "Maybe you could wait your turn? Because I was here first."

Mrs Strickland ignored me. "I recognise you, don't I?" she said to Mrs Hughes. "From the bookshop? I'd love to get your take on what's going on today." She smiled again, and held out her phone toward Mrs Hughes like a microphone.

I shuffled from one foot to the other, and glanced down at my own phone.

It was old and scuffed. Thanks to my gymnastics and a torn pocket, the screen was now cracked. I wasn't going to impress anyone holding it out like a microphone, like Mrs Strickland was doing. I stuffed it into the unripped pocket and brought out my notebook instead. I flipped it open, turned to a fresh page, and said loudly, "Mrs Hughes!"

A bit too loudly. She flinched.

"Sorry. Um. Can I ask you my questions first?"

"Oh, I—"

"Don't be silly, Jasper," Mrs Strickland said. "I'll ask the questions. You're welcome to stay and listen if you want."

Mrs Hughes looked from Mrs Strickland to me with a small frown.

I showily patted Dougal. *Your dog likes me! I'm so nice and not at all pushy! Talk to me first!*

"You're probably going to get a lot of people wanting to talk to you," Mrs Strickland said in a confiding tone. Mrs Hughes didn't look particularly thrilled at the idea. "Why not get it all done in one go?"

Mrs Hughes sighed and glanced between us again. "That sounds fair. What do you want to know?"

Mrs Strickland smiled, and angled herself so that Mrs Hughes had to turn away from me to face her.

Aaaand I was sidelined. With Dougal.

No problem. I could still get the story.

Mrs Strickland wanted to ask the questions? Fine by me. She'd ask better ones anyway, I didn't mind admitting it. She had way more experience. This was a great learning opportunity.

"When did you first hear about the body?" Mrs Strickland said. "Take me through it."

"Well, we'd just come back from Dougal's walk, when Ray and a couple of workmen came running out of his house like something was chasing them. The workmen got in their van and left—speeding, I might add—and Ray was standing there in his front drive, staring into space. I thought he was going to faint. I ran over, and he said there was a dead man in his house."

"Did he say whether he'd killed the man?"

"No. He called the police."

"Do you think he killed the man? Do you know him well? Is he the type to kill? Would you say he was nice, quiet, kept to himself?"

"Ray is very nice, and quiet. I don't think he's a killer."

"Hmm."

"I mean, he could be," Mrs Hughes said reluctantly. "Anyone could, really."

"Interesting. Let's circle back to that one. What happened when the police arrived?"

I scribbled furiously in my notebook, turned to a fresh page and kept scribbling. It was a barely legible mess, but it would make sense when I read it back and typed it up, I was sure.

Oh, damn. I needed my phone after all. There was no way I could put together an article, run to my car, drive home, type it all up on my MacBook, and get it over to Ralph in an hour.

I switched my notebook for my phone. It was only a little

bit cracked. Please work, I thought. I brushed the grit off it, tentatively pressed the home button, and the passcode prompt came up. Brilliant.

I opened up my notes app and the screen went black.

I jabbed the button again. Still black. I pressed and held the power button down and waited a second or two. Nothing.

Goddammit.

Okay.

Back to the notebook.

I switched again, looked up, and realised that Mrs Hughes and Mrs Strickland were nowhere to be seen.

I looked around wildly. Where the fuck were they?

I followed the low murmur of voices around to the front of the house, where the two women were deep in conversation.

My shoulders slumped. My first headline opportunity, poached before my eyes.

This was the most exciting thing to happen in Chipping Fairford since there was a big battle in the 1300s over by the water meadow, and I'd managed to screw it up.

I was pretty sure that Ray was having a worse day. But still.

I kicked glumly down the drive and stood staring at Ray's house. They'd set up crowd-control barricades at the bottom of his drive. Blue-and-white police tape was festooned around like tinsel.

The front door opened and two police officers came out, deep in conversation, briefly showing activity in the house behind them before the door closed.

It was as if the clouds had parted and the sun came out.

Liam.

I ran across the road. I'd hit the opposite pavement and

was heading for the gap between barricades when I saw another officer coming in to intercept.

Maybe putting on a burst of speed to try to get to Liam first wasn't my best move. But it had been a *day*, okay?

I collided with the police officer, who bodied me backward while shouting in my face, "Sir, I'm going to have to ask you to step back and stay behind the line!"

"What line?" I said.

She lifted her chin, hitched a thumb at herself and said, "This line."

"Oh. But I just wanted—"

"Back!"

"Oh my god, I'm not...you don't have to *scream* at me."

"Please back away."

"Right. I will, but can I just—"

"Sir? Back away."

"Yes. Any second. Quickly, though, can I have a—"

"Back up, please, sir."

"Seriously?"

"You can't come past the line."

"You've made that very clear, thank you. I am complying. I'd like a chance to—"

At this point we were nose to nose, and I was getting fed up at being yelled at by someone I was ninety percent sure was in the year below me at school.

And I think I kissed her older brother once.

"Fuck's sake," someone said. "Jones. Bring him to me."

I sucked in a breath, looked up, and my gaze clashed with Liam's.

Bring him to me.

It was like my fanfic.

I went bright red, I knew it. My cheeks throbbed.

"You want me to let him onto the crime scene, sir?"

Constable Jones said—yes, Katie Jones, definitely went to school with her—her voice going up in surprise.

Liam clenched his jaw. "No." He strode down the drive, his friend strolling after him.

Constable Jones gave me a warning glare before she stood aside to let them cross 'the line'.

"Hi!" I said breathlessly when Liam stopped in front of me.

"Why are you so red?" he said.

"No reason. It's hot. Am I red? Hello," I said to the woman beside him. She was a couple of inches shorter than Liam, had grey-streaked black hair in a long plait, and a flat stare that immediately made me want to confess to every crime I'd ever committed, even the ones in my head.

"Give me a minute, Detective Sergeant," Liam said to her. He gripped my shoulder, turned me, and walked me a few feet away. "Jasper," he said in a tight voice. "What are you doing?"

"Reporting! I'm gathering information for the article I'm writing for the paper."

"It looks like you're bothering my officers."

"I'm not bothering anyone. She started yelling at me."

"Listen," Liam said, walking me along the pavement.

"I'm listening."

"I'm in the middle of an investigation here, and I can't have you causing trouble."

"No trouble. Just questions. One or two, that's all. Um. Ray. Is he a suspect? Or?"

Liam stopped walking and stepping into my personal space. My breath caught. "Jasper," he said.

"Yes?"

"Go home."

"Yes. Questions first, though."

Liam shook his head sharply. "No. That's not how this works."

"It definitely is."

"I'm busy. You can't crash a crime scene like it's a party and start demanding answers and attention."

"Liam, that is literally what journalists are supposed to do."

"No, they're supposed to go through the proper channels. Those channels do not include bothering officers who are trying to do their jobs, or thinking that knowing the SIO gives you any kind of privilege."

"SIO?"

"Senior Investigating Officer."

I made a mental note. "I don't think I've got any privilege here." He raised a brow. "You wanted me. I mean. You called me over."

"To tell you to go home."

"Can you take me seriously for, like, a second? Please?"

He looked at me. "No."

And normally I'd ignore that, but the tone of disbelief in his voice on top of the shitshow of a day I'd had made me do something incredibly stupid.

I shoved him.

Placed my hands on his chest like I had that day in the pub, and shoved him.

Except I did it hard.

He rocked back, and his eyes widened.

They bugged.

His eyes bugged. Almost clean out of his head.

Because this wasn't the pub. This was a crime scene, he was working, and I'd just assaulted him.

"Shit," I said, and ran.

9

$\mathcal{S}$o. Quick recap of my craptastic day.

I wasn't available like a 'proper journo' for the first news story I'd ever had a chance to write, and Ralph had to pull out the big guns in the shape of my arch-rival Mrs Strickland.

I let Mrs Strickland cut me out of an interview that I was in the middle of conducting and I didn't even notice when she did it, because I was too busy fussing with the phone that I'd just broken while trespassing.

I had a legit police contact, and I failed to get even one exclusive detail out of him.

Instead of being available, rushing over there, successfully interviewing people, and getting a quote from a contact, I'd assaulted a police officer, ran from the scene of the crime, and now I was hiding in my house.

It wasn't a great hiding place. Liam knew where I lived, and I was expecting him to come and arrest me at any moment.

I sat glumly in my desk chair, staring at my computer. I'd pulled up the *Inquirer's* website, and there it was. Already.

An article, by Karen Strickland: "Scandal at Sycamore Close."

Good title.

I didn't bother reading it. Not today. Eventually, I'd print a copy, get my highlighters out, and try to break it down and learn from it.

But today?

No.

Today, I didn't have the heart for it.

I closed the browser, opened up my fanfic, and stared at the blinking cursor where I'd left off.

Right.

Warlord cupping my manly bulge.

I sighed, and poked at the return key.

Blank line.

Blank line.

Blank line.

I kept going until the words had scrolled up and the screen was empty.

There was zero chance of the warlord cupping my manly bulge.

There was, however, a very strong chance that the warlord was going to storm my citadel, wrap me in chains, and haul me off to the dungeon.

Liam was a proud man. A proud, determined, humourless man who wasn't going to take me shoving him around in front of his officers lying down.

He was going to arrest me. I was almost sure of it.

When I was fourteen, I ran wild. Or as wild as you could get, living in Chipping Fairford where there wasn't all that much to do.

Unfortunately for me, back then I'd been dazzled by the new boy at school, Evan Bennett, and when he said, "Hey,

Jas. Meet me tonight and we'll go tag some shit, yeah?" I'd said yeah.

I didn't actually know what he meant by *tag some shit*.

I did know that Evan was from Islington in North London, everyone thought he was cool because his mum worked in the music industry, and everyone in my year at school wanted to be his friend.

For some baffling reason, he'd chosen me for this adventure. I wasn't about to say no. I was the new boy last year, and thus far no one had shown any particular enthusiasm for being my friend.

I climbed out of my bedroom window just before eleven o'clock, landed hard in the flowerbed, and spent the next twenty minutes trying to zhuzh up my mum's peonies, which I'd comprehensively crushed.

When I got to the bus stop where he'd told me to meet him, I discovered that I wasn't the only one invited. It was me, Evan, and Adam Blake. I glowered at Adam. He glowered back.

We were both the weedy kids everyone picked last for football. Adam at least had a couple of inches on me and was okay-looking. Despite being fourteen, I had barely entered puberty. And I had a new bout of acne coming. I could feel it simmering on my face.

Amalie Galloway sauntered up while Adam and I were still sniping at each other. Evan was texting on his phone, bored. Looking back, I realised Evan was testing out members for his new crew.

None of us made the cut.

What happened was this: Evan led us all to the town square, stopped in front of the ugly millennium monument which was basically a tall flat slab of Cotswold stone with

A.D. 2000 chiselled on it, and pulled a couple of cans of spray paint out of his backpack.

I didn't want to do it. Adam really didn't. Amalie just rolled her eyes at Evan. And Evan, seeing that he'd culled three potential crew members, shrugged and sprayed the monument anyway.

That was when someone shouted, "Oi!"

Evan threw the can at me. I caught it and watched as Amalie hared off one way and Evan went the other.

Adam screamed at me, "Drop it, you idiot!"

Another person shouted. "*Adam?* So help me, if that's you—"

"Fuck," Adam said. "It's my loser cousin." He bolted. I ran after him.

Adam's extra couple of inches worked to his advantage. He pulled ahead. I puffed behind him, then the back of my flapping hoodie was snagged in a firm grip, and I was hauled to a halt.

I tripped over my feet and hit the ground with a thud. The police officer, Adam's loser cousin, swore like I'd never heard anyone swear before and tripped after me. He landed on top and I squeaked like a dog's chew toy.

"Fucking fuck," the officer said, lifting off and flipping me over onto my back. I gaped up at him. Hard blue-grey eyes lasered me from head to toe. "You okay?"

I opened and shut my mouth a few times.

"Hey," he said firmly. "Are you hurt?"

I shook my head.

"You're okay?"

I couldn't seem to engage my brain, so I gave him a thumbs-up.

He grunted, and pulled me to my feet.

At that point, Adam had circled back and started yelling at us.

"Let him *go*, Liam. God, you're so *embarrassing*."

"I'm not the embarrassing one, you little shit," the police officer snarled.

Liam.

I wasn't about to point it out to anyone, but out of the three of us? I was the embarrassing one.

I stared down at my jeans in wonder. I was so damn hard.

It must have happened when Liam had pulled me up. If I'd landed face first on that thing, I'd have snapped it clean off.

"Kid. Hey."

"Jasper," Adam said. Now that he'd stopped shrieking at Liam in a voice that broke as often as mine did, he sounded utterly bored.

"Hmm?" I glanced up vaguely at both of them, back down at my misbehaving dick, and back up at Liam.

Me looking at it made them look at it.

Adam snorted. Liam ignored it. He didn't flinch, there wasn't a ripple of reaction, nothing.

Which was a relief. I hated being mocked, and getting a boner in front of some random police officer who was also Adam Blake's loser cousin seemed like a surefire way of being humiliated.

I didn't even know what the hell my dick was thinking, to be honest.

Liam yelled stuff at Adam about how he should arrest him and throw him in the cells overnight, Adam talked him down to giving us both a caution, and my mum was steaming mad when she had to come and pick me up from the station.

If you wanted to be picky about it, I suppose you could argue that as it was a caution, technically Liam hadn't arrested me.

I didn't think I was going to be that lucky today.

Brand-new Constable Liam Nash catching a child holding a can of (not his) spray paint was a very different situation from Detective Chief Inspector Liam Nash getting shoved by an adult journalist on a crime scene.

God, I was an idiot.

My doorbell rang.

Shit.

I could just...not answer? It was tempting.

Tempting, yes, but there was no avoiding my fate. I stood up bravely. I straightened my shoulders, strode to the door, and snatched it open.

I stared at Liam.

He stared back at me.

He looked determined and focused.

I really wasn't getting out of it this time, was I?

Fine.

I put my wrists together and stuck my arms out in front of me, ready to be cuffed. "I'll come quietly," I said.

"I've already heard the noises you make, Jasper," Liam said. "I highly doubt that."

I cocked my head. "Are you flirting with me?" I asked cautiously.

"No," he snapped.

"Oh." I looked down at my wrists, then back up at Liam. "You can do it, you know," I said. "I won't resist."

He glared at me.

I was doing it wrong, wasn't I? "Do you want me on my knees? Hands behind my head? Or am I supposed to be facedown?"

His cheeks darkened. "For god's sake," he said, and barged in, slamming the door shut behind him.

I followed him into my sitting room. He strode into the middle of the room and turned sharply on his heel. He dug a hand in his bulky jacket pocket and pulled out a bright yellow Post-it note. He held it out, flapping it impatiently when I didn't move.

"What is that?" I said.

"What does it look like?" He came over to where I was dithering in the doorway, and slapped it against my chest.

He didn't move his hand.

I glanced down to where it rested against my washed-out old Adidas t-shirt, long fingers spread wide. My heart kicked in response, like it was trying to fling itself into his hold.

He held his hand there, flat on my sternum, for another long, simmering second, before he stepped back. The Post-it note stuck.

Hoping that he hadn't felt my pulse leap just because he touched me, I peeled the note off my chest and read the scrawl.

It was a phone number, with a name written beneath.

"That's the person who can answer some of the many, many questions I know you are dying to ask me," he said.

I beamed at him. "You came all the way to my house to give me a *source*?"

"No." He looked caught out. "It was on my way. I was driving past. It was quicker to stop by and give it to you than start up an endless back-and-forth text conversation when you'd keep asking questions anyway. And it's not a *source*. It's the number of our media officer."

I continued to beam at him. It wasn't on the way at all. I could get the media officer's number off the police website.

"Stop it," he said.

"Thank you, Liam."

He grunted.

"And I'm sorry for shoving you," I said.

He brushed my apology off with a half-shake of his head.

"Can I safely assume that you're not going to arrest me?" I said.

"For what?"

"Uh, assaulting a police officer?"

Liam rolled his lips in, suppressing a quick grin. "Is that was all the business at the door was about?" he said.

"All what business?"

He stuck his arms out, wrists together, and said breathily, "I'll come quietly."

I slapped his hands down.

Liam very slowly arched a brow.

On any other day, I'd have quailed under that look. Or got an erection. Probably both. But not after him imitating me.

"I did *not* say it like Marilyn Monroe," I said. "Of course I thought you were here to arrest me for assault. I shoved you."

"Right. This?" Liam closed the gap between us and pushed me like I'd pushed him. I swayed on the spot. "This is not assault."

"Okay. Good to know. I didn't actually think it was—" I had definitely thought it was, "—but I do know that *some* people take themselves very seriously and might have a problem with being physically dominated in front of their minions. Some people might be the vindictive type who need to arrest innocent men in an attempt to shore up their fragile egos."

Liam smiled, sharp and mean. "They are my hard-working officers, not my minions. And this?" He pushed me again. A little harder, this time. I shifted my weight and allowed my back to gently hit the wall. "This isn't 'physical domination'." He did the annoying air quote finger thing. "This is what a spoiled brat does in the playground to get attention."

"If I want your attention," I told him dismissively, "I know a much better way to get it. And I can physically dominate you any time I want." Which was almost never, as in fact I wanted the opposite. But right now? Yeah. I could do it right now. "Any time."

He laughed at me.

"Oh." I smiled sweetly. "You don't think so?"

"No, I don't. I think..."

He trailed off into silence as I took my t-shirt off. I did it sexy, too. I reached back, making sure my biceps flexed right in front of his face, caught the collar, and drew it up and over.

His eyes went from my bunched arm and dragged down my naked torso to where I ran my fingers along my waistband.

"Don't you dare," he said.

I pushed my sweatpants down.

But only an inch.

He was so busy watching, he didn't see my next move coming.

I got him in a headlock.

"Jasper!" he roared.

I shifted my grip, bent him over, and leaned down to say in his ear, "Do I have your attention, detective?"

"You're going to have my boot up your arse if you don't cut this shit out," he snarled.

"I'd rather you put something else up there," I told him. "But that sounds fun, too."

"Oh my god." He choked out a furious laugh. "Jasper."

I let him up.

He straightened. His hair was mussed, his cheeks were red, and his eyes were bright. I honestly couldn't tell if he wanted to kiss me or kill me.

"Now *that*," he said. "Counts as assaulting a police officer."

10

"*Y*eah?" I said.

He stepped into my space. "Yeah."

"You're not going to arrest me for it."

"Why is that? Do you think you're special? Do you think I'm going to give you a free pass?"

"Wouldn't be the first time," I said casually.

"That's a fucking lie," he said, poking a finger in my chest.

Wow. This was my new favourite thing. Baiting Liam. "Um, no. You tried to arrest me when we first met. Adam talked you down."

"Adam didn't, my supervising officer did. I was all for arresting you little brats. She wouldn't let me."

I narrowed my eyes at him. "I don't believe you. I think you didn't do it because you were scared of Mrs Blake."

"I am not afraid of my Aunt Ellen," he ground out.

I pulled a disbelieving face. "None of that matters anyway. You still won't arrest me."

Liam bit his lip and dragged it out slowly between his teeth. "Don't test me, Jasper."

Oh, I was going to test him. And poke him. And get him all riled up.

This was *amazing*. I'd been trying to get his attention for years.

Who knew all I had to do was take my shirt off and insult him to his face?

It wasn't the sophisticated seduction I thought a man like him would need, but pissing people off was very much within my area of expertise, and I was on a roll.

"You're a raging egomaniac, Liam Nash."

He was so close, I could feel his body heat sinking into my bare skin. "Yeah? And?"

"And there is no way you'd arrest me, because then you'd have to explain to all of your friends and colleagues at the station, and on the official record, that I got you in a headlock because you were too busy looking at my abs. These ones right here." I smoothed a hand over my stomach.

Liam looked.

If he clenched his jaw any tighter, he was going to crack his teeth.

I leaned in. "Got you again," I said softly.

He raised his gaze and our eyes locked.

Hmm.

I *may* have gone too far.

I went further. "You can touch if you want. And don't worry. I won't put you in a headlock while you're distracted."

"How about *I* put *you* in a headlock?"

I shrugged. "You can always try—"

He lunged.

"What the fuck!" he bellowed three seconds later from his position facedown on my sitting room carpet.

I sat happily astride his thick thighs, holding his hands, wrists crossed, at the small of his back.

As a police officer, Liam was trained in how to wrangle rowdy drunks on a Saturday night down at The Lion. As a fitness professional, I was trained in Muay Thai, among other disciplines.

He didn't have a chance.

He bucked a few times, trying to unseat me, and yanked at his arms. I leaned some more of my weight onto him until he subsided.

"Jasper," he said quietly, after a throbbing and rage-filled silence. "Get off me."

"Okay. But are you going to be calm when I do?"

"Now." His voice was a low, no-nonsense growl.

I rose up onto my knees and let his hands go. The instant I gave him room to move, he thrust up beneath me, knocked me over, and tried to pin me.

The air was loud with our gasps. Well, mostly his.

"What the fuck!" he said again. I had him bent over the sofa, his face in the cushions and one arm locked up and behind his back. He kicked out.

I avoided it easily. "That wasn't calm, Liam."

"Get off me," he said. "Right now."

My entire body prickled with goosebumps at his tone. Without thinking, I did as he said.

Instead of having another go at turning the tables, Liam straightened before sitting on my sofa.

I stood there, staring at him wide-eyed.

He slouched back in a relaxed sprawl and contemplated me.

I couldn't read his face at all. I wasn't great at reading peoples' faces at the best of times. With my pulse hammering, my body primed from a tussle, and Liam right there with his eyes on me, I didn't have a hope.

He opened his mouth to say something.

I panicked. Before he could speak, I whipped my sweatpants and boxers down. Just in case that something he'd been about to say was along the lines of, *Well, good talk, must be off.*

He smiled at me.

I smiled helplessly back. I was so lost for this man.

Leaning forward, he slid a hand around to the back of my thigh, and tugged me to him.

I tripped on the sweatpants bunched around my ankles. He caught me easily, steadied me, and said, "Take these off."

I did. And then I was standing there in front of him, stark bollock naked.

Again.

"That's better," he said. "Now come over here and sit on me."

I regarded him doubtfully.

I'd squash him.

In my head, I was a creature of beauty and grace, and I'd slide onto his lap in a delicate flurry of slender limbs. In reality, I wouldn't look remotely like that. My cheeks heated.

"Hey," Liam said. Both hands went to my thighs and he drew me closer. "Like this." His left hand slipped down to my knee and squeezed gently. He guided me to bend my leg and place my knee onto the sofa cushion beside his hip.

I wobbled, lurched forward, and bounced my pec off his face. "Oops. Sorry, I—hhhnn." I moaned and went limp as, instead of shoving me back for being a clumsy oaf, Liam teasingly bit my chest and sucked, hard and quick, on my nipple. I gawked at him.

He laughed up into my face. "Your eyes are ridiculous,"

he said, reaching up and tracing a thumb along my cheekbone. "So big and round. You look like surprised Pikachu."

"You...you know who Pikachu is?" I stuttered. "You know about *memes*?"

"Yes," he said dryly. "I know about the internet. Now, focus. You're supposed to be sitting on me."

I blushed again, awkwardly braced a hand beside his head, and swung my left leg up onto the sofa until I gingerly straddled his lap.

Liam stared thoughtfully at my dick, which was all but screaming for attention and approximately two inches from his face. I was rigidly up on my knees, not wanting to crush his thighs. "Sit," he said.

"I'll squash—"

"Jasper, sit."

"Oh my god, I'm not a dog and I'll squash—"

"I know you're not a dog, and you didn't worry about hurting me when you were throwing me around a few minutes ago. Now do as I say, and sit."

I shivered. "Yes, but—"

He gripped my hips and pulled me down.

I reluctantly settled, watching his face anxiously for a wince.

He shook his head once, then slipped his hands from my hips down and around to hold my butt.

I gasped and flexed.

Liam made a low sound of approval. "Like that, do you?" he said, stroking my arse in firm, slow circles.

My dick kicked. "It's okay." I went for a casual tone, and I landed somewhere between desperate and fuck-me-now.

"Reach behind you and hold onto my thighs," he said, "and then lean back a bit. I want to see you. Let me see you. Yeah. That's good."

Like this, my torso was stretched tight and laid out for his viewing pleasure. I went light-headed with excitement as he mapped the lines of my six-pack, then gripped my waist, hard, and stroked his thumbs down along the defined edges of my V-cut.

My stomach muscles twitched. He did it again, and then again. Something at the base of my spine loosened and I sagged between his hands. He hummed. One hand went around to cup my butt and the other spread flat under my navel, pressing down possessively.

My breath caught and I arched into it.

He took his hands away, and just looked at me.

I liked it at first, preening a little, but it went on and on and he didn't say anything. His eyes were hot and dark.

He *looked.*

I shifted, uncomfortable. Liam made an *ah-ah* sound. I froze.

"What do you want from me, Jasper?" he said.

That was easy.

I wanted a confession of his eternal and undying love.

An invitation—no, a *demand*—that I move in with him, at once, as we start our lives together.

A marriage proposal.

Kids, maybe? I hadn't decided yet. Definitely a dog.

A few decades of shagging each other senseless, then curling up on the sofa and watching movies. I'd really like it if he let me set him up with a workout plan, because middle age wasn't that far off for him and it payed to plan ahead.

I wanted him to want me half as much as I wanted him.

"An orgasm would be nice," I said, because while I wasn't smart like Adam, I wasn't a complete idiot, either.

He continued to look at me.

"Or two," I said. "If you've got the time."

Why did he keep looking?

I sat up, ignoring the *ah-ah* noise this time, and went to brace myself against his chest. He caught me before I could touch him. After a brief tussle, I subsided and let him hold my hands in one of his.

"What you said last time sounded fun," I tried.

He raised a brow. "You want my boot up your arse?"

"On the phone," I clarified. "What you said on the phone."

He raised the other brow.

Desperate to fill the silence, I gasped out, "Um, the bit where you said you wanted to hold me down and jerk me off. And then c-come on me."

I couldn't believe I'd actually *asked* someone to hold me down.

"That's what you want?"

"Why? I mean, it was your idea. I was going along with it. Those were your words, not mine," I said, glancing down.

"Let's do it, then—" he said, and laughed into my mouth when I lunged at him and kissed him. He held the side of my neck and said, "But, Jasper?"

"No, no," I said. "Talk later. Kiss now."

He firmed his hold and said sternly, "Jasper."

I heaved a sigh and slumped forward, pressing my forehead to the back of the sofa behind him. "What?"

"You get that this will be just the once, yes?"

"Really? The 'one time to get it out of our system' cliche?"

"No. That's bullshit. One time because I'm here, you're here, and I fucking want it. You do too."

He wasn't wrong. I glared at the sofa cushion. "Sure," I said.

"I don't want a relationship with you. That's not what this is."

My chest twisted. "Got it."

He skated a light touch all the way down my spine and back up before squeezing my nape. "Don't take it personally. I'm not looking for a serious relationship with anyone right now."

I nodded. The sting of his words faded somewhat, until he added, "Even if you were my type. Which we've already established you're not."

I pushed upright, stared at his arrogant face, then did something I knew I'd regret.

I slid off his lap and stood up.

I bent over to grab my sweatpants and shot him a glare when I heard him suck in a breath, presumably at the sight of the spectacular arse he would *not* be entering any time soon. "You know where the door is," I said over my shoulder, and walked out.

I'd made it to the foot of the stairs by the time I heard the sofa creak.

I was halfway up the stairs when I realised he wasn't, in fact, getting up and letting himself out, but following me.

I turned to face him and pointed over his shoulder. "Door's that way."

"Get up those fucking stairs."

"Uh, that's what I'm doing, thank you very much."

"Right now," he snapped.

I jumped, and took a step back.

He took a step up. "I was trying to be nice," he said.

"Well, you're shit at it."

"Oh, I know. I've heard that before."

I backed up another step.

He followed. "You're my little cousin's best friend."

"Yes?"

Liam's voice was steady and firm, like he was laying out the reasoning for a case. "You're too young for me."

"Okay, seriously? I get it, my god. You don't need to follow me—"

"We want different things."

I had no fucking clue what he wanted.

"You're clingy and there's a good chance that if we do this, you'll get too attached."

I had bad news for him. I was already about as attached as I could possibly be.

Also about as pissed off.

"And yet—" he'd made it to the step below me, "—you're going to turn around so I can watch your ridiculous fucking peach of an arse bounce while you get up those stairs, walk into your bedroom, get on your bed, and take what I'm going to give you."

My anger evaporated as I stared down into his eyes. Stern, stormy, and absolutely with no self-doubt whatsoever.

Was it...was it age? Did you grow into something like this, this arrogance and certainty?

Would I ever be this confident?

I couldn't imagine myself being like this any more than I could imagine myself waking up one morning, opening my email, and discovering that I'd won a Pulitzer Prize for journalism.

And I had a great imagination.

I whirled around and bolted up the stairs.

Liam laughed behind me, and came up at a much more sedate pace.

Still quick, though.

I flung myself onto my bed, panting into the duvet.

11

---

*A*fter a long moment, I said, "Are you standing there *looking* at me again?"

His voice was hoarse when he replied, "Of course I'm looking at you. Who wouldn't?"

"Until today?" I muttered. "You." I jerked when cool fingers wrapped around one of my ankles. He pulled, gently. It wasn't enough to move me, but it was enough to make my dick drag over the duvet.

"What was that?" he said.

"Nothing." Shut up, I told myself. Shut *up*. Now is not the time to remind him that he has a long history of ignoring you.

Liam didn't say anything. He let go of my ankle, and then he didn't do anything.

"Oh my god." I squirmed against the duvet. "What are you *doing*?" I'd have thought that he was reconsidering the whole thing and on the brink of walking out, except I *felt* his attention on me like a physical thing. I squirmed again, half in embarrassment and half in arousal.

The friction felt amazing against my dick, which was by

this point throbbingly hard. I tried not to do it, but I couldn't help it. I ground down, pushing my hips into the mattress to get some relief. I did it again, and then again, working in tiny tight circles that I pretended to myself he wouldn't notice.

"Shit," Liam whispered.

I froze.

"Oh no," he said. "Keep doing that."

"What?" I said, and spread my knees wider. I dipped my back, and thrust against the bed in a slow, thorough circle. "This?"

"Yeah."

I could do it. Lie there, spread out before him, and hump the bed until I came. It wouldn't take much. It would be almost like the fantasy I'd had the last time we kissed. With the key difference being that, in the fantasy, Liam was touching me.

I rolled over onto my back and stretched out as temptingly as I knew how.

Liam was standing in the doorway. Tall, broad-shouldered, solid. His sandy blond hair was haloed by the light on the landing behind him. He was still wearing his coat.

As I watched, he shrugged it off.

"Ooh, yes," I said with enthusiasm. "Undress for me!"

He let his coat drop, and he paused. "I don't like orders," he said.

I barely managed to suppress my snort.

The man *loved* orders.

He loved being the one *giving* orders. Luckily for Liam, I was very into him giving me orders. I could only assume he already knew that, considering the fact he'd been bossing me around for the last twenty minutes.

I smiled at him and shuffled backward to prop myself up against the pillows.

After a brief hesitation, Liam unknotted his tie, drew it through his shirt collar, and dropped it beside his coat. He unbuttoned his shirt collar, rolled up his sleeves, and came over to the bed.

I watched him hungrily as he sat on the mattress. I wriggled over and stretched out, pressing into him. Twisting at the waist, he planted a hand either side of me, and leaned down.

I leaned up eagerly for his mouth.

He drew back just before our lips touched.

"Lie down," he said.

"Okay, but you know I'm not actually a dog, though? *Sit*, Jasper. *Lie down*, Jasper."

He didn't smile. I sensed his amusement anyway.

How was he so steady? My heart was still thundering away, my breathing was loud, my voice was even louder.

I leaned up, trying to kiss him again. He held himself out of reach.

The sudden rush of uncertainty must have shown on my face. Smiling, he leaned in and whispered against my mouth, "Lie down for me."

I flopped flat to the bed.

He made a sound of approval and followed. Caging me between his arms, he hovered over me, kissing me softly.

It didn't stay soft.

He tilted his head, lifted one hand to my cheek, and held me as he pressed his tongue into my mouth. I whined at the commandingly sexual way he slid his tongue over mine. No one had ever kissed me quite like that. I involuntarily curled up at the sensation, my legs drawing in.

He kissed me and kissed me. Long, languid strokes of his tongue, dizzying and relentless. I was drowning in it, in him.

He stopped as slowly and gently as he'd started, taking the kiss down from fierce and demanding to gentle brushes of his lips over mine. He lifted away.

I panted. My lips felt hot and swollen. I licked them and gazed up at him, dazed.

His eyes burning into mine, he stretched out over me, heavy and solid.

I all but melted into the duvet beneath him.

Until I realised he was still wearing his shoes, and these were the clothes that he was wearing at a crime scene a few hours ago.

I heaved him up and off me.

Liam landed on his back with a hard whump and an astonished expression.

"I can't do this!" I said.

A complicated series of emotions rushed across his face. It settled on hard and blank. "Right," he said.

"Oh. We are definitely doing *this*—" I patted his hard dick and made him hiss, "—but your clothes have to come off. And, dude, you're still wearing your shoes."

"We are definitely *not* doing this if you call me dude ever again."

"Noted."

I scrambled down the bed, flashing him what I hoped was a great view of my butt, which he seemed to have a bit of a thing for, and straddled his shins. I got to work unlacing his shoes. He took his knots seriously. I tugged and picked at one but it wouldn't come undone.

"Jasper," he said. "Let me do it."

"I've got it." I really didn't want to give him a chance to change his mind, and I felt the sex magic of the moment draining away by the second. "Hold still. I've got it. I've—oh."

He sat up, slid his hands under my arms, and hauled me back. I was lying on top of him with my back to his front, and he'd locked his legs around me.

"I said—" he bit the side of my neck, "—let. Me. Do. It."

I shuddered in his arms. "Liam." I sounded wrecked already. "Please."

He groaned into my neck and rubbed against me. The feeling of clothes against my naked body was divine and— ew. *Ew*, no. Still crime scene clothes.

I shuddered again. Not in a sexy way this time. "Liam," I complained. "You're wearing crime scene clothes! And your shoes! On my bed!"

"Ah," he said, and shook beneath me. He rolled me off him. "I had no idea you were so fussy."

I went with the roll and landed on my stomach again. I propped myself up on my elbows to watch as he undressed. Absently, I pushed into the duvet. That felt nice. I—

He stopped unbuttoning his shirt long enough to reach down and grab my arse. He squeezed until I gasped. "None of that," he said. "Learn some patience."

"Learn some patience?" I managed to force out when the indignation faded. "Patience? *Me*?"

I had been waiting for this moment for *years*!

He'd got his shoes off, his shirt was loose, and he was unbuttoning his fly.

"I can guarantee," I said, "that I am the most patient man you've ever met in your whole damn life." I trailed off into silence when, holding my gaze, he unzipped his trousers.

I swallowed hard.

One side of his lips lifted.

He did not get his dick out.

Instead, he returned his attention to his shirt. He methodically took it off one shoulder, then the other, and then—

"Why are you doing this to me!" I moaned, pressing my forehead into the duvet and squeezing my eyes shut. "Why are you so slow? I could have stripped you naked in a quarter of the time it's taken you, Liam. Seriously, I—oh, shit."

He must have thrown the rest of his clothes off as soon as I looked away, because the mattress dipped and I felt him against me. Finally.

All of him.

"Oh," I said quietly. "Ohhhh…"

"Yeah," he said into my ear, and moved over me, settling.

For a moment we lay there together. I reached out to him with every part of my being, drinking in this moment— his heat, his weight, his heart beating into my back.

This.

This was what I wanted. For the rest of my life.

Liam slipped an arm under my chest and pushed his hand lower. His fingers bumped the head of my cock. He made a filthy sound. "You're very wet," he said.

"Can't help it," I said. "I've been turned on for hours. You're so slow." I sounded drunk.

"Maybe I like it slow."

I flexed into his touch, hoping he'd grip my dick and give me something to fuck into but he moved his hand away and braced his arms either side of me instead. My spine dipped involuntarily and I rubbed against him.

His breath shattered over the back of my neck. He kissed my shoulder and I moaned.

He shifted over me, once, twice, and then I felt his cock, thick and hard, slip between my cheeks.

I stilled. He opened his mouth and bit, light but with intention, at the very base of my neck.

Deliberately, Liam thrust against me.

I felt him catch against my hole and I threw out a hand, reaching behind to grip his thigh. "No," I said.

Liam stopped moving. "No?" he murmured, kissing my neck.

I didn't have condoms and I wasn't going to last through a conversation over whether or not he had one. The instant he put anything inside me, I'd come, and it would be over. I wasn't ready for that. I wasn't ready.

I shook my head.

"That's okay," he said. "I thought you probably wouldn't want…" He hitched his hips away. "That's okay."

He slid both arms under me, banding them around my chest and abs, and turned us so I was lying with my back to his chest again.

I gasped. "This is better without your clothes on," I said. His hot skin was pressed against mine. His cock lay against the small of my back.

"Yeah," he said. "I love the way you feel against me. Your body is insane."

"My body is my job," I told him, and whined when he finally, oh thank god, *finally*, touched my cock.

He just held it.

"*Liam.*"

"What?" he murmured against the side of my neck. His other hand swept up to cup and squeeze my pec, rubbing hard over my nipple.

I writhed against him.

"If you want it," he said, "you have to work for it."

"Um…?"

He flexed his hips, pushing me up and making my dick slide through his fist.

"Oh," I said. "Yes. I can do that."

"Yeah, you can," he said as I undulated in his arms, languidly pushing up and then relaxing, then pushing, then relaxing. "God, your arse is doing amazing things to my cock."

I let my head fall back and we moved together. He stopped playing with my pec and dragged his open hand up to lay it over my throat, fingers spreading possessively wide. My lips parted and I began to pant. Liam ran his thumb along the edge of my jaw.

If he stuck it in my mouth, game over.

"You feel so good," he said.

I felt myself unfurling at his approval.

"I wish I could see you like this," he said. "Watch you from above, see you moving for me." His hold on my tightened. "Can you imagine it?"

I imagined that from above, I looked like a giant, desperate hussy, writhing all over him. I imagined I'd die with embarrassment. I made a worried noise.

"Ever had mirror sex?" he said.

"Like...sex with a mirror? Or...no, do you mean sex in front of a mirror? Or...?"

There was a brief pause, and then he said, voice quivering with amusement, "Sex in front of a mirror."

"No."

He tightened his fingers on the upstroke and squeezed the head of my dick. "And the other one? Jasper? Have you had sex with a mirror?"

"What? No. Can you do that?"

"I suppose you can. Why not? People have sex with cars."

People did *what*? "Huh?"

"Yep." He let go of my dick and pressed it into my abs. "It's called object sexuality."

I pushed up, then gasped and stilled when the hand on my throat firmed.

"I want you to imagine it for me," he said in a low, dirty whisper.

I'd always known I'd do anything for Liam, but I hadn't seen this one coming. "Having sex with a mirror? Or a...a c-car? How would I do that, then?" Only one thing sprang to mind. "Do I...um? The exhaust pipe, right? I, like...? Get in a sort of squat and put my—"

The hand on my throat became a hand over my mouth.

"Mirror sex," he said. "I meant imagine watching, in a mirror, as I made you come for me."

Everything below my bellybutton tensed.

"Mmm. You like the sound of that," he said, moving his hand away from my mouth and resettling it over my throat. I arched into it.

"More than the sound of sex with a car." He was still pinning my dick. I shifted restlessly. "Liam."

"I want to see you," he said abruptly.

I broke from his hold, turned over, and lay on top of him. "How's that?" I said, and pecked a kiss on his surprised lips.

He pushed me flat and slid on top. "Perfect," he said. His head tilted and his gaze roamed over my face.

I was smiling like a fool, I knew. I couldn't stop it. "Hel-lo," I said.

Being Liam, of course, he didn't say hello back. He leaned down and kissed me.

I opened my mouth eagerly.

"Uh-uh," he said. "Wait for it."

Scowling, I grabbed at him, framing his face with my hands and trying to draw him down.

He caught my wrists and pushed them into the pillow either side of my head.

I felt my eyes go wide. It was a move I'd busted out a couple of times when it seemed right, but no one had ever used it on me.

I liked it so much.

I made an embarrassing sound like a purr and rolled beneath him. The crests of Liam's cheeks darkened, and his eyes turned fierce. He tightened his fingers.

I gasped, my mouth falling open.

"That's it," he said. He kissed me—a teasing flicker of his tongue, dipping in and out before I could chase it. He sucked on my bottom lip, then closed his teeth around it and pulled gently. "Shh," he said when my breathing grew rough. He pressed his lips to mine, and sank his weight into me.

I'd screwed my eyes shut against the intensity of the moment, but I didn't want to miss a second of this. I forced them open, and caught Liam watching me with an absolutely baffling look on his face.

"Liam?" I said between kisses. "What—oh."

He shifted his weight and pushed a hand down between our bodies. It felt almost cool in contrast to the heat we were generating. I had a metabolism that burned calories like a fighter jet burned fuel, but it wasn't all me; Liam was flushed, hard, and focused. His eyes were bright and his body against me thrummed with tension.

"Oh, let go, will you?" I said. "What are you holding back for? You can have me, however you want, I'm *yours*, just...*please*, Liam. Do something!"

A wicked, filthy smile curved his lips. "I'm making the

most of this," he told me. "And I don't like being rushed. You'll get it when I'm ready, and not before."

My mind reeled at his sheer arrogance while my body went pliant beneath him. I felt almost disconnected, like that one time I meditated too hard and thought I was about to astrally project. I lay there, buzzing with arousal, watching his face dreamily.

Liam took hold of my cock and stroked me slowly with a firm, no-nonsense touch. I rocked up into his grip.

"Beautiful," he said, and did it again, and again.

"Liam," I managed to say.

"What, sweetheart? What do you need?"

He was distracted, his hand working me steadily, his eyes locked on my cock as it pushed through his fist, appearing and disappearing. My abs were rhythmically tightening and releasing as I isolated the muscles, curling up and down, up and down.

He called me *sweetheart*. I threw an arm over my eyes and moaned. "Liam, please let me touch you."

"Touch me, then."

I went straight for his arse. He released my cock, arranged us to his liking, and began to move over me.

I gasped and dug my heels into the bed at the feel of his cock dragging alongside mine. I couldn't stop making noise. Whines and gasps. Broken, shattered words that didn't even make sense. I stared up into his eyes and completely lost it.

"Ohhhh. Uh. Uh. Ahhh. Oh, fuck. Liam. Liam. F-f-fuck..."

Liam shook against me. He was laughing, bright and honest, and loud. "Jasper," he said, and I beamed at the fondness I heard there. "My god, you could ruin me."

I could ruin him? What? I released his delicious arse and ran my hands up his back, relishing the feel of his muscles working to bring us both pleasure. I moved them up, stroking over the breadth of his shoulders, to hold the sides of his neck. "I'm...I'm..."

"Yeah?" He bit none-too gently at my mouth, then licked over my stinging lip. "You going to come?"

I nodded frantically.

He did not speed up, like a normal man would. Oh no. Not Liam. Instead, he slowed down. He lifted some of his weight away and I moaned in disappointment, reaching for him. He kissed me and said, "Shh. Be good. I'll give it to you."

He changed the angle of his thrusts, increasing the power as he drove against me, watching my face.

I choked and arched when his cock caught against mine in a way that showered a prickling cascade of sparks over my entire body, from my scalp to my toes.

Liam bent down, rested his lips against mine—not a kiss —and said roughly, "Come on, Jasper. Do it. Come for me."

Every muscle in my body tightened brutally before releasing, and I was gone.

I heard myself crying out, I felt myself shaking. I saw Liam's almost startled face in painful detail before he wrapped me up in his arms and held me, held me, held me as I came apart.

12

I sprawled on Liam's chest, clinging hard because the tension was already beginning to return to his body, when the faint buzzing sound that I'd thought was my ears still ringing from all the noise I'd made, revealed itself to be his phone.

He disentangled himself, swung his legs over the side of the bed, and sat there.

The phone cut out. It started again. Liam sighed.

I pushed up to my elbows. Tentatively, I laid a hand on his back, between his shoulder blades. I squeaked when he twisted sharply, pushed me down, and kissed me hard.

"Oh," I said when he pulled back. "Oh? Are we—mmm."

He cupped my face and kissed me again.

By the time I'd regained my wits, he'd left the bed, snagged his trousers from the bedroom floor, hauled them up over his bare arse, and was shrugging on his undershirt.

"You can stay," I said. "Please stay. We can—"

"No. I have to go." He sat down to pull on his socks. His phone started buzzing again. He tipped his head in the direction of his coat, which still lay in the doorway where he'd dropped it. "That's work."

"How do you—"

"Jasper. Of course it's work. If it isn't, it will be soon enough. My shift might have ended, but this Underwood case is a big deal. I only stopped by on the way to the station."

It wasn't on the way! I wanted to shout. *You came here for me. Specifically for me.*

Liam stamped into his shoes, slung his shirt on over his undershirt, and pulled his coat on top.

He patted his pockets once, looked over at me, and nodded. He strode out the door.

I sat there on the rumpled bed, my mouth hanging open.

He...*nodded*?

That was his idea of goodbye?

To the man he just *came* on?

A nod? Was he serious?

What the *actual* fu—

Liam stalked back in and over to the bed. He slid a hand around the side of my neck and up to grip my hair. He dragged my head back, and kissed me.

And that absolute bastard had to do it softly. His grip was unyielding. His lips were gentle as he stroked over my trembling mouth.

I was still reaching for him when he let go and walked out again.

He didn't come back.

I managed to control myself and wait at least an hour before I texted him. While I wanted to text something along the lines of, *Will you marry me?* I settled for, *That was fun! Let's hang out some time!!!*

It was low-key. Friendly. It wasn't even sexual, unless he wanted it to be.

I didn't want to come across as too desperate. An hour was chill, wasn't it?

If I was chill, Liam was subzero.

He didn't return my text that night.

I turned my phone volume up, carefully checked to make sure that notifications were enabled so I didn't miss his reply, and fell asleep waiting.

As soon as I woke up the next morning, I fumbled at my phone screen. Nope. Still no text.

It was fine, I told myself as I dragged my exhausted butt out of bed.

Liam was a busy man on the best of days. Considering the drama of his new case, it was perfectly reasonable that he hadn't acknowledged my text quite yet.

My first class at the gym was at eleven. After I'd been for my morning jog—a quick ten kilometres to get the blood pumping—I showered, hopped in my car, and drove to The Chipped Cup.

"Morning, Jas," Amalie said from behind the counter. Shouted, really. She was steaming milk for the customer ahead of me, and the giant steampunk-looking machine that I'm not allowed to touch because of that *one time* the knob fell off when I was having a go, made a hell of a noise.

I'd timed my visit to land after the morning crush as people snagged a coffee on the way to work, and before the busy mid-morning period when retirees, parents, and work-from-homers came in.

The Chipped Cup wasn't the only place in Chipping Fairford to get a coffee, but it was the best.

"What can I get you?" Amalie yelled, still steaming milk. "The usual?"

"Yes, please. To go, though. And can I have a black Americano as well?"

"Yup." She brought a cappuccino over and popped a plastic lid on the takeaway cup. She handed it to the woman at the counter, waiting impatiently with a wary eye on the bus stop outside. The bus rolled into view and the customer bolted, clutching her huge drink. I assumed she'd paid already, as Amalie didn't give chase.

While Amalie made the coffees, I inspected the pastry case. I was willing to bet that Liam had a sweet tooth.

I glanced up, and Amalie had her eyebrows raised, watching me.

"Treat day already is it?" she said. "Want a cookie?"

"Doughnuts, please," I said. "A box. Wait. Are they any good?"

Amalie's eyes widened as she set the drinks on the counter. "Excuse me? Are they any *good*?"

"Yes? I mean, which would you say are the best? Yours? Or Krispy Kreme's?"

Did I have time to zip over to the local Tesco? I knew they had a Krispy Kreme cabinet there.

"Oh, Krispy Kreme," she said.

"Huh."

"No, Jas. Mine are the best. *Mine* are. If I even *hear* about you eating Krispy Kremes, I'm going to come over to your house, and—"

I held my hands up, laughing. "Woah. Sorry. They're not for me, I've never eaten a Krispy Kreme in my life and I'm not about to start. These are a present."

"What kind of present?" she asked. "Do you want a birthday candle? We sell little single ones for cupcakes."

"It's not a birthday present. It's a...sort of. Uh. It's a Happy Wednesday present."

"That's sweet," Amalie said. "Except you know it's Tuesday, right?"

I waved a hand. "Can I have some or not?"

"Okay. Well, doughnuts are a great choice for any and all occasions. Tell your friends and colleagues. Now, which ones do you want?"

I looked at her blankly.

She took pity on me and listed them out. "Maple bar, Boston creme, good old-fashioned jam doughnut, glazed ring?"

"...jam?"

"All jam? A dozen jam doughnuts?"

No, that would kill him. I could definitely see Liam ploughing his way through all twelve. "Do you do smaller boxes?"

She bent down, slid out a flat and folded white bakery box from under the counter, and popped it up with practiced ease. She set it down. "I'm going to give you a three-pack. Let's go with one jam, one glazed ring, and a Boston creme. That's covering your bases." She efficiently loaded up the box and put it alongside the drinks. "Who's it for?"

"Adam," I lied.

She snorted. "Adam's even worse than you are with that whole body-is-my-temple shit. Don't tell me, I don't care." She held out the card reader, and I tapped it.

"Thanks, Ames," I said, and headed out.

"Hope your mystery man likes them," she called after me.

I shot her a grin as I shouldered the door open. *Me too.*

～

THE POLICE CORDON AT THE TOP OF SYCAMORE CLOSE HAD already been removed. Probably because the residents would only put up with being told they couldn't park in their own damn driveways for so long.

I turned at the junction and decided to pull over at the top of the street and walk the rest of the way to Ray's. I parked, got out of the car, and zipped up my hoodie. It wasn't raining, for what felt like the first time since Christmas, but it was cold enough that my breath plumed in front of me.

I grabbed the doughnuts and the two-cup tray of coffee and headed down the road. I was going to stay on the opposite side until I got a good look at the constables. I didn't fancy being screamed at by Katie Jones for being too close again. Once was enough.

As I approached, I saw that there was still a visible police presence outside Ray's house. The barricades and tape were still up, and a couple of bored-looking constables lurked in Ray's drive. Lights blazed in all Ray's windows, bright and hard against the dull morning.

I wondered if Ray had spent the night there? No, they wouldn't let him, surely? I shuddered at the thought. No way would I be able to sleep in a house where there had been a dead body not hours ago. I'd have gone over to Adam's. Did Ray—

I stopped dead.

Oh, shit. Adam.

I'd forgotten to give him a heads-up about Ray.

Well, he knew by now. I hadn't told him, but someone else would have. The staff at the Premier Lodge were even worse gossips than people at the gym.

The sound of voices prompted me to resume my approach. Ray's front door was open, and Liam came out with a couple of crime scene technicians in white jumpsuits, carrying...crime-scene looking stuff. Large toolbox-looking things. Tripods. Camera bags.

My stomach tightened at Liam's familiar gruff tone and I picked up the pace in case he went back inside before I caught his eye.

The crime scene techs wandered down the drive and got into one of the five cars parked at the side of the road. Liam turned to go back inside, but before he got any further, he went still then glanced over his shoulder straight at me.

I remembered in time that I had both hands full and instead of waving, I yelled cheerfully. "Hi!"

Liam strode down Ray's drive and ducked under the tape.

He shook his head at me when I started to cross the road. I stopped obediently and waited as he stalked over to where I stood in front of Mrs Hughes' house.

"Morning," I said.

"Jasper."

"I brought you a treat," I said.

He spoke over me, "Jasper, this better not be what I think it is."

I hesitated as I tried to read his expression. It was a tough one. He looked annoyed and frustrated (so far, so Liam) but there was something else there that made my stomach tighten again.

Not with arousal. This was more like dread.

"If you're worried that I brought you a camomile tea," I said, "then worry no more. You like your coffee black. I remembered."

He stared at me.

I lifted and lowered the bakery box. His eyes didn't even flicker. "And these are doughnuts."

"If you remember me saying that's how I like my coffee, do you remember me saying that I didn't want to go on a coffee date?"

"This looks like a date to you?" I smiled.

"This looks like last night's hook-up tracking me down at my place of work—"

"Oh my god," I said. "Last night's hook-up?" My voice went up and Liam winced. "Hook-up, Liam?"

"I told you it was a one-time thing."

Hook-up? I mouthed silently.

His cheeks tinted pink and he firmed his jaw. "What else would you call it? No-strings sex, no expectations of a relationship. One and done."

"Wow."

He scowled. "I'm not trying to be an arsehole here."

"I can't imagine what you'd do if you were trying," I said. "Wait for a car to come by and push me into traffic, maybe?"

He heaved an exasperated sigh and scrubbed a hand over the back of his neck. "I knew I shouldn't have given in. I knew you'd start thinking—"

"Wait, wait."

"What?" he snapped.

"Given in?"

"Yeah?"

"You gave in?" I said.

"Yeah."

"To me."

He raised his brows. "Yeah."

"Okay, but do you remember how you were the one who sought me out?"

"What? I did not, you're making—"

"No, no," I said. "I'm not making anything up. You came

to me, Liam. Twice." I glared at him. "Deny it. Go on. To my face."

"I came to your house twice, yes. I wouldn't get dramatic about it and say I sought you out."

"You did, though. I didn't invite you over. The first time, there I was, minding my own business, hanging out in a towel. You rang the doorbell, stuck your tongue down my throat, and ripped the towel off me."

He shifted closer. "*You* ripped it off."

"Maybe I was hot, did you think of that? It's irrelevant, since you were already kissing me. You had me up against the door!"

"Jasper—"

"And the second time—"

"The second time, when I came over as a professional courtesy and you randomly took your t-shirt off?"

"I was hot! Again! I have a fast metabolism! You were the one who got all up in my business."

"You got me in a headlock."

"You made me sit on you."

His shoulders heaved with a short laugh and he smiled. It didn't last long. "Jasper," he said kindly. "I told you it was a one-time deal. You agreed."

"I did agree, yes. Thing is, what I was agreeing to being a one-time deal was the sex. I didn't realise you meant having a conversation and being friendly was also a one-time deal."

"I did mean the sex," he said.

"All right, then." I thrust the doughnuts and coffee at him.

"You know you look like you're bribing me?" Liam said.

"For what?"

"For information. You're a journalist, aren't you?"

"Hah." I wished. Most of the time. "This is me being

nice. Don't you have nice people in your life who do things like bring you hot coffee on a cold morning? I'm being friendly. This is what friends do."

"Except we're not friends." My face must have done something weird, because Liam softened his tone. "You're Adam's friend. I've only ever known you as Adam's friend. What you and I are is...we're acquaintances."

I could *not* formulate a response. I couldn't.

He went on, "Can you honestly tell me that being friendly—being friends—is all you want from me? Because if so, I'll say yes. In a heartbeat. If not, the answer is no. Believe it or not, I don't want to be a dick, Jasper."

"I've got bad news for you on that front. You are a dick."

"I don't want to lead you on. It's not fair."

"Then maybe next time you see me, don't kiss me? Because saying, *No thanks, not interested* one minute, and then the next minute humping me into my mattress until I cry sends a really mixed message."

"I won't kiss you again."

I narrowed my eyes at his confidence. "We'll see."

"I won't. My reasons for not wanting to start anything with you are good reasons, and they stand."

I thought about his attention on me last night, his focus. About the way his hard hands were gentle as he ran them over me, mapping my body thoroughly and possessively. Almost adoringly. I blushed at the thought, but...it fit. He was *gentle* with me. Like I was precious. I thought about his kisses, about how they went from teasing and carnal to soft and thorough.

"Even after last night?" I said, sounding lost.

"Yes."

I swallowed hard. "Okay. I suppose you can't make it any clearer than that."

He regarded me in silence.

"Happy Wednesday," I said, and thrust the coffee and box of doughnuts against his chest.

He took hold of them reflexively. "It's Tuesday."

"Happy Tuesday," I muttered, and walked off.

"Jasper!" Liam called after me.

I turned around.

"Thanks."

"You're welcome."

"And for the doughnuts and coffee."

It took me a moment to work out his meaning. I tried to smile but couldn't quite manage to scrape one up. I lifted a hand, and walked away.

I felt his eyes on me the whole time.

*a*dam strode up and down my kitchen. "Jasper," he said, "it was amazing. I always knew it would be good between Ray and me, but holy shit. Holy *shit*." He stopped and whirled around, an expectant look on his face.

"Wow," I said.

"More than wow," he told me, and resumed pacing. "Way more than wow. I've had a lot of sex, but that?" He stopped again, this time on the opposite side of the kitchen table from where I was slumped. He flattened both hands on the table, leaning into them to say with intensity, "All we did was kiss and grind a bit, and that was the best I've ever had. Ever." He straightened up. "In my life."

"Sounds amazing," I said. It came out flat. I tried again. "I'm so happy for you!" Nope, still pretty unconvincing. "Yay!" For fuck's sake.

Adam was so wrapped up in rhapsodising about Ray that he didn't notice my pitiful attempts at celebrating the upward trajectory of his love life.

It was (definitely) Wednesday morning, and he'd been waiting for me when I came back from my daily run.

I'd woken up and glared at my ceiling for a full five minutes before I rolled out of bed and sullenly dragged on my waterproof running kit. It was still dark and I didn't even have to check outside to know it was raining—it was clattering hard against the window.

I stretched in the hall to warm up, let myself out of the house, and set off at a steady pace. It was a slog.

My morning runs usually helped me set the mood for the day. I'd look around, listen to the birds, watch the sun come up, say hello to any early dog-walkers. Even if it was raining, I didn't usually mind.

Today, I minded.

Today, my mood was already set and had been from the moment I opened my eyes.

My mood was shite.

I gritted my teeth and forced myself on through dark and miserable streets, rain lashing my face even though I'd pulled my hood up and cinched it so tight all you could see was my nose.

Liam had hurt me. The worst part of it was, I'd set myself up for it.

What had I thought, seriously? Taking him coffee and doughnuts like a fool. He'd probably laughed at me when I slunk off.

No, he wouldn't have.

He'd have chalked it up to one more incident of Jasper making a prat out of himself, forgotten all about it, and gone on with his day.

At the time, I hadn't thought it was anything other than a friendly gesture. I was still riding high after our connection. The endorphins were still cascading through my body.

With a little distance, I felt like an idiot. I had no excuse.

He'd *told* me one time, I'd agreed to it, and then not twelve hours later, I'd grabbed for more.

I was a hopeless, foolish man even more in love with the arsehole who was quite happy to hit it and quit it, and there wasn't anything I could do about it.

When I finished my miserable run and got back to the house, I smelled coffee and heard the whizz of my Nutribullet. Since only my parents and Adam had a key, and my parents had never once dropped by unannounced, it was safe to assume it was Adam.

I kicked off my wet trainers, slung my dripping anorak on a coat peg by the front door, and squelched in wet socks and running leggings into the kitchen.

Ten minutes later, I was still sitting there in my wet clothes, every now and then sipping at the protein shake Adam had made me, while Adam continued to relive the magical kiss he'd shared with Ray Underwood.

It was hard not to compare it to my magical kiss with Liam.

For me it, had been magical.

For Liam, it was a *hook-up*.

"Jasper?"

"Hmm? Oh. Right. Yay! You two were meant to be! I'm so happy for you! At long last, true love wins!" I raised my fists in the air.

Adam's eyebrows slowly rose. "Thanks. But I stopped talking about Ray and how he shut me down after the kiss about five minutes ago. I asked if you were going to the gym today."

"Oh. Yeah. I've got a couple of classes later this afternoon. No clients. I'll probably go in after lunch."

Adam surveyed me. "You okay?" The eyebrows lowered,

and he sent a pointed look at my barely touched protein shake.

I grabbed it and downed it. "I'm great," I said, and burped. "That's the stuff."

He narrowed his eyes. "Are you going to tell me what happened?"

I froze.

"I know something happened," he said.

"I should go and get out of these wet things." I pushed up. "I'd hate to catch a cold."

"Okay," he said mildly. "And then you can come back here and tell me what's going on with you."

"I'll tell you right now and you can be on your way. Nothing! Everything's wonderful."

Adam's eyes narrowed further.

Adam is tall and perfectly proportioned, with red-gold hair and the kind of hazel eyes that look like dark gold. Liam is also tall, but he's rugged, his hair is a sandy blond, and his eyes are blue-grey. There isn't really a family resemblance, other than their shared gingery-ness, and the way they can stare at you until you have to look away. Or explode. Or, possibly, come in your underwear.

I did my best to return his gaze with a nonchalant, nothing-to-see-here kind of smile. After five seconds of throbbing silence, I huffed and glanced down.

"I'm gonna go and shower," I said.

"Yep. You go shower. Don't bother trying to come up with a big fat lie or anything while you're in there, either. I'll get the truth out of you if I have to pin you down and twist your nips until you cave."

I cupped my pecs protectively. I was *sensitive* there and he *knew* it. "I'll slap you in the balls if you try."

He grinned at me. "Can't slap me in the balls when you're too busy squealing about your tits."

I glared. "You'd have to pin me first, and if Liam can't manage it unless I *let* him, then you don't have a chance."

Oh, shit.

"Liam, huh?" Adam sounded grimly unsurprised.

"Gotta go," I said, and ran for the shower.

IT WAS TOO MUCH TO HOPE THAT ADAM WOULD BE GONE WHEN I came back downstairs. I did linger in the shower, just in case. I also tried to come up with a lie, but it was hard to be creative with a broken heart.

I soaped myself up, rinsed myself off, washed my hair, and decided to fuck the lotion. Who needed touchably soft skin? Not me. I dragged on my comfiest fleece-lined sweatpants and thermal long sleeve t-shirt, and schlepped my way downstairs.

"Oh," I said. "You're still here. Great."

Adam was sitting at the kitchen table. He'd pushed the chair back, had his legs stretched out, and was scrolling on his phone.

"Aren't you supposed to be at work?" I said.

He was wearing his uniform. Purple trousers, a white shirt, and a purple tie. A purple blazer was slung over the back of his chair. I don't know how the staff at the Premier Lodge were supposed to take themselves seriously when management made them dress like pimps from the '70s.

"Later," he said, still scrolling. "The good news is, since you don't have to be at work until this afternoon, we can hang out and have a lovely long chat."

"Cool," I said. "Except I don't want to."

"Yes, you do. I unloaded about Ray driving me nuts. It's your turn. Tell me all about it. You'll feel better."

Okay, he wasn't wrong. I did want to tell him all about it. I just couldn't.

"Jasper, you know there is no chance in hell I'm leaving while all this is happening." He sketched a graceful circle in the air. I assumed he was referring to my face.

I tried to smile.

"Stop that," Adam said in alarm.

Fine. I let my face crumple. And then I let my body crumple, all the way into a chair, and then I folded over and laid my face on the table. I sighed.

"I know you're upset about Liam," Adam said gently.

I heaved another sigh. "I'll get over it." I'd never get over it.

"What did he do to you?"

Made me see God and all his angels. "Nothing."

"Mm-hmm." Adam leaned over, cupped my cheeks, and lifted until my chin was propped on the table. I stared up at him. "You know he's a dick," Adam said.

"Runs in the family."

He grinned. "What did he do?"

I wanted to tell Adam. I really did. But I refused to out Liam just to make myself feel better. I had to tell Adam something, though, or he wouldn't leave it alone. "Eh," I said. "We had a professional disagreement."

"What?" Adam seemed oddly surprised.

"I might have sort of, uh. Assaulted him. At Ray's."

Adam blinked.

I told him the sad story of my failed journalistic career. Highlights only: screamed at by Ralph, trespassed and nearly landed on a dog, got scooped, screamed at by Constable Jones, assaulted a police officer, ran away.

"Huh," he said. "That's what this is about?"

"Yeah."

"You're upset because Mrs Strickland scooped you, and you shoved Liam?"

"Pretty much?"

"Oh. Well. That's a relief."

"It is?"

"Yeah. I thought it was because you and Liam hooked up, and instead of being thrilled that a great guy like you would lower his standards enough to let Liam anywhere near him, Liam went right back to being an idiot."

I dragged my horrified gaze slowly up to Adam's knowing face. "What?" I said faintly.

Adam picked up his phone and turned it to me. A text conversation was visible on the screen.

ADAM

What did you do to Jasper, dickface?

LIAM

Nothing. Don't waste my time.

Why?

What's wrong with him?

Did he say something?

Is he okay?

I moaned. "He's going to think I told you!"

"Told me what, exactly? That you hooked up? Or that he's bi?"

"*You know he's bi?*"

"Okay, this is the part where you don't get mad at me."

I sat up. "Is it? Because it sounds like this is actually the part where I do get mad at you. You *know* Liam's into guys?"

"Yeah, kinda."

"Since when?" I demanded.

"Since I walked in on him getting a blowjob from one of his rugby mates when I was sixteen." Adam shuddered. "Gross."

"Why didn't you tell me!"

"Same reason you haven't told me. Liam's sexuality is Liam's business. Also, he's my cousin. Which brings us right back to *gross*. Besides, I didn't want you to obsess about him any more than you did back then."

I hunched in on myself. I really had been obsessed. I'd had no sense of self-preservation. Or subtlety. Every time I ran into Liam, I'd get tongue-tied. Fall over stuff. Blush. Say something inappropriate.

Not much had changed, now I came to think of it.

For all my fascination with Liam, I hadn't thought about him sexually until I was seventeen.

That was when I started trying to flirt with him. Even thinking he was straight didn't stop me. It didn't go great. By then Liam was a twenty-seven-year-old police officer climbing the ranks, with a posh-girl fiancee.

"At least I wasn't obsessed with One Direction," I said.

Adam wrinkled his pretty nose. "I wasn't obsessed," he said.

"So obsessed. You wrote out all the lyrics to their songs. By hand. In a special notebook."

"I did *not*."

"What else did Liam say? Give me your phone. Did he tell you we hooked up?" I was starting to hate that word. "Or...did he phrase it differently?"

Adam let me snag his phone and scroll through the rest of the conversation.

ADAM

No, he's not okay. I know it's your fault
because you're the only thing in the world
that makes him this sad.

LIAM

What's wrong with him?

ADAM

I'm in his kitchen right now and he's not
drinking his protein shake. He eats every
two hours. He's like a lumberjack. He's an
eating machine. He's just staring at it and
it's freaking me out.

Adam had attached a photo of me from half an hour ago.
I looked faintly green under the bright kitchen lights. I had
dark circles under my eyes. My shoulders were slumped,
and I was gazing off into space.

"Thanks, Adam," I said. "Like he didn't already know I
was pathetic, he needed a visual?"

LIAM

Is this a joke?

ADAM

No. I take Jasper's happiness very seriously.
Don't fuck around with him.

It wasn't planned. It happened, we're both
adults, and I made sure he knew what it was
going in, okay?

YOU SLEPT WITH HIM OH MY GOD WHAT
THE FUCK LIAM THAT WAS A FIGURE OF
SPEECH!!!

There were a few more messages from Adam, but Liam
had left them all on read.

"Tell me the truth, now," Adam said seriously, taking his

phone back. "Do I need to go over there and kick his arse? Because I will."

I couldn't help laughing. "I'd pay to see that, you know?"

Adam wouldn't actually try to hurt Liam, but watching the pair of them try to tussle for top spot while not pissing off their mums by damaging each other would be comedy gold.

"Yeah?" Adam stood up. "No need to pay. It's on the house. Come on. Let's go."

"Sit down," I said, trailing off into giggles. "I appreciate the offer, Adam. But you can't make him want me back."

"Uh, I don't think I need to? He clearly does."

My smile twisted. "Nah," I said. "I'm not his type."

Adam stared at me, then said, "Pfft. You are exactly his type. Why do you think he's such an arsehole around you?"

"Because he wants me so much, is it?"

Adam bugged his eyes out at me.

"I know I'm not his type. He told me to my face."

"He lied," Adam bounced back.

"He said he didn't want a relationship." I held up a finger. "And I was too young." Another finger. "And I wasn't his type."

"He's as bad as Ray." Adam's lips tightened. "I thought men in their thirties were supposed to have their shit together. After all that sweet-talking, you still let him near you?"

I flashed back to Liam holding me, whispering into my ear as I writhed on top of him. "Yeah," I said. I added miserably, "I'd do it again, given a chance."

"No, you won't."

"Pretty sure I wouldn't be able to stop myself if the opportunity came up."

"*I'll* stop you. I'll buy you a chastity device. I know a

great online store. I'll lock you in it, and I'll keep hold of the key. The next time Liam tries anything, he'll have to come through me. Unless he gets on fucking bended knee and asks nicely, then he's not getting his hands on you."

"Sometimes, I wonder if you know how incredibly domineering you are," I mused. "I really don't think most people announce they're going to lock their best friends in a chastity device. I just don't."

"Of course I know. You let me get away with it all the time."

"Not this time. I'll pass on the chastity device, thanks. It's not necessary, anyway. What we had was a one-time thing. He made it clear." I blew out a hard breath, and stood up. "I'm going to go for a run."

"You've already been."

"A proper one. I've got to shake off this mood. There's no point sulking. Nothing's really changed, after all, has it?" I smiled brightly. "Liam Nash doesn't want me. I'll live."

14

"*I* *have bad news,*" *Commander Liam Nash of the Milky Way Alliance Space Fleet announced through the ship-wide audio system.*

The mess hall of the battlecruiser was packed with Space Marines from all over the galaxy. We had been fighting the giant alien bugs from Andromeda for a hundred years, and were down to a handful of ships.

Earth and her galactic allies were close to being snuffed out for good.

Everyone in the mess hall stopped eating to listen to the broadcast.

"The latest firefight with the Bugs crippled critical life support systems," Nash continued. "We are venting oxygen."

"That can't be good," I whispered to Captain Adam Blake. He shushed me.

"As it stands," Commander Nash went on in his lovely, and yet hard and uncaring voice, "we have just enough to make it to Venus. Once there, we will dock for repairs and everyone will get a month of shore leave."

I smiled at Captain Blake.

"*Unfortunately,*" Nash said, "*not all of us are going to make it.*"

My smile faded.

"*There isn't enough oxygen to sustain all hands for the duration of the trip. Some of you will have to be left behind.*"

I frowned at Blake. "We're in space. How can we be left behind? There's nowhere to leave us."

"*The only fair thing,*" Nash said briskly, "*is to hold a lottery.*"

"*Wonder what the prize is?" I said to Blake.*

Two hours later, I stood alone on the cold metal deck of the cargo hold. My send-off party was on the safe side of the viewing window.

It was a good turnout, at least. All the officers were there, with Commander Nash front and centre. They all wore ceremonial dress uniform.

"*I just think you need to consider the fact that I'm very good at holding my breath," I said. "I couldn't hold it all the way to Venus, obviously, but I could breathe really shallowly.*"

"*A big strapping man like you takes up too many resources,*" Commander Nash said. "*My engineers have run the numbers. You are too tall and muscly. If you were a slender and pretty twink like Private Ray Underwood, who was exempt from the lottery because of being slender, pretty, and important for general and non-specific reasons, then your name wouldn't have come up as viable. But you're not. So. Here we are.*"

"*Okay, but don't you think it's worth checking the maths again? Can't hurt, can it? Because it seems ever so slightly unbelievable that I'm the problem here, and that taking me out of the equation is going to save the entire battlecruiser, the galaxy, and the human race? You did say some of us weren't going to make it. Not, you know. Just one of us. Just me.*"

"*And yet this is the situation in which we find ourselves,*" Nash said. "*Computer simulations, my engineers, and I have all decided that you are expendable. Do you have any final words?"*

"Oh my god, please don't push the button?"

"Humanity thanks you for your sacrifice," Nash said. "Your name will go down in history. Bon voyage."

The officers all saluted.

Nash hit the button, venting me out of the airlock and into space.

I took a sip of coffee, and spat it back out. Ugh. It was cold. I touched the other two mugs on my cluttered desk. One of them was still warm. I gave it an experimental swig.

Lukewarm, but drinkable. I sipped it absently as I read over my latest story.

It had started out great.

I was an eager new space recruit, making a name for myself in skirmishes with the evil aliens. I was doing so well that Captain Blake had nominated me for an award.

Summoned to the Commander's cabin for a medal and *lots* of praise, I was flustered and yet thrilled when it was revealed that the Commander was *the very same man* I had surrendered my virginity to on a space station the night before I reported for duty on the battlecruiser *Fairford*.

So far, so sexy.

And then...what the fuck?

I was supposed to be setting up the scene where Liam confessed that he'd never been the same since he claimed my trembling and nubile body that night. He couldn't stop thinking about me, he was hard from dawn to dusk, and as soon as he'd lead the Milky Way Alliance to victory over the Bugs, we would marry and explore the universe together.

But instead, he vented me into space?

I closed the file and dragged it straight into the MacBook's little trash basket.

I pushed back from my desk, gathered up the clutter of coffee mugs, and wandered to the kitchen.

Standing at the sink, I drank two large glasses of water, one after the other. I ate a banana and a handful of nuts, and marched back to the computer.

Enough messing around.

No more Liam Nash fanfic. It was time to get serious.

Mrs Strickland had scooped me and got her breaking-news article published on the website, but you know what?

She could go ahead and keep her breaking news. I was going to write a long investigative article.

If I did a good enough job, I bet I could talk Ralph into printing it. My journalistic career would be out of the gate, and running.

I knew exactly where to start.

Ray worked as an independent graphic designer and he was bound to have a website with contact details for potential clients. I did a quick Google search, found a phone number, and dialled.

It rang a few times before he picked up. "Hello?" he said.

"Hi! Hello, Ray. I mean, Mr Underwood. I'm ringing from the *Chipping Fairford Inquirer*, and I'm writing an article on the discovery —"

"No," Ray said.

"—of the dead body in your house, and I'd really like it if I could—"

"I'm not interested, sorry."

"—have ten minutes of your time to get an eyewitness account of—"

"Hey," Ray said.

"Yes?"

"I am not giving any interviews. Now or ever. This whole

thing is an absolute nightmare and I'm trying to put it behind me."

"Oh."

"Please don't call again."

"I wouldn't, I—oh." He'd hung up.

That didn't go great. I thought for a moment, then dialled another number.

"Adam!" I said brightly.

"What's up?" Adam said. "I'm at work, by the way. Keep it quick."

"I need you to get me an interview with Ray."

Adam snorted.

"Adam, c'mon."

"Ray won't talk to me after we kissed last night, you know that. In fact, me trying to set something up would guarantee he'd never talk to you. Call him yourself and ask nicely."

"I did that two minutes ago. He said no."

"Did he say anything else?"

"He said the whole thing is an absolute nightmare and he's trying to put it behind him."

"Hmm."

"Yeah, I know. I'll think of something else. I don't want to make him go through it all again. He sounded pretty definite anyway."

"I could still ask...?" Adam said reluctantly.

"Nah. No worries. Thanks, Adam."

We said goodbye and I slouched back in my chair, swinging it from side to side thoughtfully.

What would Mrs Strickland do?

What would Ralph tell me to do?

What would Jasper the award-winning investigative journalist do?

He would get in his car, drive over to Ray's, park in his drive—a bad-bitch power move—and march up to the front door.

He'd knock on the door with supreme confidence, charm his way inside, and proceed to ask insightful questions, such as...well, he'd have a notebook with the questions jotted down. He'd be ready. Because he was prepared. And a professional.

He'd grill Ray until Ray had told him absolutely everything (including how he *really* felt about Adam) and then, once Ray was pumped dry of information, Jasper would leave him, shaken and unhappy, reliving his nightmare.

Jasper wouldn't care, though, because he would have got the story, and—

Wow. Jasper the award-winning investigative journalist was a terrible human being.

I shuddered.

I'd find a better way to approach the story. I was creative, damn it! I could do this!

I opened up a new document and settled in for some focused, serious brainstorming.

An hour later, I read the last page of the document back.

"Bring him to me," the feared warlord Nash said.

I struggled in my chains as I was dragged to the bottom of the throne steps, then shoved to my knees, but not in a sexy way.

Nash spoke over my head. "One last time, King Adam. Renounce your right to the throne, or I will execute your favourite peasant."

King Adam tossed his shining curls. "I will never renounce the throne. It is my sworn duty to rule over the good people of Fayreford. I will never let the kingdom fall into darkness!"

"Why does he need to renounce it, though?" I said. "You're

sitting right on it. You're there. Maybe we should all take a
moment and consider—"

"Silence, mewling peasant."

"That's a bit...I didn't mewl. *Such a gross word. I'm just*
saying that, logically, I don't think it's necessary."

The warlord nodded to his second-in-command.

"Let this be a warning to you all," he boomed.

His fierce general smiled at me as she hefted her war axe in a
two-handed grip, swung it up in a glittering arc, and—

I sighed, dragged the document to the trash can, and
went to the gym.

I HAD THREE CLASSES BACK TO BACK. MELANIE HAD CALLED IN
sick, and after the two classes of my own I had scheduled, I
had to take her yoga class. It went well, I thought. Everyone
seemed impressed when I did the splits. After a spin class,
Legs, Bums and Tums—during which Mike the uncoopera-
tive policeman was as sorry as I'd promised he would be—
and the yoga, I was starting to feel it.

I decided to drop in to the weights room and finish my
day with some lifting, in the hopes that I'd make it home,
crawl into bed, and fall straight to sleep.

I was grunting at the leg press when Kevin Wallis came
and thumped down in the machine next to mine. He'd been
talking to a group of his friends, all of them guys a few years
younger than me, and I'd ignored the noise as they laughed
and hooted.

"All right, Jasper?" he said cheerfully.

"Hey, Kev. How's it going?"

"Eh. You know."

"Yeah," I said.

"Same old, same old," he said.

"Uh-huh." I focused on the opposite wall, and continued my set.

"Except for the dead guy in a tub thing earlier in the week. That was new."

I turned to stare at him. "What?"

"What?" Kevin's neck veins bulged and he grimaced as he struggled to lift the weight.

"Dead guy *in a tub*?"

"Yuuuuuhhhhh." The weights clanged. "Whee," he said. "That one was *tough*."

"Take it down a notch. You shouldn't be straining that hard."

"Yeah?"

"Yeah. So. Tub? Dead guy?"

He adjusted the machine, tested it out, and then said between reps, "Yeah, been working for Craig Henderson, you know? The handyman?"

"Henderson's Handymen, No Job Too Small?" I saw the van around town a lot.

"Yeah. Lemme tell you, some people are taking the piss with that. Had this one woman call us to come and change her lightbulb. And another one—"

"Oh my god. Were you one of the workmen who were there when Ray found the body?"

"Hah. Craig reckons as *he's* the one what found it." He grunted and lifted. "It was us, though."

"Kev." I turned to him. "Can I interview you?"

"Me?"

"Yes!" I said. "Wait. Has Mrs Strickland spoken to you yet?" I still hadn't read her article.

"No." Kevin shivered. "I had her for GCSE English. Scares the absolute shit out of me, that woman does."

"Same."

"Why do you ask?"

Okay. Okay. Don't get overexcited. Play it cool. "Kev, I want to do an exclusive interview with you."

He stopped lifting and looked intrigued.

"I'm a journalist," I said, and only blushed a bit.

"Side hustle?" Kevin said. "Nice."

"I want to do an article for the paper. If you were there when it all happened, I'd love to get an eyewitness account." I was confident I could get Ralph to print an exclusive interview with one of the men who found the body. It wasn't Ray, but it was the next best thing.

"All right, sure. Don't see why not. Can't do it now, though. My dad's expecting me home for supper."

"How about tomorrow? When do you start work? Can we meet before?"

Tomorrow was Thursday. The *Inquirer* went to press on Thursday afternoon and was distributed on Friday morning. It was going to be incredibly tight, but I might be able to swing it.

"Don't have a set time," Kevin said. "Tomorrow we're supposed to start painting some guy's house over in Lakeside, and he won't be there to let us in until eleven or so."

"Fantastic." I could interview Kevin for an hour, see what I got, go and tell Ralph to stop the presses by lunch... "Eight o'clock at the Chipped Cup?"

"Eight?" Kevin looked appalled. "In the morning?"

"I'll buy you a muffin."

Kevin looked unconvinced.

"And a croissant," I said. "With bacon."

"All right."

15

This was my big break and I wasn't going to mess it up.

I went for a quick morning run, brewed coffee while I was in the shower, and gulped down my protein shake as I rushed around, throwing things into my messenger bag. I grabbed a notebook, my iPhone and charger, three pens because I always seemed to lose them, a handful of protein bars, and my extra-large water bottle.

By six o'clock I was ready and waiting outside The Chipped Cup when Amalie's brother, Charlie, opened up. As soon as he let me in, I claimed a table in the corner.

Yes, I was a couple of hours early. I needed all the time I could get to prepare.

I bought myself a coffee I didn't want because otherwise Charlie would throw me out, flipped open my notebook, clicked my pen, and started scribbling some notes.

I'd heard plenty of gossip from colleagues and clients at the gym, and last night I'd read Mrs Strickland's article. Even putting it all together, it didn't add up to a whole lot of information.

What I knew thus far was that Craig and Kevin had been hired by Ray to lay a new carpet in Ray's bedroom, and in the process of doing so, they'd stumbled upon a dead body hidden under the floorboards. Adam had told me that Ray was tight-lipped about it, but Adam had gone to Ray's house and seen the scene of the crime once the police had let Ray go back home. I'd asked him to describe it. He'd told me there wasn't anything to describe. It was a hole in the floor.

I now knew from Kevin that the body was in a *tub* in the hole. *That* hadn't been in Mrs Strickland's article.

I didn't blame Ray for not wanting to talk about it. I wouldn't, either, if I'd spent however many years sleeping in a room with a dead guy crammed in a tub under my floor.

By the time eight o'clock was approaching, Charlie had made me buy two more coffees to keep the table, and like an idiot, I drank them. I have a low tolerance for caffeine. After a cup at home and three cups at the coffee shop, I could feel my eyelashes vibrating.

I chugged more water to try and dilute the coffee blazing through my veins. My bladder twinged, and I realised my mistake.

I could drink a lot, but even I couldn't hold that much liquid for hours. I'd probably drunk close to three litres since I'd rolled out of bed before dawn.

I squirmed in my seat.

Yeah, this was a problem.

I slipped my phone into my pocket, grabbed my note-book, and left everything else at the table. Chipping Fairford wasn't exactly a hotbed of crime. It would all be there when I got back.

Probably.

My bladder twinged again and I rushed up to the counter.

"No," Charlie said before I even opened my mouth.

"I haven't asked yet," I said.

"You're practically doing the pee dance, Jasper. No. The toilets are for employees only."

"Charlie, I will *pay* you. How much?"

"Twenty pence."

"Really? Cool. That's all it costs for the public toilets down by The Lion."

Charlie looked at me.

Right. "I won't make it there." I really was dancing on the spot now. I eyed Charlie. I eyed the doorway to the back. If I had to, I'd make a run for it, lock myself in the loo before he could stop me, and apologise after. "Charlie. I'll...wash dishes."

"We have a dishwasher."

"I'll cover the rest of your shift! I know how to use the machine."

"If you so much as touch my baby, Connolly, you'll be banned for life," Charlie snapped. He was the one who'd yelled at me the most when I broke the knob off their five-thousand-pound espresso machine.

"I'll clear the tables, then! Mop the floors! Empty the bins!" I tried really hard not to scrunch up my face in distress.

"Oh, dear god. *Fine.*"

"I'll—oh, really?"

"Just make it quick."

"Thanks!" I beamed. "Can you watch my stuff while I'm gone? No? No worries. It'll be fine, I'm sure. Back in a mo."

It had never taken me so long to drain my bladder in my entire life. It just kept coming. What the fuck.

Painfully aware of every second, expecting to get back

and find Kevin had been and gone and I'd missed my window, I zipped up, washed my hands, and bolted to the front of the shop.

Kevin was standing at the counter, chatting to Charlie.

"Hi, Kev," I said.

He blinked at my sudden appearance on the wrong side of the counter. "Hi, Jasper." He nodded at Charlie. "He says they don't serve bacon here."

"They don't? Weird. I could have sworn they did. Must have taken it off the menu."

"We have never served bacon here," Charlie said.

"Are you sure? I must be misremembering. Never mind." I said to Kevin, "Sorry about the bacon, mate. I'll buy you whatever else you want instead."

Kevin's eyes brightened.

"Here you go, boys," Charlie said, bringing the tray over to our table once Kevin's panini was toasted. He unloaded it, grinning.

"Thanks, Charlie," I said.

"Oh, any time. *Any* time. We like big spenders around here."

"Uh-huh."

"Can I get you anything else?"

Kevin surveyed the spread. He'd ordered a ham and cheese panini, a cheese croissant, a cheese danish, and two chocolate muffins. He opened his mouth.

"No," I said. "We're good."

"You sure now?"

"Yep."

Charlie could keep on grinning. Kevin just blew through two week's worth of my coffee and treats budget. Charlie wouldn't be seeing me *or* my money for a while.

Kevin turned his attention to his breakfast banquet and was steadily mowing his way through, when someone came and sat himself down in the chair opposite. I glanced around, startled. There were plenty of free seats.

The man was short and stocky, with salt-and-pepper hair and a genial smile.

"This is Craig," Kevin said. "My boss."

"Craig Henderson," the guy said, reaching over the table and holding out a hand. We shook, and he sat back. "The one who found the body."

Kevin rolled his eyes.

Craig didn't notice. After a quick assessment of Kevin's spread, he said, "I'll have the same, thanks," and looked at me expectantly.

My mouth dropped open.

"Kev said you were offering breakfast in return for an exclusive interview?" Craig's voice was light, his smile was friendly, and his gaze was beady. "It's a bit short notice, of course, and I had to move some things around. You're lucky we could spare the time."

I debated whether or not to tell him to pay for his own damn food, and came to the conclusion that a journalist had to do what a journalist had to do.

"Be right back," I said, and marched up to the counter.

I ordered, much to Charlie's delight, piled the tray high, dumped it in front of Craig, and sat down.

Craig looked at it, then up at me. "Where's my coffee, mate?"

I gritted my teeth, picked up my pen, and clicked it menacingly. "Let's get through some questions first, shall we? I'll get you a coffee to wash down all that food once we're done."

He held my gaze speculatively.

I had to stare down clients who really, really didn't want to dig deep and power their way through the last set on a daily basis.

One of them was a fearsome, forty-something judge.

She had three children under the age of eight, very little free time, a tendency to blister my ears with foul language when I refused to let her off the final push, and a high-five that could knock you back a step when she did it.

The likes of Craig Henderson did not impress me.

"All right," he said, and delicately peeled the wrapper off muffin number one.

I cleared my throat and flipped my notebook open. "Okay," I said. "What—"

"This is how it all went down," Craig said through a mouthful of muffin. "You *do* want all the details, right? Because I don't want to sit here wasting mine and Kev's time if all you're going to do is write an article that barely mentions I was there, and skims over the important stuff."

"I wouldn't call it a waste of time when you get a breakfast banquet out of it," I said. "Yes, I want all the details. I assume you already talked to Mrs Strickland?"

"Yeah." He sniffed disapprovingly. "Only asked my name and said could I confirm what her source had told her, that I'd found the body stashed under the floor, and it wasn't recent. The moment I confirmed it, she hung up. I was in the middle of talking, and all. Rude."

"She was covering breaking news for the website," I said with a dismissive wave. "This is investigative journalism. This is going to be in the paper."

Craig brightened. "Front page?"

"I can't promise anything, but that's what I'm shooting for. So. What—"

"I get a call from Ray Underwood, right? You know Ray?"

"Oh, yeah." I knew all about Ray. For years, I'd listened to Adam rhapsodising about Ray's beautiful eyes, about his perky little butt Adam wanted to spank, his pretty face Adam wanted to gaze down at, his lush mouth Adam wanted to put things in, his twitchy energy Adam wanted aimed at him. Yeah. I knew Ray. "Not personally, though," I added. "I know of him."

"Nice bloke. Bit nervy sometimes, bit of a pushover, but a nice bloke. Not stingy with the tea and biscuits like some people can be. Gave us Hobnobs. The chocolate-covered ones. Anyway, Ray calls and asks us to come over, rip up his old carpet for him and lay a new one. We show up nice and early, right on time, and it doesn't take too long to get the old carpet up. But here's the thing." Craig leaned forward and looked at me meaningfully. "I knew something wasn't right. Straight away."

I was jotting notes in my notebook, and I made an interested noise.

Craig sat back from the table. "I got a sense for these things."

I glanced at Kevin. He gave me a tiny shrug.

"It was like a goose walked over my grave," Craig said. "The minute I set foot in that room, I musta known, deep down, that there was a trapped spirit."

"What about you, Kev? Any bad vibes?"

"Nope. We just got to it. I like the demo jobs, so Craig was scrolling through Insta while I got stuck in."

"Anyway," Craig said. "We move the furniture to the far wall and when Kev goes to start ripping up the carpet, we find it's *sealed down*."

He gave me another of those meaningful looks.

After a moment I said, "I'm taking it that's not normal?"

"Nah. Ray asked the same. Tacked down, for sure. That's

normal. But this wasn't tacks. This was like a sealant. It was all glued down. Now, my thinking is—" he ripped a croissant in half, then changed his mind and went for another muffin, "—that it was to keep in the smell. That's my opinion, though. That's what I reckon. Whoever put that poor bastard in the floor was gonna be paranoid someone would notice."

I shifted on my chair. We were getting to the good stuff. "Kevin said something about a tub?"

"Yeah, yeah. I'll get to that. We're talking about the carpet still. Kev gives it his best, but when he can't rip it up, we have to start cutting into the seal. It was weird stuff. I've got a theory on that, and all."

Another pause for dramatic effect.

I had to give him his due, Craig was delivering more than my breakfast bribe's worth of entertainment. When it came to facts, he hadn't given me anything I didn't actually know already.

"I reckon it was homemade sealant," he said. "Made by the murderer."

"Huh."

"You don't get shit like that down at B&Q or Homebase, is what I'm saying."

"Right. And...the body?"

"Yeah. By the time Kev's got the carpet cut back from the wall it's lunchtime and we go to the pub. We get back at what, Kev? Two? Half two?"

"'Bout that," Kevin said.

I made a note. "How did you actually discover the body? Who even thought to look? It was under the floorboards, and you were there to lay a carpet. How did you come to lift the boards in the first place?"

This was all a lot more boring than you'd think the discovery of a dead body would be.

"Ah," Craig said. He grinned, and hooked a thumb at Kevin.

"Aw, Craig. Don't say anything," Kevin said. "Mr Underwood might have a go at me if he finds out it's my fault."

"Your fault?" I perked up. This sounded like an exclusive.

"Ray's got one of those old steamer trunk things in his bedroom," Craig said. "Vintage. And before you ask, I don't know what's in there, because it's locked. Heavy as shit, though. Anyway, Kev and I got it up and were carrying it over to the other side, and Kev dropped his end. Near shat myself, I did. Thought it was going to go right through the floor and drop into the room below, land on Ray. His office is right beneath the bedroom."

"Not good," I said, scribbling furiously.

"I know. I've got insurance but I don't know if it would get me out of manslaughter."

It wouldn't have mattered one way or the other. If he'd killed Ray, Adam would have murdered him.

Craig continued, "Like I said, Ray's a nice bloke but he's a bit of a fusspot. He noticed it right off. The boards, I mean. Kev damn near bounced the boards right off the beam, he dropped it that hard, and they creaked something awful when you put any weight on them. For a bit, I thought Ray was too nice to bring it up but when we got back from the pub he mentioned it, and I told him I'd fix it."

Craig shoved the final bite of muffin into his mouth and held up a finger.

Kevin had already finished. He looked a bit wistful as the muffin vanished.

Craig dabbed his mouth with the paper napkin. "So we

went to take the floorboards up. And this is where it gets creepy again."

I waited eagerly.

"The nails," Craig said, "were unusually loose."

I continued to wait eagerly.

Craig raised his brows.

Oh. "And that's creepy?"

"Yeah. Once you nail boards down, unless you pull 'em back up for access to pipes and stuff, what you gotta to keep popping them back up for? *Suspicious.* As if that wasn't bad enough, when I got the boards up..."

"Yes?"

"Weirdly deep underfloor."

I nodded, eyes on my notebook as my hopes of a good story withered.

Other than the tub, I had a homemade sealant, unusually loose nails, and an extra-deep space under the floorboards.

And Kevin dropped his end of a steamer trunk and nearly manslaughtered the unsuspecting Ray.

I really hoped Craig was being theatrical and saving the good stuff to last, because none of this was really going to blow Mrs Strickland's breaking-news article out of the water.

I sighed, realising that I had a whole lot of nothing.

And I wouldn't be able to afford the coffee shop for a month.

"That's when Ray spotted the tub," Craig said. "Just think. If he hadn't poked his head in the hole and had a quick look around, I'd have re-seated the boards, and he'd have spent the rest of his life sharing his room with that dead guy lying there not four feet from his bed."

I shuddered. "Can you describe the tub?"

"Big, obviously. I didn't see the full length of it, but it was big enough to stuff a body in. With a bit of folding, of course. It was opaque, too. Kind of yellowed. Looked old. You could see something was in there, but not what. Ray thought it was Christmas decorations."

"Who opened it?" I asked.

Kevin sat up. "Oh! Me! That was me. Ray and Craig were talking about what was in there and Ray was leaning toward leaving it, and I thought it'd be a shame not to know. So I popped the lid."

"Then *you* were the one who technically discovered, it, Kev," I said. "Tell me—"

"*I* knew at once," Craig said loudly, "what I was smelling. In my line of work, you come across more than a few corpses."

"Really?"

"Yeah. Mostly cats and birds, though. Couple of squirrels. Nearly always up chimneys. This was my first person."

"Kev?" I asked. He was looking vaguely miffed at Craig.

"Bat," he said.

"Huh?"

"Found a little mummified bat once. Cute little thing. I felt really sorry for it. I buried it in a shoebox at the bottom of my dad's garden."

I smiled. "Was it one of those pipistrelles, or—"

"*Mummified*," Craig said, "is exactly how I'd describe the body."

Okay. This was news! Finally! I knew the victim hadn't been murdered recently, but mummified was something else.

"Oh, yeah," Craig leaned back, relaxed now that he had my attention again. "Yep. It was all leathery and withered. Dried out. It was not fresh, is what I'm saying. It wasn't, y'know. Oozing or anything. My guess is, any oozing it did would have been soaked up by the cat litter."

"…cat litter?"

"I didn't really notice it at the time, what with the dead body and all, but there was other stuff in the tub. Whitish-grey stuff. We were talking, me and Kev. We think it was cat litter."

My stomach rolled uneasily and I took a couple of deep breaths. "Okay." I cleared my throat. "If you had to guess, how old would you say the body was? Would you say it was ancient, like an Egyptian mummy from a museum, or…?"

"No, no. Couldn't be that old. It was wearing jeans. Now I come to think of it, though…" Craig scratched his jaw. "Maybe it isn't old at all. That thing looked like the apricots my wife dries in her dehydrator. Would a dehydrator work on a body? If you built a big one? The murderer could have done that for storage purposes. Dry the victim out, pop him in some Tupperware. Keep for a good long while like that."

I wasn't squeamish. I wasn't. Especially when it comes to the human body. Exercising doesn't always go without a speed bump here or there, especially for the elderly. Accidents happen. I've seen bodies in distress. I've helped calmed things down and sort things out. It's part of my job.

Apparently, I drew the line at dead folk. I was starting to sweat. My stomach turned at the thought of a human-sized dehydrator doing its thing, slowly sucking…the, uh…the juices…

A glass of water was banged down by my elbow, making me jump. Charlie glared down at me.

"Don't you dare puke on my floor," he said, and stalked off.

I sipped the water gratefully, and cleared my throat. "Uh. Where were we?"

"I found the body," Kevin said.

"Kevin took the lid off the tub and *I* found the body," Craig said. "I was closest."

"Then what happened?"

"Kevin screamed," Craig said.

"Craig threw up," Kevin said.

"I did not!"

"You did."

"How would you know what I did? You ran so fast you were already out of the house before I got up off the floor."

Kevin looked proud.

"Ray freaked out, is what happened," Craig said. "He's lucky I was there. I helped him down the stairs, had him sit on the doorstep to gather himself, and the police came. That's about it."

I flipped back through my notebook and read the sparse notes I'd made after talking to Mrs Hughes.

"Mrs Hughes from the bookshop lives over the road from Ray. She said she saw the pair of you run out the house and drive away. She said you were speeding."

Craig hesitated. "We were late for another job. And unless she or her little dog clocked it with a speed gun, that's her opinion and nothing more."

"She also said that Ray was the one who called the police."

"I can't speculate as to whose call went through first, but let me tell you, I was on the phone the minute we were out of Sycamore Close."

"And what did you do after that?"

Craig hesitated again.

"Pub," Kevin supplied helpfully.

"Kev needed something to settle his nerves," Craig said. "He was in a right state. Nothing like Ray, but still."

I couldn't imagine what Kevin in a right state looked like. He was the most placid guy I'd ever met. Ray, on the other hand, I could easily imagine freaking out.

"Right, then," Craig said. "Do you want a picture before we go, or not?"

"Of what?" I put my notebook down.

Craig pointed between him and Kevin. "The discoverers of the body."

"Yes! Good idea." I hadn't thought of that, but it might give me an edge when I pitched it to Ralph. I didn't think I needed an edge, though. I'd got some exclusive and unsettling information that hadn't made it into Mrs Strickland's article. If the police had told Craig to keep the extra details to himself and he'd decided to give it all up for a breakfast banquet, I decided, that was on Craig.

Craig stood, checking his watch. "We've got to be off to Lakeside for our eleven o'clock, but I parked out back. Does a shot of us in front of the van work for you?"

Ah. Free advertising for Craig. I didn't argue. I didn't exactly have the time to set up any kind of photoshoot. I'd barely have the time to write the article and get it to Ralph before it was last week's news.

"Oi," Charlie yelled when I went to follow them out. "Get back here, you've got work to be doing. A deal's a deal."

Shit. I'd forgotten about that. "How about tomorrow?"

"Jasper."

"Fine. I'm going to pop out for a minute with these two and get a couple of photos, and I'll be right back." I slung my messenger bag on the counter and pushed it toward him. "Collateral."

I bolted before he could argue—and he would—and hurried after Craig and Kevin.

I snapped about twenty pics, declined to let Craig choose his favourite, and watched them go.

"Listen, Charlie," I was already saying when I marched back in. I was going to hold up my end of the deal, but I was going to negotiate. Article first, then I'd come back and do whatever Charlie wanted. "I am on a deadline here, and—oh."

I stopped dead when I saw Liam standing at the counter.

He raised his eyebrows at me.

Say something.

Say something!

Anything!!!

I opened my mouth and something definitely came out, but it wasn't so much a word as a sound.

One second I was Jasper the intrepid journalist, ready to crash through any and all barriers to get his story to the presses. The next second, I was reliving that moment when Liam was pressing me into my mattress and moving over me, watching me, and—

I moaned.

It wasn't loud, or like a porn moan, but it was not a normal sound to making in a crowded coffee shop, that was for sure.

Liam closed his eyes briefly, nodded to Charlie, and collected his coffee. He said to me as he passed, "Morning."

"Hi," I breathed, and *kill* me. Just—

"What," said Charlie, "the fuck was that?"

"Shut up," I said.

I did my best to convince Charlie to let me come back later to do the mopping or tray collecting or whatever menial tasks he'd been stacking up for me. He wasn't having any of it.

I rushed around, cleared and wiped down every unoccupied table, emptied the bins, and emptied and reloaded their little dishwasher. I cleaned the employees' toilet, cleaned the window, mopped up two spilled drinks, told Charlie that next time I'd go and pee in the back alley behind the shop and he couldn't stop me, and left.

I was cutting it fine.

16

I sat in my car, fumbling desperately at my phone.

I hadn't realised how late it was. Charlie didn't let me go until lunchtime, and I was beginning to have doubts about whether or not I was going to be able to make it.

Yes!

Yes, I was. No quitter talk. *Dig deep. You can do it!*

I gritted my teeth and thumbed in another few words.

There were people out there—and this boggled my mind—who wrote entire books on their phones.

Books.

Tens of thousands of words upon words.

With their thumbs.

I couldn't do it. Call me a size queen, but when it came to a screen, I needed more than two inches. And as for typing? I'm a physical man. I yearned for the rattle and clack of a keyboard. I needed the feedback, I wanted to *feel* the words exiting my body.

iPhone keyboards were not made for the likes of me.

No matter how careful I was or how slowly I typed, autocorrect got right up in my business every third word. The first draft of my article was an underwhelming one hundred and fifty words long, and I'd been pecking it out laboriously for the last twenty minutes. I'd fogged up the windows. It looked like I was having way more fun in here than I actually was.

I wasn't having any fun at all.

Being a journalist was turning out to be way harder than I'd imagined—and this was with a killer story.

Okay, fuck the phone.

I tossed it onto the passenger seat and switched on the ignition, blasting warm air through the vents to clear the windows. The phone bounced, landed in the footwell, and skittered out of sight under the seat.

"And fucking stay there," I muttered at it. I leaned forward and swiped a clear patch on the windscreen. It was probably enough to see out of, but I was a nervous driver on the best of days. "Come on, come on." The moment it was properly de-misted, I was off.

I had two options here.

I could go home, bang out a first draft, shoot it over to Ralph, and hope he opened his email when he saw it was from me, or...

I flipped on my indicator.

Or I could swing by his office before I wrote the article, and talk him into it first.

Ralph's office was in the centre of town. His wife ran one of those shabby-chic shops that folk from London love so much, full of charming old wooden buckets, dainty ornamental stone benches, dove cotes and the like. The *Chipping Fairford Inquirer*'s newsroom was above it.

The closer to the centre of town you got, the harder it was to park, especially during lunchtime and the early afternoon. I made an executive decision. Would Ralph be angry if I noodled my car down into the tiny carpark at the back of his wife's shop? He had been in the past, so, yes.

But he'd have to look out the window and see me to be angry. I was willing to take the risk.

I waited for a florist's van to stop blocking the turn, and nipped down the narrow road. I parked the car, scooped my phone out from under the passenger seat, slung my messenger bag over my shoulder, and darted out.

I could have gone in through the back, but I didn't want to push my luck.

I ran around to the front of the building. The entrance was a tiny little foyer with a right into the shop, a left into the bookshop next door, and the stairs dead ahead.

I jogged up the stairs and rapped on the door. *Chipping Fairford Inquirer* was stencilled in gold on the frosted glass in a fancy script complete with curlicues. I tried the handle and the door opened. I popped my head through.

"Ralph?" I called.

The squeak of wheels preceded Ralph's appearance as he scooted his office chair backward across the wooden boards and peered cautiously around the corner. "Jasper."

"Hi!" I strode in. "Am I interrupting anything?"

He scooted back out of sight and I followed.

"Just lunch," he said, waving a hand at the food laid out on the desk. He'd got it from the deli two doors down. I recognised it.

And I wanted it.

My stomach groaned passionately.

Ralph looked horrified and blocked my view of his food, as if he thought I'd lose my self-control and fall on it.

I was tempted. I hadn't actually eaten anything at the coffee shop and my blood sugar was dropping rapidly.

"I'm going to make this quick," I said. "Stop the presses, I have an exclusive!"

I'd always wanted to say that.

"About what?" Ralph said suspiciously. "If it's another article about bees, Jasper, I'm sorry, but people aren't that interested."

"It's...no. People should be interested in bees, by the way, but no. It's about the Sycamore Close case!"

Ralph's eyes widened and he sat up sharply. "You know who did it?"

"Uh, no?"

You know the victim's name?"

"No?"

"You got Underwood to give up the goods?"

"No."

"You sweet-talked Nash into giving up the goods?"

"What? *No.* Why would you even think that?"

"I heard about you bribing him with doughnuts. Rookie mistake. Bribes happen in private." He winked.

"What? I wasn't bribing him, it was Happy Wednesday— Tuesday! It was a Happy Tuesday treat. And who on earth told you about that?"

He tapped his nose. "Sources, kid."

Ralph liked to pretend he had a network of informants, but this was Chipping Fairford. Once again: the discovery of the body in Ray's house was the most exciting thing to have happened since a battle in the 1300s. So. Seven centuries.

"What sources?" I said.

"Facebook. Hotbed of gossip. If you actually looked at it once in a while, you might be able to write stories people are interested in reading."

"Right. Well, I wasn't bribing Detective Chief Inspector Liam Nash with doughnuts, or with anything else." I ignored the way Ralph sat back in his chair and tucked his arms behind his head, grinning wide. I *knew* I said Liam's name weirdly, okay? "That was me being friendly."

"Cultivating connections, huh?"

I glared at him. "Yes."

Ralph sat up. He leaned his elbows on his desktop and looked over the top of his bifocals. "What have you got? And sit down. You make me nervous when you loom about like that."

"Sorry." I grabbed the chair from behind the spare desk, wheeled it over, and sat down. I put my knees together and drew my arms in, hunching a little. "I just came from an interview. With eyewitnesses."

Ralph looked thoughtful. "Ah. The handymen?"

"Yep. Craig Henderson and Kev Wallis of Henderson's Handymen."

"No Job Too Small," Ralph finished absently. He rubbed his jaw. "Could work. Strickland already contacted Henderson. She couldn't track down the other one, though. Left a few messages, but by then the piece was up on the website."

"Kev Wallis. I know him from the gym. He spoke to me. I got an interview with both of them. Pictures, too."

He nodded, looking impressed. "Pictures. Good thinking."

I didn't tell him it was Craig's idea.

Ralph wiggled the mouse and his computer screen lit up. He sucked his teeth. "I dunno, Jasper. It's half one. I've got the weekly issue all laid out and good to go to the printers..."

"I've got new information that Mrs Strickland didn't get."

"What?" Ralph sat forward.

I shook my head at him. "What's the deadline? What's the latest you can hold off?"

He looked at me. "Four," he said abruptly. "Think you can turn it around?"

I nodded at once, even while I was still doing the calculations. Oof, that'd be cutting it fine. "I'm thinking it should go on the front page," I said.

If you're gonna go for it? Go hard.

"Let me see the pictures." He gestured for me to hand over my phone.

I unlocked it, swiped to the album, and passed it across the desk.

"Eh," he said. "Be better if it was a dead body, or Underwood. Or better yet, Underwood *with* a dead body. These will do." He handed the phone back. "Your screen's cracked," he said.

"I know. I dropped it. Don't worry about it."

Ralph drummed his fingers on the desktop, then flattened his hands. "Do it," he said. "Write me an article. Five hundred words."

I punched the air. "My first commission!"

"Nope. Nuh-uh. Not a commission. *Per*mission."

I scowled.

"Send it over before four and I'll have a look at it. If it's good enough, it'll be in the paper tomorrow." He stared at me. "What are you waiting for? Shoo."

"Yes!" I jumped up and stuffed my phone into my back pocket.

"Text me the photos. Email the article by four. No later."

"Consider it done."

DEEP BREATH IN. DEEP BREATH OUT.

Deep breath iiiiiiiiin.

Deep. Breath. Oooooooout.

The article, which I'd thought would be so easy to write when I was interviewing Kevin and Craig, was refusing to cooperate.

But!

There was no need to panic.

And I wasn't panicking.

Maybe if I wasn't sitting here at my computer doing my calming breathing exercises, I would be. But I wasn't. Because I was breathing, and I was calm.

I'd texted the photos as soon as I got in. I'd grabbed myself a protein shake and two bars, and the fruit bowl for good measure, kicked off my shoes, and rushed straight to the computer.

That was about as far as I'd got in an hour.

It was ridiculous. Five hundred words. I could toss out five hundred words in fifteen minutes. I'd timed myself.

Five hundred words about Liam, and dragons, and Space Marines, and Liam, and shagging, and Liam and whatnot.

I *could* do non-fiction, too. I could.

I flipped through my notebook, jotted a quick outline—ugh this was like school—and told myself to just start.

I ground my laborious way through the article, anxiously watching my word-count progress bar tick up one reluctant percent after the other.

I skimmed it back and winced. It was...hmm. A bit dry? It needed a little something. I needed to punch up the words, really tell a *story* here, really grab the reader.

Zhuzh it up a bit.

I pushed back from the desk, dropped to the floor, and worked through a set of pushups. Physical activity always helped me think.

After the pushups I rolled to my back and did some sit-ups.

Some burpees. V-sits. A few Russian twists. I grabbed my kettlebell and swung it around a bit until I'd really worked up a sweat, and—

Shit.

I rushed back to the computer.

"Ahhhh," I said when I checked the time. It was half past three. What the fuck?

I re-read my zero draft. It was...honestly, it was too late to restart.

The bones were good?

I gave it some sparkle. Tossed in a few exclamation points, some italics. That made it look more interesting.

I read through it another hundred thousand times, words lost all sense and meaning, and at five to four, I had to face facts.

It was crunch time.

The Word document throbbed at me from the computer screen.

It was absolutely covered with comments and markup. Gritting my teeth, I deleted all the comments and accepted all changes. There were still a lot of red squiggles.

I'd hoped to run it through Grammarly and proofread it before it went, but I was out of time. I didn't even have long enough to run a spellcheck.

Well, Word got it wrong half the time anyway. There probably weren't that many mistakes.

"Are we go or no go, Connolly?" I said. "We are a *go*. Come on. Come oooooon! Yeah! You've got this. Wooo!"

I couldn't believe I just woo-ed myself.

I started a new email to Ralph and attached the document.

"Yeah! Do it! Do it! Hit that button. Press send. Come on, you can do it. Go!"

I pressed the button.

My muscles went tight, my stomach lurched, and I collapsed in a sweating heap.

Good job I was already sitting down.

Wow.

Did that feel good? I couldn't tell. I checked my pulse, then folded at the waist when my vision whited out.

This was all perfectly normal, I was sure of it. This was like endorphins.

Well, no.

I was very familiar with endorphins.

This didn't feel like an orgasm, or the satisfaction of a good lifting session, or a hard run. It didn't even feel like the satisfaction of writing another Liam Nash fanfic.

This must be what *intellectual* endorphins felt like. It was different, that's all. I'd get used to it.

Feeling queasy, I stood cautiously and tottered to the kitchen. I prepared and ate a healthy salad with skinless grilled chicken breast, chased it down with three Snickers bars from my secret stash because desperate times call for desperate measures, then I went and had a shower.

I turned the shower on hot, climbed in, and stood under the spray until my brain was happily numb and my skin was rosy warm. I pulled on my comfiest sweatpants and t-shirt, climbed into bed, and took a nap.

When I woke up, I found an email notification on my phone. The email was one line long, and it was from Ralph.

It's at the printers.

"Yay," I whispered into the silence of my room.

---

17

*T*he next morning I was scheduled to take a Box Fit class, followed by an Introduction to Weightlifting class. I wasn't needed at the gym until ten, giving me more than enough time to get my run in, do some stretching because I'd slept in a knot and woken up feeling like I aged a century overnight, and swing by the newsagents.

I stood in front of the shelf where they kept the newspapers. We had quite the eclectic selection here in Chipping Fairford—everything from *The New York Times* and *Vanity Fair* to the *The Sun* and the *Angling Times.* Tacked on at the end, there was a small stack of the *Chipping Fairford Inquirer.*

I stared at it.

Circulation was low and, according to Ralph, dropping every quarter. He'd said that the print run was at about five thousand copies these days.

I stared at my name. I didn't love the headline, but it wasn't like I'd had a chance to workshop it. I vaguely remembered tossing into the subject line of the email in a frenzy of panic.

"Local Handymen Discover Body in Local Murder House," by J.C. Connolly.

I was glad I'd gone with initials for my byline. I'd die before I told anyone what the middle initial stood for, because it was stupid, but J.C. Connolly looked much more professional than plain old Jasper Connolly, who people knew as a personal trainer from the gym.

I pulled my phone out of my back pocket, and called Adam.

"Hey," he said, sounding sleepy.

"Are you still in bed?" I demanded.

"Some of us need more than five hours a night, you know. Some of us need our beauty sleep. What do you want?"

I hadn't told Adam about the article yet. I hadn't told anyone, as I hadn't wanted to get my hopes up only to have Ralph cancel it because something more interesting came along. Or because he read it and thought it was crap.

"Switch to FaceTime," I said.

"Ugh. No."

"Come on, Adam. I've got something to show you."

Adam sighed noisily and toggled his camera on. His cheeks were flushed a rosy peach, his coppery hair looked perfectly styled even though I knew that was his version of bedhead, and he was sitting on his sofa in his flat, slumped over a bowl of granola.

"That had better be reduced-sugar granola," I told him, and didn't even feel a twinge of guilt about my three Snickers bars.

I'd *earned* them.

"Yes." He shovelled a mouthful in. "Of course it is," he said around a big lying smile.

I was his personal trainer. We'd see if he was still smiling about it when I added an extra three sets of squats to our session later.

"Look at this," I said, and flipped the camera.

"What am I looking at, exactly? Because it looks like you're at the newsagents."

"I am!"

I held the phone closer to the papers.

"Jasper!" Adam yelled. "You're on the front page!"

"Oh my god, calm down," I hissed.

"No! This is a big deal! I'm so proud of you!"

"Sorry," I said when someone nudged me out of the way, reaching around to grab a copy of *The Telegraph*.

I moved down the aisle to the magazine section, and toggled the camera back to my face, grinning at the tiny Adam on my phone. "Thanks," I started, and then froze when someone said, "Morning, Ray."

"Did someone say Ray?" Adam said.

Of *course* he heard that.

"Shhh." I ducked and scurried around to the other side of the aisle where they stocked random stuff like stationery, balloons, and ant traps. I went on tiptoe and peered over the top shelf.

Ray was at the counter. He was talking to the owner, Miss Lawson.

"Over there," she said, pointing right at me.

"Shit." I pretended to be very interested in the box of batteries I found myself standing in front of.

"What's going on?" Adam hissed. "Is that Ray? Is Ray there? Turn the camera. I want to see."

"Will you shush?"

"Why are you hiding?"

"I don't know, okay? I *panicked*. I don't know, it feels weird that I wrote about him and now—oh god, he's coming over. Why? What does he want? Adam, what do I do? I—"

I broke off and stood there, wide-eyed, watching Ray's approach.

I was holding the phone up already, so I surreptitiously thumbed the camera to toggle forward.

Our gazes clashed and Ray hesitated.

We looked at each other for a moment. Then he said, "Excuse me," and grabbed a three-pack of batteries from the box. He turned and walked away.

Air leaked out of me.

I watched as Ray paused by the Cadbury Creme Eggs, seemed to have a mental debate that lasted approximately five seconds, then grabbed one.

"What's he doing?" Adam's voice said.

I took it off camera and lifted it to my ear. "Standing in the queue. He's buying batteries, and a Creme Egg." Ray leaned to the side and took something from one of the small stands by the till. "And a packet of chewing gum. He's an impulse buyer, and—oh no."

"What?"

"He grabbed a copy of the *Inquirer*." I gave a nervous giggle, then went rigid and stared fixedly at the batteries as Ray wandered past on his way out of the shop. I sagged. "Okay, he's gone."

"Jasper?" Adam said. "Is Ray going to be upset by the article?"

"Um. Hard to say? He's a highly strung kind of guy?"

And I called his house a murder house.

I went and stood in the small queue with a packet of triple-A batteries—didn't hurt to have some in my junk drawer—and a copy of my very own of the *Inquirer*.

"Jasper," Adam prompted.

"It was an interview with Craig Henderson and Kevin Wallis, the handymen. Their take on things. That's all."

And I called his house a murder house.

"Cool. Okay. See you at the gym later?"

"Yep."

"I'm so proud of you."

I beamed. "Thank you!"

Adam disconnected and I was still smiling widely when I tapped my card to the reader. Miss Lawson didn't smile back. I didn't care. It was going to take more than that to ruin my day.

I nearly bumped into Ray again outside the shop. He was standing to one side of the door, reading the newspaper, with a smudge of chocolate at the corner of his lips. The Creme Egg hadn't lasted long. As I watched, he snorted and crumpled the paper up into a ball. He dropped it into the litter bin and walked off.

Okay, *that* didn't feel great.

ALL IN ALL, MY EXPERIENCE AS A FINALLY PUBLISHED journalist left a lot to be desired.

Ralph paid me fifty pounds for it. I hadn't expected a lot, but I had expected a tiny bit more.

That would teach me to get something agreed on beforehand next time.

It wasn't all bad; the fifty pounds came in the form of a gift card to the coffee shop. Even though Craig and Kevin between them had blown through a month's budget, I still came out with a profit.

Because I knew my parents didn't read the *Inquirer* —they were the *Financial Times* and *The Telegraph* people—I took a copy around for them on Friday afternoon. They both said they'd have a look, but they never mentioned it again. Either they read it, shared Ray's opinion and put it in the bin, or they forgot.

They probably forgot. It was fine.

My parents had made their feelings on my life choices more than clear when I failed to pick a career that pulled in a hundred thousand pounds a year. I could hardly expect them to suddenly change their minds because I'd got something printed in a local newspaper.

Saturdays were always busy at the gym. As well as classes, I had back-to-back clients until five. By then, I was more than ready to chill for the rest of the weekend.

I staggered home, showered, and got into my comfies. I took a big bottle of water over to my writing corner and poked the spacebar on my MacBook to wake it up.

I hadn't touched it since I'd sent Ralph the final (who was I kidding, first and only) draft of the article on Thursday, and my email client was still on screen. I grimaced and closed it.

This left the article on screen instead, with all its red squiggles shouting, *You've made a mistake, right here!*

As it turned out, Ralph didn't do a spellcheck or a proofread either. It was fair to say that one or two cockups had made it through, and those mistakes were now immortalised in print.

I was sure I'd hear all about it from Ralph when his number one reader and Chipping Fairford's self-appointed grammar police, Terry Stoddard, sent in his usual annotated copy of the paper with all the mistakes circled in red pen.

I'd suggested that Ralph hire Terry to go through it all *before* printing, but they had some sort of long-running feud, and Ralph swore he'd rather strip naked and do a one-man tango down the high street.

I closed the article and opened up a new document.

It was time to get serious now. I needed to capitalise on my success and brainstorm some ideas for another article. Think about what mattered to the community.

What did people want to read about?

It was easy; all I had to do was pin that down, and the ideas would flow.

I stared at the cursor.

They'd flow.

All of the ideas.

Like a river. A bountiful river of creativity.

Okay. My creativity river was flowing like a glacier.

I had to shake it loose, stop overthinking it, get the blood pumping.

I leapt out of my chair, did some lunges and squats, and sat back down. I closed my eyes, set my hands on the keyboard, and started typing…

At long last, I had been summoned to the warlord's tent.

I was shaking and nervous, yet determined to do the right thing. I would stab the blackguard through the heart, in the name of King Adam and the conquered people of Fayreford, one more kingdom swallowed up by the dark greed of the barbarian warlord Liam Nash.

I would look down on him as I fulfilled my destiny, and I would laugh in his face as he expired at my feet, smitten by the deadly beauty of Fayreford's Avenger.

I would toss my hair out of my eyes and sneer and say, "And you thought I was a simple soldier. You handsome fool! But, no. I am a highly skilled assassin, with no mercy, and nothing but loyalty to my king and my people in my heart. Despair of the day you cast your lustful gaze upon our kingdom!"

Or something like that.

I had been chosen, along with other favoured friends of the king, as hostages for King Adam's good behaviour. We had been traveling for weeks, dragged along on foot behind the warlord's mounted soldiers. Now, finally, I was summoned.

Nash sprawled on a rough-hewn bench, lounging with the remains of a feast spread out on the low trestle table before him.

"Bring him over here," he said, sounding bored.

I put up a show of resistance—not too much, though—as his second-in-command shoved and wrangled me forward. She thrust me down to my knees at Nash's feet.

"Leave us."

Excellent. Everything was unfolding perfectly.

It was just me and Nash in the dark and candlelit tent, with lots of furs and weapons and stuff around. Shadowy, iron-bound trunks. Piles of treasure. The usual ill-gotten loot.

Any minute now I would snatch the knife from my boot, plunge it into his wicked heart, and—

Nash gripped my chin in his hard hand and turned my face up to the light. He tilted it this way and that, eyes like wicked steel boring into mine.

I did my best to boldly glare back at him but my gaze fell before his as my breathing sped up.

He stood slowly, bringing his groin level with my face.

I went cross-eyed trying to focus on it.

"Well, then?" he said softly. "What are you waiting for? I know you want to try it."

"Oh, fine," I said, and undid his breeches.

Nash frowned down at me. "By all means," he said. "Pleasure me with your pretty mouth if you must. But what I meant was, go ahead and try to kill me with the knife you have hidden in your boot."

Awkward.

"For which treachery I will of course be having you executed at dawn as a warning to all of your fellow hostages."

"Executed? That seems a bit harsh, doesn't it? I haven't done anything."

Yet.

"You didn't come here to kill me then?"

"...of course not and frankly I am offended. What? No. I wouldn't know how. I am but a lowly foot solider. Who farms. Wheat. I am a wheat farmer. Most of the time. And was conscripted into the army."

"Conscripted."

"Yes. Forced to serve."

"By your best friend the king."

"...yes. He can't be seen to have favourites, especially amongst the peasants."

"Then you're not a favourite?"

"Me? Pfft. No. I'm nobody."

"If you're nobody, I don't need you as a hostage."

"And by nobody, I of course mean I am dear to the king's heart. Dearest of all, I would say. Apart from his concubine, Ray. I am an excellent and deeply valuable hostage. Whomst King Adam would be greatly miffed if you executed at dawn, even if I did try to kill you. Which I wouldn't. Even though it would be justified. Maybe. I don't know, I never studied ethics and stuff. Just...okay, so my baseline philosophy is, don't be a dick. That's about as complicated as that gets. Anyway. Where were we?"

I had one hand on his firm backside and the other still in his breeches.

"Your lies will not save you," he said. "Fortunately, your king already has. I summoned you here to tell you that you have been successfully ransomed and will be returning to Fayreford. I have no further use for you. You'll have to walk the two hundred miles back, of course, we can't spare a horse. It'll probably take you a *month. If, that is, you survive the burning sun, the Canyon of Doom, the orcs encamped on the Blasted Wasteland, and then the wolves in the Forest of Despair. You've got your boot knife, though. Sure you'll be fine."*

"What?"

"You're free to go. Any time you like. Or now, that would suit me better. I'm expecting company."

He eased himself from my grip and went to lounge seductively on his bed of furs.

I was still on my knees, hands in the air from where I'd been holding him, and I gawked as the tent flaps opened to reveal a tall and willowy young man. He was dressed mostly in chiffon scarves and sexy gold chainmail that was more holes than anything else. It wouldn't stop a spoon. He sauntered in and crawled onto the bed like he owned it. "Who's the filthy captive?" he said in a purring voice, straddling Nash.

"Oh. Is the random peasant still here?" the warlord said. "Ignore him. He'll go in a minute."

I pushed up to my feet. "I'll just—oh. No preliminaries? Straight to it? Must have planned ahead." The warlord's date had ripped his chiffon trousers off and sat on Nash. They both moaned as he began to move. His moaning was a bit fake, if you asked me. "Excellent. I'll...yep. Carry on."

I rushed out so I didn't have to hear the moaning, and—

Oh for fuck's sake.

I think I preferred it when Liam shot me out of an airlock to actually writing about him shagging *someone else*.

Who was this guy, anyway?

Where did he even come from? He could go right back there, thanks.

I was supposed to be overcome with passion when the boot knife was wrestled mercilessly from my desperate grip and I was sexily conquered on the floor of the tent.

Not get summoned, released into the wilderness, and forgotten about.

I was busily deleting the nonsense word by frustrating word when the front door opened and shut. "Jasper?" Adam called out. "You here?"

"Yes!"

"Good. Okay. Are you ready for this?"

"Probably not."

"Close your eyes. Don't ask questions. Just do it."

"Don't be naked. It'll never work between us. I'm in love with your cousin."

He gave a short laugh. "Not naked. In love with Ray. Close your eyes!"

I did as I was told. Adam came in and walked up to me. I felt his body heat as he came close, then sensed him standing off to one side of my desk.

"Okay," he said. "Open."

I did. "Adam!" I gasped.

He was holding a huge frame up against the wall, above my MacBook.

He'd had my article blown up and framed.

"Ta-da," he said.

My eyes stung and I bit my lip.

"Oh no," he said.

"I'm okay. I'm okay!"

"This is not what okay looks like, Jasper," he said, and propped the frame against the wall. He grabbed my cheeks and angled my head back, looking down at me with concern. "What's going on?"

"Nothing! My life is spectacular!" I gestured at the framed article and made an incoherent noise. "Thank you, seriously."

He tugged the sleeve of his hoodie over his hand and

gently blotted my face. "Uh-huh."

My life *was* spectacular. I loved being a personal trainer, I was making progress as a journalist, I had a great writing hobby which would get back on track any day now...and I was getting over Liam.

I *was*.

18

I was not getting over Liam.

It was almost two months since that after-noon I'd thought he was coming to arrest me and we'd ended up in bed.

Two. Months.

I could recall in exquisite detail the sensation of his heavy body moving over me, his heat, the flash of his eyes. I could still feel his lips on mine.

I remembered it all, no matter how hard I tried to forget.

I'd cut myself off from writing Liam Nash fanfic. Matters hadn't improved there, either. One morning I'd read back my latest attempt, realised that it wasn't healthy that I kept writing myself out of my own stories, whether I was getting vented into space or watching some other guy get it from Liam, and went cold turkey.

The turkey was so cold, it was in a deep freeze; I hadn't even opened up a document in weeks. Not even to write an article, which had freaked Ralph out.

He was used to fending off my pitches on a regular basis. After I'd gone quiet, he called me into his office.

"All right," he'd said, leaning back in his chair and peering at me over the top of his glasses. "I'll bite. What's happening? Why aren't you bugging me anymore? What's wrong?"

I'd dropped in on my way to work. "Nothing," I said, fiddling with the strap of my gym bag.

He sighed. "Will you please sit down and stop looming?"

"Uh, actually, no. I have to be at the gym in twenty minutes."

Ralph blinked. "Right. Well. What are you working on?"

"Nothing."

"Nothing?"

I shuffled. "Yep."

"I don't believe you," he said after a long minute. "You're working on something. Something big."

"I'm really not," I said with a shrug.

"You finally get your front page, you finally get into print, and, what? That's it?"

"I'm kind of busy right now. With life and stuff. I've got a load of new clients, I'm teaching a couple of new classes." I shrugged again. "I don't have the time."

"Okay." He still looked suspicious. "Well. Keep your eyes and ears open out there. I'm ready to hear any pitches you come up with."

"Thanks," I said. "But unless another body is discovered in Chipping Fairford, I probably won't be bothering you for a while."

"Can't imagine that happening twice. All right. Get going, then."

Unlike the Liam fanfic, I hadn't made the deliberate decision to stop trying to write for the paper. It just sort of happened. Being honest with myself, I was having doubts.

They'd been circling for a while. Did I even want to be a journalist anymore? People changed. Dreams changed.

Out of the fanfic and the journalism, I definitely missed the fanfic the most.

I missed fictional Liam almost as much as I missed real Liam.

I missed, most of all, the days when the thought of Liam wanting me back had been pure fantasy.

Now that he was no longer married, now that I knew he was into men, that he was into me—at least physically—and yet I *still* wasn't enough, it was a special kind of torture to run into him when I was out and about.

Over the past couple of months, I'd seen him at the pub with his old rugby mates. I'd bumped into him in the Co-op once. More than a few times, I'd seen him driving around town.

There had been an electric moment at the gym where I nearly embarrassed myself to actual death when I turned around in the locker room, all unsuspecting, and came face-to-butt with a half-dressed Liam.

He'd been changing and chatting to a friend. Slammed with the unexpected vision of all I yearned for, out of nowhere, I'd frozen, and stared.

After I'd made some sort of inappropriate noise.

His friend scowled at me. Liam turned to see what his friend was scowling at. I turned purple with embarrassment and ran out.

I'd run straight back in when I remembered I was only wearing my jockstrap and my trainers.

It wasn't a great moment.

That had been last week, and I'd been fighting the urge to rewrite the sorry event into a sexy gym story ever since.

I had a feeling I was going to lose that fight. The story was an itch under my skin.

And I liked it.

It was a positive sign, I decided. A sign of healing.

I'd taken a break and my ego (my heart, oh my heart) had got over itself. In another couple of weeks, I'd be back to wanting Liam in a totally normal and distant way, happily writing stories and knowing that I would never have him.

I might not be over Liam quite yet, but I was on the right track.

I was in a good mood.

Unlike Charlie, who was on the other side of the coffee shop counter, glaring at me. "You want what?" he snapped.

"A triple venti mochaccino frappe with extra ice, whipped cream, a squirt of the chocolate sauce, and a wafer, please. Oh. And can I have a smile on top?"

"Amalie!" Charlie yelled. "One of your idiot friends thinks he's being funny. You deal with him."

"I'm busy!" she yelled back. "Is it Jasper?"

He smirked at me, shouting, "What tipped you off? Was it when I said idiot?"

"Hey, now," I said.

"Just give him a coffee," she bellowed.

Charlie raised his eyebrows at me.

"And a smile?" I said.

"No." He stalked off to make the coffee.

I bent my knees and leaned my forearms on the counter as I perused the chalkboard menu.

It was April, and they'd long phased out the wintery and Christmas-themed treats. They'd started selling Easter goodies last week. I was tempted to try a gingerbread Easter bunny with pink-and-white icing, or a Cadbury Mini Egg-studded brownie.

I decided to go for it. I deserved a treat. So did Adam, who was meeting me here in a few minutes.

Adam had been going through his own issues with Ray. Like me, he'd got close and had a taste of happiness, only to have the object of his affection shut him down. We were dealing with our disappointing love lives very differently. I moped over Liam; Adam flaunted himself at Ray.

A lot of Adam's flaunting happened right here in the coffee shop. It was the only place Adam could engineer an 'accidental' meeting, since Ray came here at the same time every day.

It was stalker-level genius, I'd told him, and not as a compliment.

It was boring, he'd replied. But he was committed. He was playing the long game and waiting for Ray to come to him.

I envied his confidence. To be honest, it would probably work. Adam could smoulder like you wouldn't believe. Sooner or later, Ray would cave, and jump him.

I was entertaining myself imagining how Liam would react if I ever attempted to smoulder at him, when something cold and wet pressed against the back of my knee.

I shuddered and lurched forward with a yelp, banging into the counter.

"Sorry, sorry," a woman said. "*Dougal*! We've talked about this."

Mrs Hughes stood behind me with Dougal. Dougal was wearing a little red harness and matching arthritis boots. I put down a hand to block him from licking my knee again. His tongue swiped my hand instead.

"I'm so sorry, Jasper. He has a thing for knees."

I squinted down at Dougal. He smiled up happily at me. "You little pervert," I said. "Knees? Really?"

Mrs Hughes laughed. "He can't resist. If he sees a bare knee—front or back—he's got to lick it. Makes for a lot of fun in summer when everyone's wearing shorts or skirts, I can tell you. He's very stealthy."

"I had no idea."

"You're tall. Your knees are usually out of reach. He just got you because you were bending."

"Jasper, stop draping yourself over my counter, it's unsanitary," Charlie said, returning with my coffee.

I straightened, eyeing the steaming cup. "Are you sure I can't have a nice frappe?" I said with a sigh. "You can skip the wafer. I won't mind."

"No. I hate doing the fancy drinks, that's Amalie's gig. She's busy. This is a perfect Americano, and you will appreciate my artistry. Look at that crema. Hi, Mrs Hughes. What can I get you?"

"Flat white for me and the usual for Dougal, please."

"Flat white and a puppuccino, coming up."

"Puppuccino?" I said indignantly. That sounded fancy.

"It's only warm milk he froths up a bit," Mrs Hughes said. "Dougal likes a treat."

"How come Dougal gets a fancy drink and I don't?" I said to Charlie.

"I like Dougal."

"Thanks. That's very flattering. Can I have another Americano for Adam, please? Oh, and a gingerbread Easter bunny and a brownie."

"When I'm done with Dougal's puppuccino," Charlie said.

He wasn't as mean as he liked to pretend. I really got on his wick for some reason, kind of like with Liam. Adam said it was because Charlie fancied me, but I didn't see it. Also,

Charlie didn't date anyone, ever. I didn't think he was into people.

"I read your article in the paper," Mrs Hughes said.

"Yeah?" I straightened.

"It was very...vivid. You certainly have a way of spinning a yarn. Much more entertaining to read than that one on the website from Karen Strickland was. Good job. "

I grinned. "Thank you!"

"Those men were definitely speeding, though. I stand by that."

Charlie returned with Mrs Hughes' order and she wandered off at a snail's pace, Dougal trudging behind. Charlie said to me with exasperation, "What was it you wanted again?"

I didn't bother repeating myself. He was already getting the bunny and the brownie out of the display case. Instead, I said, "You know, for reference, I was actually being served *before* you let Mrs Hughes and Dougal queue jump."

"Queue jump?" Charlie looked around at the quiet coffee shop. "What do you think this is, Starbucks on Piccadilly Circus? Are you in a rush? Off to the London Stock Exchange before your shares plummet? You'll get your order. Stop complaining."

He filled a tray with the coffees and the treats, waited for me to tap the card reader, and whisked off.

"Charlie," I called after him, "you put an extra brownie on my plate."

"The extra one is yesterday's. It's stale. I was going to put it in the compost bin. You may as well have it."

"Aw," I said. "Thanks."

"Go away," he said, biting back a smile.

"Okay." I went and sat down at an empty table and

tucked into my free brownie. It was definitely baked today. I could tell a fresh brownie when I had one.

Adam came in with his usual fanfare, drawing the eye of everyone in the shop. It wasn't like he flung the door open and stalked in or anything, but he had whatever *it* was that made people look. Not that he ever deigned to notice.

He threw himself down in the chair opposite me and sprawled out.

I pushed the coffee and the gingerbread bunny over to him.

He grunted, slouched lower, and cradled the cup in his long fingers. He closed his eyes and sipped, sighing with satisfaction. When his lashes fluttered open, he caught me staring. Slowly, he licked his lips. "Am I turning you on?" he said in a deep voice.

I shuffled in my seat thoughtfully. "Nope. Everything's nice and limp down there, thanks."

Adam let out a crack of laughter.

"I'm immune to your sexy mojo," I said.

"Good." He shoved my ankle with his foot. "Why were you watching me like that?"

"I was wondering if I could pull off that sort of move."

"What move?" He was genuinely confused.

I tenderly picked up my cup, kissed the rim and took a long, pretend sip. I sighed like I was coming down from an orgasm.

Adam glared. "I don't do that. And no, you can't pull it off. You look constipated. Why do you want to drink coffee sexy anyway?"

"Why do you think?"

He rolled his eyes.

"I was wondering, earlier. Before you came in. Is it that

Liam still sees me as immature? Should I try to tone it all down? Try to be more sophisticated? Smoulder a bit?"

"If what you did at the end of that little performance was a smoulder—"

"It was."

"—then hard no. And don't you ever tone yourself down. You're perfect. Babe, Liam is a Neanderthal. He's not even going to notice you trying to do sexy things. Think way, way simpler. There's no need to make it complicated. Bend over in front of him. He won't be able to resist."

That didn't sound very romantic. I poked at the crumbs on my plate, picked them up on the end of my finger, then stuck it in my mouth. "Huh," I said around my finger. "And don't call me babe."

Adam turned his attention to his Easter bunny, and I brooded.

After thirty seconds of brooding, I got my Moleskine notebook and a pen out of the front pocket of my gym bag.

L is a Neanderthal, I wrote. I wasn't stupid enough to write his name unless it was safely protected by a password on my MacBook. Then I scratched it out and wrote, *L is a caveman. I am the helpless time traveller captured by a rival tribe and brought to his camp to trade for a share in the spoils of the mammoth hunt. It's a harsh world. Locked in ice. Battered by storms. Will we make it through the winter? Who knows? I am shivering in my Under Armour. One minute I was in the twenty-first century, the next I was transported here, trapped forever in the dark dawn of mankind.*

I sat back and gazed ahead, lost in the Ice Age. I wondered what the coffee shop looked like ten or twenty thousand years ago? I glanced around. Or even further back, millions of years ago in the time of dinosaurs.

Oh?

I dropped down a line in my notebook.

L is a dinosa—no. I scratched that out quickly, shaking my head.

It was getting close to mid-morning and the coffee shop was filling up. There was a queue at the counter. I sat up straight when I caught sight of a familiar figure.

"Adam," I said. "*Adam.*"

"What?" He was scrolling through his phone.

"Ray is here," I said.

You'd think I'd shoved a stun gun into his balls and hit the go button, the way he jerked in his seat. He banged the table with an elbow and everything rattled.

My eyes widened. "I said Ray is here, not Ray needs saving from velociraptors, now's your chance to shine. Oh my god. Can you pretend to be cool for a second?"

"Shut up. Yes, I can. Photographers and fashion houses have payed me thousands and thousands of pounds to be cool."

"How much will it cost to get you to bust some of that out now? Because I'll pay."

Adam glared at me.

I leaned over the table and poked his nose.

"Do that again and you lose a hand," he said. There wasn't much heat behind it. He was already scanning for Ray. And when I say scanning, I mean his eyes went unerringly to Ray.

"Shit," Adam said, and slid down in his seat. He crossed his arms over his chest, uncrossed them, crossed his legs at the ankles instead, and said to me in an urgent whisper, "How's my hair?"

I gave him a thumbs-up. "Really bringing your tousled curl game today. Ten out of ten."

He flashed me his dimples. "What's he doing?" He was stubbornly refusing to look for himself.

"Oh my god. He is...holy shit. He is a *minx*. Adam. Check it out. He is standing in the queue and oh, *oh*!" I pretended to cover my eyes. "Has the man no *shame*? He's *on* his *phone*."

Adam gave me a flat, unimpressed look.

I grinned back. "As much fun as it is watching you regress to the fourteen-year-old nerd I remember with such fondness, I have to get to the gym." I pushed my chair back from the table and stood up. "Are you going to be able to control yourself around him?"

"Yeah," Adam said. "But quick, before you go, kiss me."

"*What*?"

"You heard. Do it." Adam fake-laughed, bright and loud, making people look. Then he hissed at me, "Touch my beautiful face and kiss me."

I stared at him like he'd lost his mind, read murder in his eyes, and obediently bent down. I pinched his chin, muttered, "Really?" as our lips got closer because this felt weird now that I'd had Liam's lips on mine, and—

Adam turned his face coyly at the last minute. I ended up kissing his cheek as he shot one of his goosebump-raising model smoulders over at Ray.

I followed his gaze.

I'd sell my spleen for Liam to look at me like either of them was eyeing up the other, I really would. Pretty cheap, too.

Amalie called Ray's attention back to his order, and Adam slumped. He went rigid again when Amalie continued her conversation with Ray over the noise of the ice machine, yelling loud enough for the whole coffee shop to hear, "You've got a nice arse, too!"

"He's got a spectacular arse," Adam said. "Perky and cute and *round*. Although why she's shouting about—"

"Oh. Dating profile, is it?" Amalie said, her words ringing as the ice machine cut off.

Uh-oh.

"Dating profile?" Adam gritted out.

"Maybe waiting for him to come to you wasn't the right play," I said.

"Bring your dates here," Amalie was saying. "Support your local coffee shop. Fuck Starbucks."

The Galloways really hated Starbucks.

"He'd better *not* bring his dates here," Adam said. "He'd better not date anyone at all."

"Adam, calm down."

Adam's cheeks were flushed. "You know what? No. I'm going to go over there and tell him, right now, to delete that fucking dating app because he doesn't need it—"

"Adam—"

"You know what dating apps are like, Jas. I bet you anything he's on a hook-up app and too naive to know it. Ray can't do hook-ups. He'll get *hurt*. He's sensitive. I'm not going to stand by and let him get hurt."

"Snap out of it." I grabbed his shoulders and shook him. "Adam, Ray can make his own choices. He's a grown man. He is Liam's age. I'm sure he's done the dating-app thing before. And even if he hasn't—" I stared deep into Adam's eyes, "—you can't just make him bend to your will."

He stared back into my eyes. "I fucking can," he said.

"You are so creepy sometimes."

He gave me a feral smile. "Yeah. Has he gone yet?"

"Yes."

Adam slumped bonelessly in his seat. "I'm adjusting my plan," he said. "Ray should have jumped me by now." He rubbed a hand over his face. "I'm going to lose it if I see him on a date, Jasper," he said.

"You'll be fine," I said.

He was, mostly.

I was the one who lost it.

We saw Ray on a date two days later.

With Liam.

19

I was waiting to be served at the bar when Liam came in.

It was a Thursday night and The Lion was loud, hot, and busy. I hadn't been out for weeks. Post-work classes at the gym were always popular and, by the time I'd done three in a row, got home, and showered, I didn't have the energy left for more socialising.

For once my schedule had lined up with Adam's and he'd suggested meeting for a pint like the wild and crazy youngsters that we were, rather than hanging out at the coffee shop all the time. What the hell, I thought. Why not?

And then Liam came in.

I saw his reflection in the mirror over the bar. He was wearing a deep burgundy sweater, dark indigo jeans, and he had a hint of gingery stubble. He'd done something to his sandy blond hair. He looked great.

I turned to face him, and gave a hesitant wave.

Liam blushed.

It was faint, but it was a blush. It wasn't an I'm-getting-annoyed-with-you-Jasper kind of blush, either. He looked uncomfortable.

I cocked my head. What was—

"Jasper, hey," Lenny said behind the bar. "Jas. Wake up, come on. I haven't got all night. Drinks."

I collected the drinks and paid. Liam moved on. I looked around for him as I went to sit with Adam and a couple of mates. I set our drinks down on the table, still looking for Liam, and eventually spotted him over in the restaurant area.

That should have made me suspicious, straight away. Nice clothes, did something with his hair, sitting in the restaurant area like the last time I saw him on a date.

But I wasn't suspicious at all.

Instead, I sat there staring at him. He was studying his phone, resting stone face in place. As I watched, he scowled and started typing.

God, I even liked his scowls.

"What are you smiling about?" Adam said, nudging me and taking a swig of beer.

I shook my head and didn't say anything.

So.

It was time to face facts.

I'd spent two months pining and writing miserable little stories about us that kept going sideways and leaving me out in the cold.

Apart from the new Liam-is-a-caveman story. That one was going surprisingly well. I'd written a furious five thousand words on it last night, and it felt fantastic.

Getting over Liam was clearly a thing I was absolutely incapable of doing. Moving on, ditto. Where did that leave me?

I gazed across the bright and busy distance.

Nobody wanted to be *that* guy, the one who doesn't take no for an answer. The thing was, apart from calling him to ask him on a coffee date, Liam was the one who'd made all the moves.

He came to my house. Twice.

He kicked things off by kissing me.

Twice.

He ordered me up the stairs, onto my bed, and took me apart.

Then he rejected me and called me a hook-up, but still.

Maybe he was regretting it.

Maybe he was thinking, *You know what? I was unnecessarily dismissive, I didn't give us a chance, and Jasper is lost to me forever. Woe.*

Maybe I should go over there and indicate that it wasn't the case at all.

Adam was adjusting his plan to seduce Ray. I decided that it was time for me to be proactive about winning Liam. I wasn't a quitter!

I stood up abruptly.

Adam glanced at me, startled.

"Going to the toilet," I muttered.

"Okay," he said. "Thanks for keeping me updated."

"Cool."

I smoothed my t-shirt down over my abs so it clung a bit better—my abs seemed to distract Liam a fair bit and I wasn't above playing dirty—swiped a hand over my hair, and made it halfway across the room in a businesslike stride before I came to a sudden halt.

I'd been so fixated on Liam, I hadn't seen the man approaching from the other side. He cut in front of me, walked right up to Liam's table, and sat down.

I stood there like an absolute muppet until someone

bumped into me and made a big deal about having to walk all the way around me to get to the bar. Turning on my heel, I marched jerkily back to my table.

I sat down.

"Ray's here," I said blankly to Adam.

"Yeah?" He broke off his conversation to a chorus of groans. Everyone knew how Adam felt about Ray. "Where is he?"

"Over there," I said, and pointed. "On a date. With Liam."

Adam made a noise like a growl that would normally have made me get him in a headlock and hold him back before he could do something stupid, but I was busy watching my future crumble to dust and blow away in the wind.

I sat there like a lump.

Of *course* Liam was on a date with Ray.

Of course.

Because I wasn't his type.

Ray was.

Of course.

"Oh, hell no," Adam said, lunging out of his seat and stalking over.

Wow, was I an idiot. And a glutton for punishment. And a fucking idiot. I threw back the rest of my mineral water and stood up.

"See you later, guys," I said to anyone who was listening —most of them were watching Adam crash Liam and Ray's date—and walked out.

I wasn't Liam's type.

I didn't really remember getting home and going to bed, which in retrospect was alarming. I'd managed to walk home, let myself in the house, get up stairs and into bed, all without any conscious thought.

When Jasper got married to his ex-wife, Verity, I'd been devastated. I'd also been a hormone-addled eighteen-year-old with a romantic streak a mile wide.

This hit differently.

Now, I was a man. A full-grown adult who'd had his fair share of knocks and rejections by this point. I'd learned how to take a hit. I'd learned how to get back up.

I always got back up.

So that's what I did the next morning.

Yes, I felt like I'd been run over by the Truck of Broken Dreams, but what the hell? I was still standing. Nothing new.

Seriously, nothing new. I was right back where I was two months ago, after Liam had told me I was a hook-up. It hadn't sunk it back then. It had sunk in now. All the way down to the bone.

I was surprisingly okay with it. I went through my morning routine. I ran. I journaled. I deleted the caveman fanfic, and brainstormed four decent article ideas. Okay, two. I went to work. I came back.

I did the same again the next day, and the next.

It didn't hurt anymore. It wasn't even a big deal this time. Nothing had happened. I just saw him out on a date with the man everyone wanted, because Ray was everyone's type.

I got on with my life.

My obsession with Liam Nash was officially over.

For real this time.

20

I stared at my enemy, my nemesis, the Lex Luthor to my Clark Kent: the cursor.

Blink on, villain, I thought. I will defeat you in the end.

My victory is inevitable.

It was Thursday morning and I was all set up at my desk in my writing studio.

Giant bottle of water? Check.

Soft crackling fire and rain sounds playing on my white noise app? Check.

Fresh, clean document? Check.

I had nothing to do other than sit here and let my imagination unspool.

I was here to brainstorm, and nothing else. This was a practice session.

Since I'd last tried to come up with some article ideas for Ralph, I'd had something of a revelation.

There was a *reason* that the fiction flowed and the non-fiction didn't.

Other than the fact it was unarguably way more fun to write about getting railed than it was trying to sex up a story about the bitter fight for parking spaces in the centre of town.

It was obvious. I couldn't believe how long it had taken me to work it out.

Very simply, I'd written hundreds of thousands of words of fiction, and...well. Ten thousand of non-fiction?

I hadn't logged the hours. That was all.

Now that I was free from my obsession with Liam Nash, I had many, many, many hours available in which to practice writing the way I was *supposed* to. In a way that would appeal to and entertain the good citizens of Chipping Fairford, rather than just me.

I knew how to train toward a skill. I'd trained my way through learning everything from yoga to kickboxing. If things got desperate at the gym, I could even stand in for Barre class. That had happened once or twice, and I wouldn't mind if it happened again. I'd loved it.

All I had to do was flip those physical training skills into the mental realm.

As of now, I was in journalist training.

And a good journalist could make a story out of anything, I told myself as I sat there, continuing to stare down the cursor.

Even carparks.

Which was a good thing. Because nothing exciting ever happened in Chipping Fairford.

Apart from that battle in the 1300s.

And Ray finding a dead guy in his bedroom floor.

I could hardly expect something like that to happen twice, could I? I'd just concentrate, open myself up to inspiration, and practice.

I lifted my hands and held them poised above the keyboard. I closed my eyes. The universe was on my side.

The universe would deliver the perfect idea. I would write abouuuuuut—

My phone rang over on the sofa where I'd put it out of reach.

Oh, thank god.

I jumped up and glanced at the screen.

It was a new phone, or at least new to me. When I went around to my parents house the other day, my mum had noticed the appalling state of my phone with its cracked screen, and insisted I have one of her old ones. She'd opened a kitchen drawer and told me to take my pick.

That drawer was stuffed. She gets a new phone every time Apple releases one, and she'd had her first mobile back in the *nineties*. In other words, it was like a phone museum in there.

The display said it was Ralph calling. It cut out before I could answer.

The universe hadn't filled me with inspiration about what to write, but here was Ralph, calling out of the blue. It was a cosmic thumbs-up, I decided. A nod. I was going in the right direction.

A voicemail notification popped up and I was about to hit play when the phone rang in my hand.

"Hi, Ralph," I said. "You'll be happy to know that I—"

"Oh, thank fuck you answered your fucking phone this time!" he yelled. "What a refreshing change! Jasper!"

Oh my god, why was he screaming at me? I winced, and held the phone away from my ear. "Yes?" I said tentatively.

"I'm about to do you a favour," he said. "The biggest fucking favour in the world, all right? It happened again, and I'm putting you on it. Don't fuck up."

"Wow," I said. "That sounds exciting. Thanks, Ralph. Putting me on what, though?"

"On the case! The story! The dead guy!"

"Someone died?" I said.

"Yeah. Guess where?"

"I'm assuming somewhere in Chipping Fairf—"

"Number fifty-two, Sycamore Close," Ralph said. "Ring a bell?"

"Ray's house?" I said. "It's not Ray is it?"

I had complicated feelings about Ray. On second thought, I had one feeling about Ray, and it was searing, boiling jealousy. So. Not that complicated.

But I didn't want him dead.

"No, it's not fucking Ray Underwood. I heard from my contact on the police that he found another dead body on the premises, same deal as last time, and called it in to the police."

"Holy crap."

"I know," Ralph said, his abrasive voice quavering with excitement. "Get your shit together, kid, get over there, and get me the story."

"I am on it!" I glanced across the room at the blown-up article Adam had framed for me. I'd hung it on the wall above my computer, having to move my *Write! Write! Write!* banner to make room. Maybe there'd be another framed article up there soon.

Maybe there would be loads.

I'd been up and down about the article since I'd hung it, especially as seeing all those spelling mistakes in a huge large font made me want to edit it and reprint it, but it must have been good. Ralph was trusting me with a breaking story when he could have asked Mrs Strickland.

"I'm sending Strickland as well," Ralph said.

"Ralph, come on."

"I don't care which one of you gets it. Honestly? I'm

hoping it's you. Strickland is good. You're not as good, but you've got a certain readability. That's what I want for the *Inquirer*. This is it, Jasper. The big one. Your big break."

He hung up and I stood frozen in the centre of the room, heart pounding, still holding the phone to my ear.

Another body in Ray's house. What were the odds? How did he keep finding them?

What were they doing there in the first place?

Was Ray really an innocent bystander, or had Adam pledged his eternal devotion to a clever minx of a socio-pathic murderer?

It was time to ask some questions.

And I'd better get my arse into gear and get out the door, or Mrs Strickland would scoop me again.

I darted into the hall and pulled on my trainers. I shoved my phone in my sweatpants pocket and shrugged on a parka over my t-shirt. My gym bag was waiting by the door, and I kept a notebook and a couple of pens in the side pocket. Grabbing the bag and my car keys from the hall table, I rushed out of the house.

I was focused. Aimed like a deadly arrow. Less than two minutes after Ralph had hung up, I was on the road.

"You can do it, Jasper," I said with conviction. I suppressed a nervous giggle and firmed my jaw. "Showtime."

I knew better than to even try and turn down Sycamore Close. I blew past the cordoned-off junction and turned down the street running parallel.

I kept a wary eye on the parked cars as I trundled down the road, dreading seeing that green VW Beetle with its chillingly misleading flower decal.

It was camouflage. It said, *I am owned by a sweet and*

whimsical driver! Not even a hint that a vicious retired English teacher was the one behind the wheel.

There was no sign of Mrs Strickland. I was here first! Unless she'd taken the other road that ran parallel to Sycamore Close.

I parked at the back of Mrs Hughes' house, took off my parka because it was a warm day and I was having a bit of a panic sweat, and tossed it onto the passenger seat. I dug my notebook and pen out of my gym bag, stuffed them in the pocket of my sweatpants along with my phone, and got out the car.

It wasn't trespass if the property owner didn't mind, I told myself as I approached Mrs Hughes' larch-lap back fence.

She hadn't exactly issued me an open invitation to cut across her lawn any time I was on official journalist business, but she hadn't prosecuted me, either.

I decided I could take that to mean it wouldn't be *too* big of a deal if I indulged in another shortcut.

I put my hands on the fence, popped myself up and over, and landed in a crouch.

"Oh, damn," I said as I straightened. "Um. Hi, Mrs Hughes. Lovely weather today."

She was in the middle of hanging her washing on the line, and was staring at me. Her lips twitched. "Morning, Jasper," she said.

I pointed at the side alley that led to the front. "Sorry. Do you mind if I...?"

"By all means," she said.

"Sorry. Won't make a habit of it. Thanks!" I ran over the lawn, pausing to pat a bewildered-looking Dougal, and made it to the gravel path before she said,

"Out of curiosity, though, any particular reason you're jumping over my fence today?"

"Uh, another dead—I mean. It's reporter business. Journalist stuff."

She gasped. "Ray found another dead body?"

"I don't know, I think so, lemme go check," I said over my shoulder, and ran.

"Don't forget, I keep the side gate locked!" she called after me.

"No problem," I called back, and scaled it. Up and over.

My phone fell out of my pocket and hit the asphalt with a smack. Face first, of course.

"Fuck." Oh, well. I'd go and raid my mum's phone museum tomorrow.

I swept it up from the ground, stuffed it back into my pocket, glanced up, and locked eyes with Liam Nash.

"Fuck," I said again, this time with feeling.

He was talking to a paramedic on the other side of the road. The paramedic was leaning her shoulders against her ambulance, ankles crossed.

Liam pinned me across the distance with blistering disapproval. His gaze raked the full length of my body, from my pink t-shirt which said *PUMP IT!!!* to my battered trainers and back up to my face, before he turned back to listen to whatever the paramedic was saying.

The front of Ray's house was cluttered with cars and official-looking people, the door was open, and people were shuttling in and out. Some of them were wearing familiar white forensics bunny suits, carrying lights and cables, and ominous black crates.

I whipped out my notebook and started jotting down some notes and observations that I could plug into an article.

I was stalling.

I had to go over there and attempt to get someone to talk to me in a moment, but it was fine to soak up the atmosphere first. Get a feel for the vibe.

"Do you think he did it?" someone said beside me.

I flinched and looked down. "Mrs Strickland."

"Jasper," she said with a weary sigh, "I've told you before, call me Karen. I haven't been your teacher for quite a while now."

"That's okay," I said. "I like to be respectful to my elders."

She narrowed her eyes. "Very bitchy," she said. "I approve."

"Cool."

We stared at each other for another moment before she said, "You think he's involved? Underwood?"

"It crossed my mind. But, honestly, I can't see it. Have you met Ray?"

"No," she said. "He refused to talk to me. Why, have you met him?"

"Not, like, to talk to? Either? I did call him the once, but he told me not to bother him again. I do know him in a secondhand kind of way?"

"Oh, yes? What are your impressions of him?" She tilted her head.

"Well," I said, thinking. "He's a nice guy. Sweet. Very pretty. Tense, though. Could probably stand to do some yoga." I was also so jealous of him I could barely see straight. She didn't need to know that.

Her eyes crinkled at the corners. "He does have a certain charm, doesn't he? Not the killing type, in your opinion?"

"Nah." Maybe?

"You don't think perhaps he's *too* sweet? The pretty ones get away with a lot, you know. It could be the perfect front."

"It could…" I said slowly.

"Food for thought," she said. "Perhaps you could write a nice article about it some time."

"I'm here to cover the breaking news."

"Oh dear," she said. "That's why I'm here. You must be the backup."

I scowled.

"Excuse me." Mrs Strickland sauntered over the road, heading for Liam.

Good luck, I thought, and then my jaw dropped when Liam went to meet her as she stood politely by the line of police tape. He angled his head down, listening.

What?

What was happening?

I speed walked over the road, making a beeline for Liam.

He must have seen me coming in his peripheral vision. It was hard to miss me in my bright pink t-shirt. He said something to Mrs Strickland, gestured at his partner, whom I had since learned was Detective Sergeant Patel, and walked toward the house.

"Liam!" His name burst out of me before I could stop it. "Detective Nash."

He hesitated and turned back. Shooting a professional smile over at Mrs Strickland, who was getting impressively stone-faced by DS Patel, he tipped his head to the side, indicating I follow him along the line of police tape.

"Detective *Chief Inspector* Nash," he said.

I nodded. I knew that. I also knew it pissed him off when I didn't use his *full* title, which was why I did it every time I saw him. Yes, it was juvenile. No, I didn't care.

He came to an abrupt stop and turned to face me.

We were on opposite sides of the police tape. I flipped

open my notebook and clicked my pen. For some reason, I was having trouble meeting Liam's gaze. I swallowed hard.

"Well?" Liam said.

I opened and shut my mouth.

He shifted impatiently.

The genius words that came out of me were, "Did you have a nice date with Ray?"

"Yes," Liam said. "He's a spectacular kisser. Now, do you have any appropriate questions, or are you just here to waste my time?"

Spectacular...? I glared at Liam's lips. They flattened into a hard line.

I wanted to lean over that tape and show him spectacular.

But, no.

Last time I was here on the job, I shoved him. I was *not* going to outdo myself by kissing him.

Even though I really wanted to.

I clicked my pen aggressively. "I have some questions," I said. "I have lots of them."

Liam waited with raised eyebrows. "Are you going to ask them?" he said eventually.

"Yes. Do you think Ray is a sociopathic murderer hiding behind his pretty looks and a sweet-as-honey persona, lulling the community as he commits evil and stashes bodies in his house then calls it in to the police to fulfil an aching need for attention?"

Liam looked at me levelly. "No."

Holding his gaze, I flipped my notebook closed. "No more questions."

We were still staring at each other when there was a kerfuffle at the front door and Ray appeared. He was pale and hunched. Even from here, I could tell his eyes were slightly unfocused.

"Nash," DS Patel called, and lifted her chin in Ray's direction.

Liam strode off and scooted Ray back into the house.

I picked up my phone, hoping it still worked, and dialled Ralph.

"Talk to me," Ralph said when the call connected.

"I want the front page," I said. "I don't care about the breaking news piece on the website. Let Mrs Strickland have it. But, Ralph? I'm going to write you an article for tomorrow's edition." I took a deep breath. "Stop the presses."

"You know the drill. I can hold it until four. I need it in my inbox by then to get it to the printers."

"You'll have it."

"And try to at least run a spellcheck if you slide it in under the wire again, okay?"

"I can't promise that, Ralph," I said. "But it will be there."

21

I needed to get the article written and sent by four o'clock. It was a little after twelve now.

No problem.

I needed an outline, I needed photos, and then I needed to get my arse home and in front of my computer.

I didn't know if photographing a crime scene was technically legal or not, so I crossed back to Mrs Hughes' house and sat on the kerb, ignoring the cold bite of stone through my sweatpants. I got my phone out and kept things covert as I snapped the scene.

It wasn't all that interesting. It was probably more exciting inside the house. Out here, it was mostly vehicles and random people milling about.

I got a few shots of the ambulance, some of the police cars cluttering up Ray's drive, the police tape, a couple of some officers, and a few of Liam. One of those showed him looking my way very suspiciously, but he didn't come over.

Once I had plenty of photos to choose from, I opened up my notes app. Typing slowly, I began to jot down an outline.

My preference, obviously, was to work on my MacBook,

but I was determined to stay on scene as long as I could stand to type on my phone, in case something happened. Another body. A wild confession from Ray. The discovery of a secret cellar with a human-sized dehydrator and a multi-pack of storage tubs ready and waiting. Who knew?

After a few minutes, Mrs Hughes came out. She told me to get off the ground or I'd get haemorrhoids, and brought me one of her lawn chairs to sit in. I was comfortably reclining in her drive with Dougal on my lap and a good number of bullet points and paragraph fragments written when there was some activity at Ray's front door.

It was Ray again, being escorted by Liam.

Ray paused on the doorstep and looked up at Liam. He wasn't as pale and shaken as earlier. In fact, he seemed downright irritated. He was arguing with Liam the whole time Liam walked him firmly down the drive and to Liam's car.

I swiped out of my notes app and toggled to the camera.

"Stay cool, Dougal," I said. "Don't draw any attention."

I angled the camera until I had Ray in frame and, feeling oddly guilty, snapped a few shots. Ooh. That last one was gold. Liam had popped open the back door of his car, set his hand on top of Ray's head, and guided him in. It looked like he was being arrested. Perhaps he was! I got a full burst of that little sequence.

I got a few more of Ray fuming out the side window while Liam talked to DS Patel and another officer before getting in the car himself and driving off.

I decided to head out as well. I lifted Dougal up off my lap, tucked him under my arm, and carted him to the front door.

"Thanks for the chair, Mrs Hughes," I said when she answered my knock. I handed Dougal over. He was a solid boy, and she sagged at his weight. "Shall I run it around to the back for you?"

"If you would, Jasper," she said. "Get anything good for your article?"

"Oh, yes." I waved my phone at her. "I've got lots of material." It was mostly speculation, but there *was* lots of it.

"I look forward to reading it in the paper tomorrow."

For some reason that made me break out in a light sweat. "Thanks!" I said brightly. "Speaking of, I'd better be off to write it."

"If this happens again, you have blanket permission to hop the fence."

If it happens again? I carried the chair back to her patio, crossed the lawn and jumped the back fence. I paused on the other side to make a quick note on my phone—*are there more bodies???*—before jogging to my car.

The traffic gods smiled upon me. I made it through town without hitting a single red light, dumped the car, ran into the house, and was at my desk within fifteen minutes of leaving the scene.

My notes app was synced and it was all there waiting for me.

I copied and pasted it into Word.

It was now two o'clock. Great. I had *so* much time. Two whole hours. I bet it would only take me half an hour to get it written. I'd choose a couple of photos, run a spellcheck, and send it over well before the deadline.

TWO HOURS LATER, I WAS SWEATING AND BREATHING HARD, folded at the waist with my forehead on the desk.

So.

Didn't take me half an hour.

I rolled my head sideways and checked my watch. It was twenty minutes past three.

My crisis of confidence had kicked in at three o'clock, when the outline that had seemed clear and strong back at Ray's had failed to coalesce into anything coherent.

This was worse than the first article. I wasn't even starting from a blank page!

By the time three forty-five ticked around, Ralph called.

"Where is it?" he said tightly.

"It's here. It's right here. I'm looking at it."

"Can *I* look at it, please?"

"Ah...no? Not yet?"

"Listen. Strickland's piece is up on the website. I kept it short. She offered me a long piece. I said no. Ask me why, Jasper."

"I'd rather not."

"Because I put my trust in you. Did you know, we sold more copies with your article than in the previous three months? Combined?"

"No. I didn't know that."

"Yeah. We did. Strickland's good. She's better than good. She could be writing for *The New York*-fucking-*Times* if she wanted, but she doesn't want. Their loss. You still shifted way more copies than anything she's ever given me. Gimme more."

"I just...Ralph, I'm thinking that maybe this was a mista—"

"Nope. No. It wasn't. Send it."

I stared in absolute horror at my outline. It had started to do that thing where the words *throbbed* at me.

"I have some great photos," I said.

"Send them, too."

"Or instead. I send them *instead*, and you let Mrs Strickland do a long follow-up piece, and we call it a collaboration. She can have the byline. I don't mind."

"No," he said. "Send it."

"What about the spell—"

"Send it!" He hung up.

I wrote like I was possessed, used up the final five minutes on spellcheck, attached all of the photos, and sent it.

Ralph called instantly. He must have been watching his inbox like I was watching the clock. "Headline!" he barked, and hung up.

Fuck. I wrote a blank email with the headline in the subject line, sent it, and collapsed.

I *really* didn't think this response was normal.

When my heart had stopped pounding quite so hard, I pushed myself up to sitting with a groan. I'd had no idea how physical this journalist gig was.

It must be just non-fiction, because I could happily write away at my stories for hours, and come out of it feeling refreshed.

Not like I'd just been through boot camp.

I stood up, creaking like an old man, and shuffled to the kitchen. I ate two bananas, drank a pint of water, then caved and went for my Snickers bar stash.

Feeling more like myself, I decided that a quick home workout to get the blood pumping and the joints lubricated was a good antidote to the nerves and the vague, nagging feeling of unease that had settled over me.

It wasn't the same unease that I'd had after sending the first article. That had been more about not wanting to fail, about not doing a good enough job.

This unease was shaded toward a guilty feeling that I

might, possibly, have been led somewhat astray by my jealousy of Ray the spectacular kisser, and there was a chance that I may have been more critical of him than was wise.

Great. Now I was thinking about Ray kissing Liam. Or Liam kissing Ray.

I didn't feel betrayed. I had no right to. We weren't dating. There were no promises between us. I had no control over or say in Liam's actions and choices.

But I was angry.

I was frustrated.

I was *right here*, if Liam wanted kisses.

Only, he didn't want them from me.

Was it because he preferred to tenderly cradle Ray's slender form in his manly arms, rather than go chest to chest and grapple with me?

Was it because Liam and I were roughly the same height —I was an inch taller—and he didn't have to bend down for it? Because when we kissed, we were eye to eye, mouth to mouth?

Beyond being a willing participant for a man who wasn't choosy, did I turn him on at all?

Having Liam tell me it was a one-time thing had hurt, but he'd said he wasn't interested in a relationship with anyone. It hadn't felt like a personal rejection of me.

Seeing Liam date Ray felt personal.

Ray, the man who Adam loved, and now Liam probably also loved and, knowing my luck, would marry. Ray, who couldn't be more my opposite in terms of appearance.

I pushed myself hard through some bodyweight exercises on my sitting room floor, building up some heat.

And this was what was sticking, right?

I was onto the kettlebell now, swinging it around.

I *did* turn Liam on.

I was pretty sure.

He'd touched me tenderly. He *had*. I remembered everything about our time together, and he *hadn't* treated me like a hook-up, like a convenience, a random body to thrust against. Not until the next day.

The bastard said one thing, and he did another.

By the time the doorbell went, I'd built up a light sweat, a righteous fury, and once again, I should have known who'd be standing there.

Once again, I didn't.

I opened the door, took one look at Liam, and shut it in his face.

22

"*J*asper Caius Connolly—"

I snatched the door open. "How the hell do you know my middle name?" He'd even pronounced it right. *Keys*. Ugh. "And can you keep it down, please? There is no need to broadcast it to the entire street. Hey."

Liam shoved me backward and muscled his way in. "I know because you told me," he said, and headed into the sitting room.

I trailed after him. "I don't believe that for a second. I've never told anyone. Not even Adam. And it's not weird, by the way, it's a family name. When, exactly, did I tell you?"

He smiled for some reason. It didn't last long. He stared at me.

I shifted uncomfortably. I was flushed from exercising. My t-shirt was damp and clinging. I was suddenly self-conscious. "What's the matter?" I said, and gestured myself up and down. "Too swole for you?"

I wanted to smack myself immediately.

Swole?

Liam's eyes tracked over me thoroughly, lingering on my chest and biceps. "Too unprofessional," he clipped out.

"I am a personal trainer, Detective *Chief Inspector* Nash," I said. "We're supposed to dress like this."

"Journalists, however, are not," he said. He startled me by reaching out to pinch the fabric of my t-shirt. He pulled it away an inch, and let it snap back. "This is very tight."

I batted his hand away. "It's sweat-wicking."

"It doesn't leave anything to the imagination," he said.

I gaped at him. "It's not supposed to, you giant prude. The tighter the better. Both for wicking purposes and to showcase the results of your hard work." I smoothed the fabric down over my damp abs. "See?"

I heard Liam swallow.

"Are you the fashion police now?" I said. "Or is it the morality police? Should my clothes be baggy?" I leaned my upper body toward him. "Should I be wearing beige?"

He narrowed his eyes. "All I'm saying is, it's not very professional for a journalist to show up wearing a pink t-shirt saying *PUMP IT!!!* to a crime scene, and expect to be taken seriously!"

I glanced down at myself. "Is it because it's pink?"

"Don't be ridiculous."

"Then what is your problem?"

"I don't have a problem. I am here as a professional courtesy—because I want you to succeed, believe it or not—to tell you that it wouldn't hurt, if you want people to take you seriously as a journalist, to take a leaf out of Karen Strickland's book and present yourself that way."

I went rigid.

That.

Was.

It.

I said through gritted teeth, "You drove over here to criticise my appearance and to tell me that I should try to be more like *Mrs Strickland?*"

"More or less," he said. "Although when you phrase it like that, it makes me sound like a judgmental dick."

"Imagine that! Are you sure you didn't mean to say I should be more like Ray?"

"Why would I want you to be like Ray?"

"Because then I'd at least be more your type!"

He frowned. "Jasper—"

"No!" I threw up a hand. "No need to explain. I get it. You will be happy to hear that I finally, finally get it. I am not your type." I shrugged like it didn't matter. "Ray the spectacular kisser is your type."

He laughed. "It wasn't spectacular, it was fine. And it was one kiss. One date."

I ignored him. "Of course he's your type. Ray is everybody's type. Not mine. But definitely yours."

"He's actually n—"

"Unlike me. And Liam, I accept it, okay? You've told me before. Over and over again. It never sank in. Well?" I laid a hand flat on his chest, and pushed lightly. "It has sunk the fuck in."

Liam's cheeks darkened.

"I'm not your type. You sampled the goods. One and done. I wasn't good enough for you to come back for seconds. Last time I did this, it worked like a charm. You were aaall over me." I grabbed the hem of my t-shirt. "But look, now I can do it and—"

Liam lunged at me and caught my hands.

I'd got the t-shirt up by about an inch. A strip of skin showed; my lower stomach, and the start of my V-cut.

I stared at him.

He stared back.

I gave the t-shirt a tug upward.

He gave it a tug down.

I let go, poked him in the bellybutton, and when he doubled over with an involuntary *oof*, yanked my t-shirt up.

"Jasper," he growled. This time he caught the t-shirt at armpit height.

I squirmed, bent my knees, and wriggled out of it. I straightened triumphantly. "What's the matter?" I said. "It's not like this does anything for you." I threw my arms out, and ignored the way my voice quavered. I was almost sure he didn't notice it.

Liam let out a harsh breath.

"These?" I stroked my abs. "Too much, right? Unnecessary." I stepped into him until we were nose to nose. Eye to eye. "I'm too tall." I pushed him back a step. "Too strong."

His hands flashed out and he gripped my sides. I sucked in a breath and my spine arched reflexively. I waited for him to shove me back, but he didn't. He was still breathing hard, like he was on mile nine of a ten-mile run. His face was tight.

I put my hands on my waistband.

His hands covered mine instantly. "Jasper," he said, warningly.

And then we went down in a thrashing heap as I tried to get naked and he tried to stop me.

I genuinely didn't know what I thought I was proving at that point, it had gone sideways so quickly.

All I knew was that I had Liam on top of me, breathing hard, his hands on my skin, his attention for me alone.

He could have walked out and left me standing there with my dick out like a pillock.

But instead, he was on me, over me.

I could have reversed our position at any time, but I let him straddle me, hold my hands down, and we were panting against each other's open mouths. He tilted his head and I leaned up for him.

Before we made contact, his phone rang.

His eyes closed as if in pain.

I pushed up desperately, but he stopped me with a gentle hand laid over my throat. "I don't have the time for this," he whispered against my lips, and was up, off, and gone.

I lay there and contemplated the ceiling.

What the fuck just happened?

My whole, *Look at what you passed up,* and, *Hey guess what, it's too late because you'll never have it again* performance lasted pretty much until he pinned me down and then once again, I went limp.

I don't have the time for this.

I rolled to my feet and stalked over to the computer. I sat down, scooted my chair close, and dragged the external keyboard onto my lap.

I opened up a new document.

"Bring him to me," I shouted. My voice boomed across the vaulted Great Hall. All the enemy soldiers, huddling like the cattle they were, shivered in fear. I thrust out an arm and pointed. "That one. The arrogant bastard over there."

Adam, my second-in-command, looked the man up and down. "Are you sure?"

"Yes! That's the one I want," I said.

"Isn't he too arrogant?" Adam asked. "Too much of a bastard?"

I threw my head back and laughed. "Ha ha ha. We shall see how long that lasts. He will serve as my war prize for the next fifty years."

"He's kind of old," Adam said. "In another fifty years, he'll be

in his eighties. Besides, you've got plenty to choose from. Apart from this one. I like the look of this one. Can I keep him?" He indicated a shuddering, slender man with brown eyes and hair who was clinging to my war prize and trembling like a delicate flower.

"If you like bland, I suppose you may," I said. "Now! Bring mine up here so that he may kneel before me and pledge his fealty."

Adam poked the arrogant bastard in the back with his broadsword.

The man scowled and shuffled forward, hampered by the shackles around his ankles.

"Commander Nash," I said, propping my elbow on my knee and my chin on my fist. "Yes! I do indeed recognise you, my arch-enemy. Hiding amongst the rabble like a common soldier? How the mighty have fallen."

"Jasper," Nash said through gritted teeth. "I'm going to kill you."

"That is Great Warlord Jasper, ruler of ten empires and... just...that is warlord to the likes of you. Address me correctly. Mewling peasant."

"I am no peasant. I am the ruler of this land, and I will vanquish you."

"Ha ha," I said, successfully quelling my nerves at the simmering fury in his beautiful blue-grey eyes. "It is you who are vanquished. Which one of us is in chains, huh? You are."

"For now."

"Forever, if it pleases me!"

"We'll see."

"Okay, Adam? Could you, like, push him down to his knees for me? On the throne steps. Right here between my boots? That'd be great. Show him his place and all that."

Adam tried, grunting and heaving down on Nash's broad and lovely shoulders, but Nash wouldn't go.

"*Maybe give him a little chop?*" I suggested. "*At the back of his knees—no! Not with your sword. With your hand, come on. What the fuck, Adam?*"

Adam re-sheathed his sword, kicked the back of Nash's knees, and grinned when Nash hit the marble steps.

"*Oh my god,*" I said, "*are your kneecaps all right? That sounded bad.*"

Nash just glared.

"*Right. Um. Swear fealty to me.*"

"*Not a chance.*"

"*You are vanquished! Accept it, wretch. Your forces are beaten. I sit upon your throne. You will yield to me.*"

"*Nope.*"

"*You will. You must!*"

This wasn't really providing the right optics for my victorious army, having the guy who lost sort of not acting like it. At all.

I stood and stared down at my helpless captive. "*We shall continue to discuss this in private,*" I announced.

"*Probably for the best,*" Nash said.

"*Thanks, but I wasn't asking your opinion. Although, yes. Indeed it is for the best. I shall claim my war prize in the most erotic and filthy of ways and you will, uh. Whimper beneath me and beg for my. Taking. For the taking. Why are you laughing? Adam, make him stop—no! Not with your sword, oh my god. Gag him or something?*"

"*With what?*"

I looked at Nash. "*I have an idea,*" *I said seductively.*

"*You stick anything in my mouth, I'm biting it off,*" Nash said calmly.

"*No, you won't. Because you'll be begging for it first. You don't get it if you don't ask me for it.*"

"*Good to know.*"

This was really not going the way I'd planned. I threw my

shoulders back and stalked out of the Great Hall, my boots ringing on the stone and everyone cowering before me.

"Bring him to my new chambers," I called over my shoulder. "Which will echo with the sounds of his ecstasy as I plunder the figurehead of this vanquished country because he asked for it so prettily."

I hurried out. That fell a little flat. I could push through. I was, after all, the warlord. He was the war prize.

It wasn't as if Adam would bring him to the chamber—previously Nash's own bedchamber—and leave us alone for a private seduction, at which dramatic moment Nash would reveal that he had never, in fact, been chained, his shackles were unlocked, and it was all a ruse.

It wasn't as if Nash had cunningly intended all along to be found amongst the captured soldiers, and was waiting to get me alone, overpower me, and turn the tide of war.

That wasn't going to happen

Definitely. Not happening. Because I was the warlord.

"Leave us," I said to Adam. He left and I swung to face the surly captive. "Ah. Alone at last, former Commander Nash. On your knees."

"You first." Nash kicked off his unlocked shackles, snatched a long dagger from his knee-high boot and closed the gap between us like a striking snake.

Guess it was happening, then.

He held the point of my chin on the flat and deadly edge of his dagger. Adding some pressure, he lifted my chin an inch. "Yield."

I stared at him. "Oh, fine," I said. "Why not? How do you want me?"

"I was expecting more fight from a mighty warlord."

"I don't know what to tell you. I am overcome by my lust for your powerful and manly form. I'm being sexually awakened as we speak, just from looking at you, in a way I have never before *looked at a man, what with being an innocent and untouched virgin."*

"Right. You hid that well, with all the talk about plundering and filthy erotic seduction earlier."

"It was a bluff. And now I am trying super hard to resist but despite all my best efforts I am fiercely aroused and compelled to accept you as my lover. So. On my back? All fours? Little hint?"

Nash smiled evilly and re-sheathed his dagger. "Do not think to trick me in a double bluff," he said.

"That is a good idea, which I definitely thought of already, but oh—"

Nash caught me by the back of the neck and dragged me against his hard, solid body. He laid his cruel lips to mine. "This was easy," he murmured against my mouth.

"What can I say? Who could possibly withstand your searing sexual magnetism?"

"Who indeed?" He claimed my mouth with his and kissed me silly. Wrenching away, he said, "Prepare yourself for the taking, war prize. Give me a minute to pop out to the Great Hall and let everyone know I'm back in charge of things again. I'll reinstall my guard, give your second-in-command to my counsellor, Ray, as a pet, march your army off the property, and then we'll get to the sex."

I pushed back from the keyboard, panting.

Okay.

Not quite the Jasper-takes-control revenge story I'd been attempting.

At least Liam didn't shoot me into space, sleep with some rando, or abandon me in a desert this time.

I leapt up from the chair, bolted upstairs and ran into the bathroom. I jumped into the shower, took hold of my cock and came in about three strokes.

It had been a hell of a day.

23

J was sitting at my kitchen table, freshly showered and in my favourite worn-out old sweatpants, meditatively ploughing my way through a plate of chicken parmesan when it hit me.

I'd forgotten to tell Adam about Ray again.

Squinting through the cracked screen on my phone, I pulled up Adam's number and dialled. I really didn't want him to read my article about his soulmate finding another dead guy in his house without me at least mentioning it first.

"What's up?" Adam said.

"Hi."

"Hello. Jasper? You okay?"

"*I'm* fine," I said.

"Don't like the stress on the *I* there. Is everything all right?"

"Can you talk?"

"Yeah, I just came off shift. I'm in the break room."

"Soooo."

"You're worrying me."

"Sorry. Opposite of what I was going for. Uh. Hmm. I'm not sure if you know this or yet, but Ray found another body in his house."

Adam laughed. "Yeah, I know. Liam turfed him out of his house again and he checked into the hotel for the night, like he did last time. God, he was a mess when he showed up here. I'm going to take care of him, don't worry. And I heard all about it from Liam."

"Oh, good. You're in the loop. I'm sorry, I should have told you earlier, but Ralph called and I had to get on the scene, then I had to get home and write the article, and then...other stuff came up. I forgot until now that I hadn't called you."

"Hey, you wrote another article! That's great!"

I hunched a little lower in my seat. "Yeaaaah?"

"You're sounding weird again."

I cleared my throat. "Yeah!"

"That's better. Is it on the website? Can I read it?"

I laughed weakly. "You can read it tomorrow. Right now, it's at the printers."

"Jasper! Another front page! You are killing it. I'll buy a copy as soon as my morning shift is over. I'll get it framed and you can have another one to hang over your desk."

I hoped he felt that way after he'd read it. Somehow, I doubted it. "So the thing is, it's about Ray."

"I imagine it is. He was the one who found another body in his house, after all. How does he keep doing it? Most people go their lives without ever finding one." Adam sounded fond.

"I know that Ray is like, your soulmate and everything, but it's not a hundred percent flattering. Toward him."

It wasn't even ten percent flattering toward him. I hunched further.

"You're not writing a puff piece, I get that," Adam said. "News is news."

I chewed my lip nervously. "Mm-hmm."

"I'm sure you did an amazing job, Jasper. I'm so proud of you."

"Okay, well. Thanks! Bye!" I hung up quickly.

He wasn't going to be proud of me in the morning when he read what I wrote about Ray.

I'd come to the conclusion that I didn't have it in me to be a deadline-based kind of journalist. This was the second article I'd fired off in a panic. I already knew it wasn't going to land quite as well as the first.

I finished my chicken parmesan, drank a pint of water, and dragged myself up to bed. I crawled in under the duvet, taking my phone with me, and navigated to the *Inquirer*'s website.

"Scandal at Sycamore Close: the Sequel," by Karen Strickland.

Good headline.

Wish mine was classy like that.

My stomach tightened.

I'd gone with something more sensational.

I could have come up with something better, but Ralph gave me thirty seconds! I sent back the first thing that sprang to mind.

And you know what?

Ralph was the editor *and* the owner of the paper. He didn't have to use my headline if he didn't like it.

I read Mrs Strickland's article.

It was elegant, pithy, and contained nothing but facts. No wild speculation *at all*.

I powered my phone off, curled into a smaller ball, and closed my eyes.

I didn't think I'd sleep after the day I'd had today and the day I anticipated having tomorrow. Somehow, I did.

"You're up early," Miss Lawson said suspiciously when she found me jogging on the spot outside the newsagents.

"I'm always up early," I told her.

She shooed me out of the way so she could set out the A-board open sign, and glared when I rushed into the shop behind her.

"All right, what are you in such a hurry for?" she said.

"Nothing, I'm fine." I stood in front of the newspaper shelf, hunting for the *Inquirer*.

"You know, all of the news is online these days." She was leaning on the other side of the counter, watching me. "If you're having a news emergency."

"Yep." I poked at a couple of the newspapers, knocked an edition of *The Sun* down, recoiled when it opened to a double-page spread of boobs, and shuffled it back into place. "These are yesterday's."

"I'm in my slippers still. I haven't stocked today's yet. Deliveries are all out the back."

"Oh." I fidgeted in place.

After an awkward thirty seconds of silence during which I stared at her hopefully and she stared back, I said, "Need any help with that? I can bring them in for you." I flexed my arm and pointed at my biceps, like a dick.

She almost smiled. "No, thanks," she said. "I have my routine. I'll get to it in a minute."

Her routine apparently involved sitting behind the counter, sipping tea and gazing placidly into space.

I picked up a magazine without bothering to check what

it was, and stood there pretending to be absorbed by *The Economist*. My pulse continued to race.

Eventually, she got up and went into the back.

I quivered on the spot.

She came back in toting a stack of papers, thumped them down on the floor beside the counter, and briefly sorted through them. She straightened, holding one out. "I assume this is what you're after?" she said. "Local Man Arrested On Suspicion of Murder. What Is He Doing With All The Bodies? Are There More???"

Oh, god. It sounded even worse when someone said it out loud.

"I haven't had a chance to read it yet—" she began, and blinked when I talked over her.

"How much?" I said.

"A pound twenty."

"No. For all of them." I waved my arms at the stack. "Every copy."

"Of every paper? Or just the *Chipping Fairford Inquirer*?"

"Just the *Inquirer*."

"I am not selling you every copy. Most of these are reserved. People have already paid for them. Besides. You do realise this isn't the only place that stocks the *Inquirer*, don't you?"

"Right." Of course. I knew that. But this surely accounted for a big chunk of the copies floating around town.

She continued to hold it out. "Do you want one or not?" she said.

"Uh. Yes. Thanks." I crossed over to the counter, tapped my card to the reader, wished her a good day, and left.

I ran to my car, threw myself in, and smoothed the paper out on the steering wheel.

It probably wasn't as bad as I'd been remembering it.

The headline was still not entirely accurate.

The picture was good, though? It really helped tell the story; Ralph had chosen one where it *did* look like Ray was being arrested. Liam had a hand on the top of Ray's head as he ducked into the car.

I read the article, folded the paper in half and set it carefully on the passenger seat.

Well.

Okay.

I was fucked.

I turned the car on, put it into gear, and drove slowly home.

I went for my usual morning run, got to the gym three minutes before my first class started to avoid having to talk to anyone in the break room, and worked the class so hard that they didn't have any time for talking, either.

Classes done, I showered, and bravely dragged myself to the coffee shop.

I could only avoid the fallout for so long.

24

"*M*orning," Charlie said brightly.

"Hi." I pretended to peruse the chalk-board menu so I didn't have to look him in the eye. "I'll have a macchiato, please," I said. "With extra...nothing."

"Extra *nothing*?"

I didn't have it in me today to add the usual ridiculous requests. "Yes. Just a macchiato."

"Mm-hmm." Charlie made me a black Americano, set a tiny gold-wrapped chocolate on the edge of the saucer, and refused to let go of it until I looked up.

"Congratulations on another front page," he said.

I shifted awkwardly. "Thanks."

"Is that Jasper?" Amalie's voice came from the back. "Jas! Stay there. I want to talk to you. I have questions!"

I tugged on my coffee cup and looked pleadingly at Charlie. He frowned, then gestured me away.

"You can hang around chatting with your friends when you're done working," he called to his sister, and got an earful in response.

I retreated to a table in the quietest part of the coffee shop and sat down.

I slumped, rubbing my hands over my face.

Had I written a speculative and very much *not* fact-based article about Ray, insinuating that he might perhaps be a serial killer, you just never know, and all because Liam said he was a spectacular kisser?

Yes, I had.

Was I proud of myself?

Nope, no, and hell no.

I'd regretted it the moment I sent it, I was regretting it more now, and I would regret it even more—hard to believe that was possible, but I was sure I'd manage—when Adam read it.

Or Ray.

I slid down in my seat and glumly unwrapped my chocolate treat.

Or Liam.

Okay. I shoved the chocolate in my mouth and got out my phone. Before I could call Adam, Ray walked in.

The coffee shop fell silent.

I hadn't noticed how busy and loud it was until then. The hiss of the steamer, the whirr of the bean grinder, the clatter of crockery, the chatter of voices...it all added up to a cosy background hum. Its sudden absence made the silence all the more startling.

Ray hesitated in the doorway, his big brown eyes widening as everyone turned to look at him. He clutched the strap of his laptop bag defensively.

This was my fault. Okay, it wasn't *all* my fault. Gossip spread like chlamydia in small towns. People would have been talking about him with or without my article. It hadn't helped, though.

Should I do something? This was so awkward, I was starting to sweat.

I should. Yes. I should do something.

I half-rose from my chair then sat down again. I had no idea what to do.

Another customer came in behind Ray and bumped him forward. Ray lifted his chin, gathered himself, and strode up to the counter.

The eerie silence and tension that had taken over the coffee shop broke.

I pressed dial, my eyes glued to Ray as he started talking to Amalie.

"Hi, Jasper," Adam said. "Make it quick, I'm working."

"Um. Okay. Hey, I was wondering. Have you read the paper today?"

"No, not yet. I promise I will, though. I'm sure it's great."

"Ha ha. No, it isn't. Do you think Ray's read it?"

"Doubt it. He was with me last night. All night." Adam sounded warm and happy. "He left the hotel a few minutes ago. To be honest, Jasper, I don't think he'll read it at all." Adam added gently, "He's not a fan."

"Yeah. Me neither."

It didn't look like Ray and Amalie's conversation was going all that well. Her expression had gone from wary to uncomfortable, and was settling into unfriendly and suspicious.

"Here's the thing, Adam," I said. "We may have a problem."

"What are you talking about?" His voice sharpened.

"Okay, shit." Rip it off, Connolly. "The article I wrote about Ray *could* be interpreted as *maybe* a suggestion that he *might* perhaps have been arrested? And also he might be a serial killer? Going on the general mood of the coffee shop, which is where Ray and I both are right now, by the way, I'm thinking that most of Chipping Fairford has gone ahead and interpreted that way."

"Meaning?"

"Meaning, everyone went quiet when he walked in, like he was the last human on earth walking into a vampire bar?"

"Like *what*? Never mind. Hang on. Misha?" His voice faded as he held the phone away and talked to one of his colleagues. He came back to me. "I'm coming over."

While I'd been the one to call Adam, I wasn't exactly keen to see the disappointment on his face when he looked at me. "Ray's talking to Amalie right now. He seems pretty cool. Chill, even."

"Ray? Chill?"

"Oblivious?"

"That I believe." Adam sounded like he was walking fast. "See you in a minute."

He hung up.

For a moment there, I actually thought that things would be all right. Ray would order a coffee—hopefully to go—he'd leave, and the drama would fizzle out.

The hotel was a short distance away. Unfortunately, before Adam showed up, the conversation between Amalie and Ray got heated. His voice rose. So did hers. She must have had a copy of the paper with her, because Ray suddenly leaned forward, snatched a newspaper up from the counter, and held it in front of his face.

His lips moved as he read the headline. The paper trembled in his shaky grip, then he threw it down.

"I wasn't arrested," he said, loud and clear for everyone to hear. "I am *not* a murder suspect!"

I slunk low in my seat. Come on, Adam, I thought. Any time now would be good.

Ray turned the paper on the counter to face Amalie, and poked it. "Do you see any handcuffs? No? That'll be because I am not being arrested!"

"It looks like you are, though. He's got his hand on your head. He's putting you in the back seat."

"Because he's a dick! I'm not a murder suspect!"

"Uh-huh."

"This is ridiculous. I'm going to sue. Defamation of character. Libel. Slander?"

"Come on, now. Liam's all right."

"Okay, one? No, he's not. He's a dick. And two? I was talking about this drivel." Ray flicked at the paper. "This nonsense. This arsehole reporter, whoever wrote it. The man I'm going to sue." Ray picked the paper up and squinted at it. "J.C. Connolly."

Yep. I was definitely fucked.

"Don't sue Jasper," Amalie said. "He's a lovely lad."

I was vaguely aware of some sympathetic looks aimed my way, which was nice, if not technically warranted at this point.

Ray, on the other hand, was still going off. "*I'm* a lovely lad," he whisper-yelled. "*He's* a slanderous muppet who just cost his employer a hundred thousand pounds!"

Slanderous muppet? Ouch. That one stung. It would have stung more if I wasn't reeling at the rest of the sentence.

A hundred thousand pounds?

Ralph didn't have a spare hundred thousand pounds lying around.

Even if Ralph did, he wouldn't pay. He'd make me pay.

"How d'you figure that?" Amalie said. "And if it's in print, it's libel, not slander. Slander is slagging someone off down the pub. Which Jasper would never do."

Ray ignored her in favour of jabbing at his phone. "I don't know the going rate for libel these days, let me fucking ask fucking Google. Oh." He stared at the phone. "That solves all my problems."

"What?" Amalie asked, trying to look at the phone.

"That is a nice chunk of money," Ray was saying thoughtfully. "I could move from this awful, awful place instead of being stuck for the rest of my life because all my money's locked into a murder house, and the idiot locals think I did it!"

"Babe," Adam said. "Where's my coffee? You're taking forever."

The entire coffee shop, including me, had been so engrossed in the drama happening up at the counter, that I don't think anyone noticed Adam's arrival until he stopped behind Ray.

Ray looked over his shoulder and frowned. "What? Adam? Was I getting you coffee? I don't remember that. Are you sure? This is all very stressful." He passed a hand over his forehead. "I forgot. Sorry. And an Americano for Adam, thanks," he said distractedly to Amalie before turning around and laying his hands on Adam's chest. "Adam."

"Yes, Ray?"

"All these people think I'm a murderer."

Adam's eyes briefly met mine over Ray's head.

It was hard to gauge his mood. I wasn't optimistic enough to think he was quite as amused as he was playing it.

I didn't think he was friendship-endingly mad. He sure as shit wasn't pleased with me, though.

"I heard," he said, returning his attention to Ray.

"And that Liam arrested me," Ray continued, shoving the paper into Adam's hands.

Adam took it and scanned it. His face did something complicated.

He was trying not to laugh.

"This isn't funny," Ray said.

"It *does* look like you're being arrested." Adam glanced over at me again.

"Well, I wasn't!" Ray said. "Unless Liam forgot to inform me of the fact. You know what? I hope that is the case, since everyone thinks he did anyway. Then I'll sue him *and* Jasper, and I will definitely be able to set fire to the murder house and go live somewhere else!"

I didn't want to be sued!

"Don't sue Jasper," Adam said, brushing a lock of dark hair out of Ray's eyes and smiling down at him. "He's a lovely lad."

Oh, thank god. Adam wasn't going to let him sue me.

"*I'm* a lovely lad!" Ray yelled.

Everyone was glued to the drama now. I wasn't the only one who jumped when Liam appeared beside Adam. "I'd rather you didn't threaten arson in my hearing, Mr Underwood," he said. "I really would have to arrest you."

"I'll burn down my own damn house if I want to," Ray snapped. "Kick back and toast some marshmallows. Grill a steak, who knows? It's my house. *Liam*. Don't worry, though. I won't be claiming the insurance. I won't need to. When I'm done suing you and Jasper, I'll be a millionaire."

The blood drained from my face so fast my vision greyed out. He was going to sue Liam, too?

Liam didn't seem bothered by the threat. "It's still illegal to burn down your house, whether or not you're trying to commit insurance fraud. And it's the site of an ongoing investigation. That would be tampering. I'd have to arrest you twice. Hey, Adam."

"You got here quickly," Adam said.

"I was coming over anyway."

"Oh, yeah?"

"Yeah, had about ten calls that a murderer was about to go off."

A quick glance around the coffee shop showed that most people had their phones out. A few were being subtle about it, but at least three were very obviously recording.

I probably should have been one of them. Except my career had just flatlined and, as yet more evidence that I wasn't cut out for this journalist gig, it hadn't even crossed my mind to.

"You're not funny, either," Ray said to Liam. When he registered the attention they were all getting, he shrank back against Adam. Adam slung an arm around his waist and tugged him closer.

"I need to talk to you again this morning, Ray," Liam said.

Everyone shifted forward a bit in their seats.

"You're not arresting him, are you?" Adam said. Loudly, for the benefit of the room.

"No."

"Why is that, Liam?"

"Because he's not a murder suspect, Adam."

"What about this?" Amalie waved the paper in Liam's face.

He didn't even look at it. "Incorrect," was all he said.

"Libel," Ray hissed.

Liam winced.

He *winced.*

Oh my god, that meant Ray really could sue me for a hundred thousand pounds.

I'd have to flee the country.

"What is the procedure when it comes to libel, Detective Nash?" Ray continued. "I'm afraid I don't know off the top of my head."

"Don't be an arse, Ray," Amalie said, sounding bored as she set two to-go cups on the counter.

"Me? I'm the only person in here who isn't an arse! Ten minutes ago, you thought I was confessing to necrophilia with one of my murder victims!"

What? Necrophilia? I never said that!

...shit.

Had I...?

I mean, I'd written the thing in a fugue state of deadline-induced panic and general heartbreak. It was bad enough accusing him—*if* you wanted to take it that way—of being a serial killer, but I was almost sure I hadn't said he'd done stuff to the bodies.

Other than kill them.

If you wanted to take it that way.

And, fine. I *had* questioned what he was doing with them, in the very broadest sense. As in, the headline said, What Is He Doing With All The Bodies?

But that was it.

"All right, all right, get over it," Amalie said. "How was I to know you were talking about sleeping with Adam?"

I slumped. Okay, the necrophilia must have come up during Ray's and Amalie's conversation, and not my article.

First bit of good news I'd had all day.

It wasn't saying much: did not accuse a man of necrophilia. I'd take it.

"More likely than me sleeping with a corpse, isn't it?" Ray said with dignity.

Amalie shrugged. "Lotta people been trying to lock that down," she said with a lascivious grin at Adam. "Yeah, I'd say it's more likely you slept with a dead guy than you snagged Adam."

I sucked in a breath. Amalie had always had a sassy streak, but that was cruel.

Ray flinched.

"Oh," she said. "Ray, I didn't mean—"

"Thanks, Amalie," Adam said tightly.

Yikes. She'd be hearing about that one for the rest of her life.

Ray squirmed out of Adam's protective hold, grabbed the coffees, then blushed and muttered, "Forgot to pay."

"On the house," Amalie said quietly.

Ray shook his head at once. "No. Thank you." He paid, then turned to Adam and pushed one of the cups at him. "Here you go."

Adam took it.

Ray focused on Liam. "What did you want from me today, Detective?" Before Liam could reply, he gestured to the door. "Shall we?"

Liam stepped aside and allowed Ray to pass.

As he did, Liam looked straight across the coffee shop to where I was sitting. His gaze clashed with mine. He looked...

He looked really...

I got up out of my seat and dithered, eyes locked on his.

Everything inside me went suddenly quiet. The panic stopped. I was slammed with the urge to go over there and wrap my arms around him, have him wrap his arms around me. I wanted to lean into his sturdy frame, put my head on his shoulder, and know that everything would be all right.

Liam's lips parted as he tilted his head. His face softened. I watched him take a deep, sharp breath.

Ray had paused at the door and was also looking at me. There was nothing soft about his regard. He narrowed his eyes for a fraction of a second, then continued on out.

Liam and Adam followed in his wake.

The noise of the coffee shop back kicked in, and so did my nerves. This was the *worst* day.

The *worst.*

I didn't think Ray really would sue me.

...would he?

He'd made a valid point, after all, in amongst all the ranting. It *would* solve his problem with his murder house.

No one wants to buy a house that has been in the news for having dead people stashed in it. No way would he be able to get a buyer to give him a decent market price. Not unless they're getting a hell of a bargain. Or they're a true crime fan.

Liam, Adam and Ray were all standing outside the coffee shop, talking. I couldn't hear them, but I had a great view as Adam lifted Ray's face to his and laid one on him.

I anxiously checked to see how Liam took it. He didn't seem particularly fazed; he rolled his eyes as Adam deepened the kiss and Ray held on for dear life. When Adam pulled away, smiling as Ray swayed after him, Liam had his professional, mildly impatient expression back in place.

Adam sauntered off in the direction of the hotel. After watching him go, Liam and Ray continued their conversation.

I did a quick search on my phone about getting sued for libel, but I didn't really know where to start. Wikipedia articles could only get you so far. Even the titles of the blog posts and articles that Google wanted me to check out were making my blood run cold. I wasn't a lawyer. I didn't know the first thing about the law.

My gaze tracked back to Liam, who was still talking to Ray.

Now there was someone who knew plenty about the law.

And his ex-wife was a lawyer.

I leapt up from the table. I'd go out there and apologise to Ray and then, depending on how that went, grill Liam about the process of being sued.

They both suddenly looked over at me.

My gaze bounced between them. Liam was grim.

Ray *waved* at me.

Oh, god.

That was a threat.

I sat down heavily, knocking into the table and making it shake. I caught my coffee cup before it fell to the floor.

He was going to do it, wasn't he? Ray was going to have me arrested, thrown into jail, and sued until I had nothing left.

I was cranked so tight by that point, I nearly screamed when my phone rang. I grabbed it, almost knocked my cup over again, and said, "Hello?"

"Oh, Jasper." Adam sighed.

"Did you read the article?"

"Yes. I bought a copy from the newsagents and skimmed it on the way back to the hotel. I'm almost there."

Silence hung between us. My stomach churned.

"It was an exciting read," he said, eventually.

"I didn't *mean* to make it sound like Ray's a serial killer."

"Didn't you?"

"No?"

"Jasper?"

"No! I didn't! I don't know what happened! Okay, yes, I do. My jealousy got the better of me, but that isn't even the main reason. I'm really, really bad at this, Adam. I'm so bad at it."

Even though I wasn't his favourite person right now, he immediately leapt to my defence. "No, you're not, you—"

"I am! I can't do it! It's the pressure! I swear to god I nearly died writing that stupid article, and now Ray is going to sue me, and—"

"Jasper. Jas! Calm down, Ray isn't going to sue. He was just kicking off."

"You can't know that," I said.

"I can know that. He won't sue you," Adam said firmly. "He's a nice guy. The best. Is he pissed off at you? Hell, yes. But not enough to ruin your life. Trust me, the worst he'd ever do is glare a bit, or say something snippy." The noise of traffic cut out. "Hang on a sec," he said.

I waited while he had a muffled conversation with someone. I heard brisk footsteps, the tapping of a keyboard, and the creak of an office chair.

"Right," he said. "I'm back at the hotel."

"I'm sorry, for what it's worth. And I'm definitely going to tell Ray that. I might still be able to catch him—oh. No, they've gone now. Never mind, I have his phone number."

"Maybe wait a bit before you try and make contact," Adam said. "At least until the police have finished processing his house and he's allowed home again. Give it some time to blow over. And don't write another article."

"I don't think I'll ever write another article," I said grimly.

Adam had to check in a new arrival and he hung up, telling me not to worry about Ray. Adam planned on taking good care of him.

That, along with the smoking hot kiss outside, suggested they were a thing now.

At least one of us had got his soulmate.

Good for Adam.

I sighed and stood up, slinging my messenger bag over my shoulder. I'd leave Ray alone to cool down, like Adam said, but I should probably give Ralph a heads-up.

Either I did it, or he'd hear the gossip about Ray's meltdown in the coffee shop, and call me up to yell at me. Today had been shit enough, thanks.

BY THE TIME I GOT ACROSS TOWN TO THE NEWSPAPER'S OFFICE, he'd already heard the gossip.

I could tell by the way he was white-knuckling the glass of whisky on his desk, which sat next to a bottle with a good third missing.

"Ralph," I said as I crossed the room. "This is nothing to worry about."

He knocked back the whisky, spun the cap of the bottle off, and poured out another glass, all the while pinning me with his beady glare. He took a dramatic sip, then said mildly, "Do I look worried?"

"A little bit."

"That's weird. Why would I be worried? I can't think of a reason. Unless..." He took another sip as he pretended to think. He snapped his fingers. "Oh! Is it because I've had fifteen phone calls telling me that Ray Underwood is going to sue the ever-loving shit out of me?"

I dragged a chair over and sat opposite him.

He was on a roll. "Is it because some kind person sent me actual video footage of Underwood threatening it, and I've played it twenty times already, and I'll be hearing those words echoing in my head until the day I die?"

"Ralph—"

"Hmm. That *is* cause for concern, isn't it? The likelihood that my empire, which I have so laboriously and lovingly built over the years, is about to come crashing down, all because I took a chance on a bright-eyed young journalist, out of the kindness of my heart? Yes, that's very concerning."

Ralph had bought the *Inquirer* five years ago after retiring from selling BMWs. His wife fondly referred to it as his retirement hobby. He was laying it on a bit thick.

"Ray won't sue," I said. "I have it on good authority. I'm going to apologise to him personally, when he's not so sore about it, and it will all be fine."

"Hah. What good authority?"

I didn't think that saying my best friend, now Ray's boyfriend, said so was going to be very reassuring. Instead, I went with, "I have a source."

"Yeah?"

"Yes."

"Who?"

"A good journalist never reveals his sources," I said automatically. Ralph very slowly raised a single eyebrow. "Right. I know." I looked down at my knees. "I'm not a good journalist."

Ralph set the glass down and threw himself back in his chair, making it squeak. He rubbed his nose. "You're not a bad journalist, Jasper, you're just..." He sighed. "You're young."

"I'm twenty-four."

"And that means you're allowed to fuck up as you find your way, all right? I'm sixty-five. I don't have that excuse or luxury anymore. I'm the editor and the owner. I knew after the first article that you're not built for a quick turnaround, but the article did well, and I pushed you into doing it again. It's on me."

I winced.

"I'm thinking it's best if you go back to writing your little general interest pieces. About bees and stuff. Get some experience under your belt. The next time I put you on the front page—"

"There won't be a next time," I said. "I quit."

"I'm not telling you to do that, Jasper."

"I know. I don't think I'm any good at this. I don't think I want to do it again. Thank you for believing in me, and I'm sorry, but I'm done."

"That is a damn shame. You've got talent. You're a great storyteller."

"I'm great with stories. This is reality. I keep trying, but I'm not so great at that." I shrugged. "I don't want to upset people. Ray was pretty upset."

Ralph cleared his throat. "My door's always open," he said gruffly.

"Okay. Thanks again. Bye."

I walked out, got in my car, and drove to the gym, leaving my dreams of being a journalist behind.

$\mathcal{I}$ had a spin class at five, and I ran out as soon as possible to avoid getting cornered by any of the seniors who wanted to squeeze extra gossip out of me. I'd planned on going home, and yet somehow I'd ended up sitting in my car in front of Liam's house, gripping the steering wheel and telling myself to leave.

By 'somehow,' I mean I had to call Mrs Blake for Liam's new address, since I'd realised I didn't know where he lived. As soon as I had it, I drove over and parked up on the other side of the street.

Liam's house was small and nothing special, situated in one of the quieter, less tourist-worthy areas of town. It was surprisingly similar to mine. Even more surprisingly, it was only a few streets over. I could run there in five minutes from my house. Less, if I sprinted.

I'd imagined him living in one of the big houses in the centre of town, made of honey-coloured Cotswold stone, and draped with purple wisteria.

Then again, divorce knocked your finances for six. He probably wasn't living the high life right now.

I didn't know if I *technically* owed Liam an apology for misrepresenting him in the article, but *technically* could stuff it. I felt bad about it. I wanted to apologise to his face.

Also, while I trusted Adam when he said that Ray wouldn't sue, I'd feel better if Liam told me Ray couldn't.

These were the reasons I'd been giving myself for coming over, anyway.

Really, I had been drawn here by the soul-deep yearning for Liam that was in my blood and would never die. I was having the worst day. I just wanted to see him.

"Which is ridiculous," I said. "You romantic prat." I leaned forward and rested my forehead on the steering wheel with a groan.

Still slumped over the wheel, I turned my head to gaze morosely out of the side window at his house.

Liam was standing on his doorstep with his arms crossed, looking right at me.

I switched the engine on, threw the car into gear, and peeled out of there *well* over the speed limit.

Once I'd turned at the end of the road, I pulled over and parked the car, my heart thundering.

Wow.

Just when I thought I'd hit rock bottom of embarrassing myself in front of that man, I found a secret trapdoor to another level of humiliation, and fell right through it.

I got caught stalking him, and my genius response was to *commit a traffic crime right in front of him.*

My phone pinged.

Oh, god.

I gingerly picked it up and tilted the screen to face me.

Jasper. It was from Liam.

That could mean anything.

It could be, *Hey. What's up?*

It could mean, *You absolute disaster of a human being. I despair of you.*

It could mean, *Get your arse back here right now. I want to arrest you for speeding in a residential area where there are dogs and cats and children, you delinquent.*

One way or another, I was fairly sure it was a summons.

Swallowing hard, I started the car and drove slowly back. I pulled over and parked at the bottom of his drive, blocking in his car. I got out and looked up at the house.

He wasn't waiting for me on the doorstep, which for some reason I'd expected. I shut the car door and walked up the drive. I didn't have to knock; the door opened before I even raised a hand.

Liam stood there, haloed by the cosy glow of lamplight behind him. I couldn't quite see his face. When he didn't say anything, I shifted awkwardly and rubbed the back of my neck.

"Um," I said.

"Are you coming in?" Liam said, when I didn't have a follow-up to my brilliant conversational opener.

"Yes?"

"You don't seem too sure."

"I'm sure."

Liam smiled, put a hand on my waist, and drew me inside.

I looked down at that gentle touch, then back up at his face. I could see him clearly now, and his expression was soft. Like it had been in the coffee shop.

He firmed the hand at my waist in a quick squeeze. "Come on. I'm cooking. Stay for dinner."

Whaaaat was happening?

Liam headed off and I trailed after him.

"What are you cooking?" I said, sniffing the air. I was starving.

"Pizza. Sound good?"

It sounded bizarre. *Hello. Come in. Stay for pizza.*

Even my wildest imaginings about Liam hadn't included such things.

"Sounds *fantastic*," I said, with way too much enthusiasm.

Liam turned to look at me, and there it was, still. His face was...fond? He gave me a thorough examination from head to toe, and back up. His smile grew.

"What?" I burst out. "What is happening? I don't—"

"Shush," he said. "Sit down."

Liam had a small central island in his kitchen, with high stools tucked neatly away. I dragged one out and sat with my hands primly in my lap.

"Wine?" he asked.

"No, thanks. I'm driving." Now didn't seem like a good moment to tell him that the last time I drank alcohol was at his wedding.

Liam took down a pint glass from one of the cupboards, filled it with water from the fancy dispenser in his fridge, and brought it over. "This okay? I've noticed you're always drinking water."

"Hydration is important," I told him. "Thank you, I—" I choked when instead of moving back, he nudged my knees apart and stood between them. He lifted my chin with a firm hand at my jaw.

I gazed up at him.

"You have the biggest, roundest eyes I've ever seen in my life," he said. "Such a beautiful deep dark brown." He ran a thumb over my parted lips and I sucked in a sharp breath. "Always so needy when you look at me."

Needy? That didn't sound flattering. "Are you being mean?" I asked uncertainly.

He shook his head. His gaze tracked from my eyes—which probably *were* big and round, because frankly they were bugging out of my head at this point—and rested on my lips. He dragged his thumb back and forth, back and forth, watching it with intense focus.

All the tension in my body suddenly released, and I made an awful wanting sound. "Liam," I said desperately, catching his wrist.

As if he'd been waiting for it, he leaned down, angling my face up. He murmured against my mouth, "Can I kiss you?"

"You can always kiss me," I said. "You must know that. You must."

"Mm."

The kiss was soft, gentle, and sweet. He had one hand at my jaw; the other cupped the back of my head. He brushed his mouth lazily over mine until I was gasping.

He pulled back and we stared at each other.

Of course that's when the oven timer went off.

Liam dropped a quick kiss on my forehead, and crossed over to the oven.

I continued to stare at him as he took the pizza out and set it on the counter. While he got out the pizza wheel and expertly sliced through it, I discreetly put two fingers to my neck and checked my pulse.

Okay, shit.

Calm the fuck down.

At the rate my heart was going, I'd burn off the pizza before I even had any.

Liam plated it up, grabbed some cutlery from a drawer,

and brought it all over. He sat opposite me and raised an eyebrow.

He'd put half of the pizza on my plate, and a quarter on his. I obediently hacked off an enormous piece and stuffed it in my mouth.

I chewed, all the time staring at him.

Biting back a smile, Liam cut himself a piece. He popped it in his mouth. He didn't look away, either.

I was in Liam Nash's house, eating more than my fair share of his supper, sitting across from him, having a stare-off.

I didn't know what to do.

What to say.

The only thing going through my mind continued to be the clanging refrain of, *What the fuck is happening?*

I kept shovelling in the pizza. He finished first, although barely.

He was enjoying my discomfort. He waited for me to finish, swallow, fidget with the cutlery, and finally open my mouth to ask what the hell was going on, before he said, "So. What brings you over tonight?"

"I wanted to apologise, actually."

He pushed his plate to the side and leaned his forearms on the island. "You did?"

"Yeah. For the article. I kind of...went off on one with that. I was not entirely accurate with the facts. I feel bad about misrepresenting you. Because of ego, I suppose. And...and stuff."

"And by 'ego and stuff,' can I take it that you mean because of hurt feelings?"

"Yeah. Like I said, bruised ego."

"I don't think you *have* an ego. I hurt your feelings, Jasper."

"However you want to phrase it, I was unprofessional and I apologise."

"I appreciate you driving all the way over here to tell me that," he said.

"You're welcome. It's only a few minutes away from my house."

"I was putting the bins out when you pulled up. You didn't see me. I watched you sit in your car outside my house for twenty minutes."

"Um—"

"I was waiting for you to come inside in your own time. Except the second you saw me, you drove away. At speed."

"Please don't arrest me."

"I won't." He smiled. "You came back, though. Why was it so hard to come to me, Jasper?"

"You're kind of intimidating."

"I intimidate you?"

"Are you kidding?"

"Yeah. I know I intimidate you." His gaze heated. "I like it."

"I'm glad one of us does," I muttered.

"Oh, I'm confident we both do."

I didn't quite know what to say to that, or how to process the strange charge between us. The air was heavy. My skin prickled. It felt like we were having sex, but we were just *talking*. I grabbed my glass of water and chugged it, slowing down when I took in the way he was watching me.

I dropped my gaze as my cheeks scorched. For lack of anything better to do, I kept drinking until I'd drained the whole pint. I set the glass down with a click.

"You're thirsty," he said.

"Lotta salt in that pizza."

"Do you want more, Jasper?"

I wasn't imagining the suggestiveness in his voice, was I?

"Pizza?" I said, twisting the glass one way and then the other, avoiding looking up. "Or water?"

"Anything."

"Water, please," I croaked, and shoved the glass at him.

Luckily he caught it before I skated it clean off the island.

Okay, that was it. I flopped forward and dropped my head on my arms. "Liam," I complained. "I don't know what's happening." I snorted with surprise when a warm hand closed over the back of my neck. Liam put the refilled water glass down beside me, then pulled me up to sitting. He used my shoulders to turn me on the swivel stool until I was facing him.

He braced a hand either side of me. I was hemmed in, caught between his arms with the island at my back. I gazed up at him.

"Do you have any more questions about the article or the case?" he said.

"No. I'm almost sure Ray won't sue—"

"He won't."

"And I quit as a journalist earlier today, so. It doesn't matter anymore."

Liam seemed surprised. "You quit?"

"Yeah. I don't think I'm very good at it, you know?"

"You..." He broke off. "Hmm. You're not bad at it. You're great at telling a story. Very vivid."

I sighed.

"You shouldn't quit, Jasper. This is a hiccup. A blip. Everyone has to learn on the job."

"Are you *encouraging* me?" I said with a smile.

He pushed my hair back. It was a gesture of pure tenderness. My hair was too short to need pushing back. "I'm giving it a shot. I want you to be happy."

Once I'd gathered my wits after that bewildering statement, I said, "It doesn't make me happy. Liam, I almost died writing those articles."

He laughed. "What?"

I nodded seriously. "It's insane. I can run a marathon in just over three hours."

"That's fast," he said faintly.

"I know. I've also entered and placed in an Iron Man competition every year since I turned twenty. I can dig deep. Push past the pressure. Find that little bit extra to power over the finish line. Finish lines are child's play for me. Deadlines, though?" I shuddered. "Also, it turns out I like writing stories. Not real life."

"You write stories?"

I stilled.

"Jasper?"

Nope. Not talking about that right now. "I'm thinking maybe I've retired from my journalistic career."

He hummed. "You have to do what makes you happy," he said. "I want you to be happy."

"Okay, that's the second time you've said that to me tonight—or ever—and honestly? It's nice, but it's freaking me out."

"I can imagine." He pushed away. I immediately missed the heat of his body. "Right. You came to apologise, which wasn't necessary but I appreciate it."

"Yes," I said, because he seemed to be waiting for confirmation.

"And you're not here to ask me questions about the case."

"No. Unless you feel like sharing any details?"

I didn't want to write another article, but that didn't mean I wasn't curious. Who the hell puts dead people in storage tubs and hides them in their house?

"I can't. I'm not at liberty to share information about an ongoing case with the general public."

"Of course not. I wasn't really asking."

"I'll tell you what I told Ray earlier today. Given the age and condition of the bodies, and how many times the property has changed hands since their estimated deaths, it's incredibly unlikely that we'll ever know who killed them. The only reason I'm even telling you this is because a good journalist would have already put that together for himself."

Maybe a good journalist would. I hadn't.

"Ray's house will be thoroughly searched and documented, and the case will eventually get turned over to a special team who deals with cold cases."

"And that's it? You find dead people in someone's house, and that's it?"

"That's it."

"Who knew that finding mummified bodies in a quiet little Cotswolds town would be this boring?"

"It's the nature of a lot of police work. Boring and frustrating."

"Is it your weirdest case ever?"

Liam grimaced. "Sadly, no. Okay. Enough about the case." He held out a hand. "Come on."

I let him pull me up from the stool. He kept hold of my hand and I assumed he was taking me to the front door until we diverted to his sitting room.

"What—*oof.*" I bounced on the sofa cushion when he pushed me down and stood looming over me.

"You asked me a couple of days ago how I knew your middle name," he said. "Do you want to know how?"

If he'd said that half an hour ago, I'd have been discombobulated by the jarring subject change. Since I'd been discombobulated *for* half an hour, it had become my new normal. I rolled with it. "I've thought about that. Is it from the paperwork when you tried to arrest me when I was fourteen? Good memory."

He laughed, then quickly sobered. "No. It's from when you, Jasper Caius Connolly, pledged your undying love to me in Adam's bedroom after I'd helped my Aunt Ellen wrangle you two drunk miscreants home and up the stairs. You then burst into tears and told me that I'd broken your heart."

Oh my god. "*What?*"

"After which, you took all your clothes off, puked on my shoes, and passed out."

My face was scarlet. Or on actual fire.

"Meanwhile, Verity, my wife of six hours, was putting the bridal car through the car wash at the garage, because you and Adam—we got you on CCTV—had covered it in shaving cream."

I slunk lower in the cushions.

"Completely covered it. And then drew an ejaculating penis in the shaving cream on every window. It was graphic."

Silence throbbed between us.

Eventually, I managed to croak out, "That certainly explains why you've always seemed to have a problem with me. I did wonder."

27

"*I* don't have a problem with you, Jasper. I never did. For most of the time I've known you, you were just my bratty cousin's weird little friend."

And the hits kept coming.

"Right up until you weren't," he continued. "That's when the problem started. The person I have a problem with, by the way, is me." Liam sat down beside me. "Okay. I'm going to lay it all out for you. Jasper, you have been a pain in my fucking arse from the moment I met you."

"...I'm sorry?"

"You would have been my very first arrest, did you know that? My supervising officer told me not to be a dick, you were just kids, and to let you off with a caution."

"Sorry again?"

He smiled and shook his head. "Not the point I'm making. When we met, you were a fourteen-year-old madly in love with Harry Styles—"

"That was Adam."

"—and a child. You two were a pair of menaces."

I sighed. "Yeah."

"Then you grew up, and for some unknown reason, your innocent hero worship developed into a crush on me that was visible from space."

Great. We were back to setting Jasper on fire with absolute mortification again.

"I used to get the piss taken out of me for it all the time. By my rugby mates. My work mates. Guys I grew up with. I hated it."

"I can imagine."

"Can you? You were a baby. I'm ten years older than you. I was a man before you hit puberty. It was embarrassing to have you mooning after me."

"Oh my god," I said in a broken voice, "*stop* it. I'm sorry."

"Hey, no. No, no." Liam sounded horrified. He slung an arm around me and heaved a few times. "Holy shit, you weigh a ton. Get over here."

"What are you trying to do?"

"Get you on my lap. Come on." He grunted and hauled. Obviously, he couldn't shift me.

"Don't get a hernia or anything," I said, and twisted. I swung a leg over him until I was straddling him awkwardly. "Like this?"

"Mm. Almost." He got his hands on my arse, and slid me closer. "Better. Right. I'm really shit at this, by the way."

"Me and my erection beg to differ, but whatever."

"At explaining myself," he said. "I wasn't trying to embarrass you."

"Well fuck, please don't *ever* try."

"That I promise," he said, and kissed me. "Where was I?"

"Embarrassed about me mooning after you."

"Yeah. Let me rephrase that."

"You don't have to. I get it. I've got it for a long time, trust me. No grown adult wants a teenager lusting after them."

"No, they don't. Let me get through this, okay? I'm a coward, and it's taken me a long time to get the balls to say all this to you. I know you thought you were in love with me back then, but you weren't. You were eighteen."

I glared at him.

"Okay, maybe you were in love with me, I can't tell you your feelings. But I was in love with Verity. I married her, and I fully intended to spend the rest of my life with her."

"You really are shit at this," I said. "Please, tell me more about your happily ever after with the perfect woman."

"We kind of dropped the ball on the *ever after* part of that," he said.

"Do you still love her?"

"God, no. She's one of my best mates, but we were terrible at being married. I love you."

"Good, because—wait, what? *What*? WHAT?"

"Can you not shout? I'm right here."

"You *love* me?"

"Jasper. Zip it. For three more minutes. Let me finish."

I was vibrating with the need to grab him by the shoulders, shake him and yell *WHAT?* again. "Sure."

"I think I've loved you for a long time now. It's impossible not to. Anyone who knows you has to love you. I've been *in* love with you since I moved back to Chipping Fairford a year ago."

"*A year*? Sorry. Carry on."

"Yes, a year. We sold the house, I moved back here and rented for a bit. Bought this place a few months ago. You didn't notice me around more?" He sounded wistful.

I snorted. "Of course I did. I always notice you."

"Yeah. Beats me why, but yeah." He reached up and

traced a gentle fingertip along my cheekbone, under my eye. "You always look at me the same way."

I couldn't maintain eye contact. "Needy," I said flatly.

"Mm. Which you know I like." He leaned up and nipped my mouth sharply. "But also...I don't know." He gave a disbelieving laugh. "You see me and you light up."

"Because I love you."

He caught his breath.

"You know I do, Liam."

"Yeah," he said, sounding shattered. He stroked my cheek, then trailed his fingers along my jaw and down the side of my neck. I shivered. "You light up for me. I don't think you understand what a big deal that is, do you?" He continued to gently stroke my throat.

I managed not to purr, but I couldn't stop myself from arching into his touch.

"You are an enthusiastic, optimistic, kind and beautiful man," he said.

I squirmed.

"You are so *bright*, all the time, it doesn't even seem impossible that you could get brighter. But you do. Every time. I show up, and..." He trailed off, drawing me closer. He kissed me. It was soft still, his lips more worshipful than demanding, but I sensed a growing edge to it. "You light up," he said again. "For *me*. Doesn't matter if I'm mean, or rude, or in a bad mood. You take one look at me, and there it is."

I shrugged. "Can't help it."

"Neither can I, although god knows I've tried." He groaned. "I tried so hard and it was no use. I kept coming over to your house on the flimsiest of excuses, mauling you, and then running out on you."

"They *were* flimsy excuses," I said. I *knew* it. "For the record, I loved the mauling and I would very much like to have another go. As for running out, you can stop doing that any time."

"I was trying to do the right thing. It was incredibly hard to do when you kept getting naked."

"Kinda my whole motivation in getting naked. Even though you said I wasn't your type. And you didn't want a relationship. And I was too young." I was ticking things off my fingers. "Only worth it once. And not your friend. Didn't have time for me. And—"

"If you want to leave," he said, eyes wide, "I really wouldn't blame you."

I settled against him, making myself as heavy as possible. "I don't want to leave," I told him.

"Jasper, I want, so very much, for you to be happy. I don't want to break your heart. I don't want to disappoint you. Above all, I don't want to be the one to hurt you. But here's what I realised after the last time I came over, and you thought that I could possibly want Ray more than I could want you." He took a deep breath, sliding both hands up the sides of my neck to cup my face. "I already am hurting you, aren't I?"

"I mean...yeah."

"I've pushed you away, and messed you around, blown hot and cold."

"There has been no blowing," I said sadly, attempting to lighten the mood, because he seemed really cut up about it

He laid a finger on my lips.

I licked it.

He smiled, a sharp warning.

I pressed my lips together and blinked at him innocently.

"And then today, in the coffee shop," he said, "you *looked* at me. You were freaking out about Ray freaking out, and I walked in. You looked up and saw me, and you were relieved. Like you were suddenly on solid ground. That's fucking stupid. I don't know what I'm saying. I *do* know I'm saying it wrong." He broke off and frowned. "You saw me and you looked like, just because I showed up, things were... better. Even though Adam was there, me showing up made that difference."

"You make everything better," I told him when he came to a stop, his cheeks dark but his gaze unwavering.

"I'd like to try. I'm not sure the reality of me will be able to live up to your expectations, but I want to try."

"The reality of you will be beyond my wildest dreams," I assured him.

"No pressure."

I smiled slowly. "You feel pressure?"

"I have a history of disappointing people, and you're the one person in the world I least want to disappoint. Yes. I feel pressure."

"How about now?" I said, rocking down onto him. "Feel any now?"

"Mm-hmm." He gripped my hips and controlled my movement. "Right where I like it."

Leaning forward to brace my hands on the back of the sofa, I bent down to kiss him.

He held the back of my neck and took control of the kiss, sliding his tongue in slow and filthy.

I kept trying to grind on him faster, harder. He kept slowing me down, kissing me deeper.

"Liam," I said, my breathing ragged. "I want—"

"I know what you want."

"Then let me have it!" I said, pulling back. "Give it to me."

His eyes were dark and his face was tense. "Not yet."

That, I wasn't expecting.

He gave a short laugh. "Are you pouting?" He brushed a fingertip over my mouth. "Yeah, you're pouting. God, I love your mouth." He kissed me again, and then pushed me off his lap.

He gave it a shot, anyway.

"You cannot move me unless I want to be moved," I told him. "I thought we'd established that? And, Liam? I do not want to be moved."

"You want a tussle?" he said.

"And an orgasm."

"I want to give you an orgasm. I want to give you many, many orgasms. Sometimes, I'll give you one after the other until you're sobbing, before you've even recovered from the last, when you don't think you can handle any more. But you will. I'll use my hand. My mouth." His lips curled in a wicked smile. "My cock. Looking at the state of you right now?" He scanned me. "Maybe one day I'll try talking you into one. Hold you down, and tell you all the things I've imagined doing to you."

"That—"

"But not today. And not right now."

"Not to beg or anything, but—"

"Jasper," he said. "I don't want it fast and hard on my sofa when I have to be in bed in an hour because I need to be up early tomorrow for work."

"Oh."

"You know how I like it?"

"Well, you're bossy."

"I am," he said. "Which is a good thing, as you seem to enjoy being bossed around."

I scoffed, and convinced absolutely no one.

"I like it slow. Deep. Hard. I want to spoil you." He

laughed. "Yeah. There are those big round eyes. That's what I want." His hands were possessively stroking over my back, gripping my waist, cupping my butt. "I want you under me, spread out for me, looking up at me. Just. Like. That." He punctuated it with small, nipping kisses. "You deserve my attention. My full, unwavering, devoted attention. And you're going to get it."

Oh my god, I wanted that so much.

He sat back and looked at me.

I couldn't come up with a response.

Smiling, more than a little pleased with himself, Liam rubbed a soothing hand over my back.

I stuffed my hand in my sweatpants pocket and whipped out my phone. I pulled up my calendar app, turned the phone to face him, and said, "I'm free whenever." I'd call in sick if I had to. "Pick a day. Any day."

He took the phone from me. "Good grief you need a new phone." He angled it one way than the other, squinting.

"I keep dropping them."

"I'll buy you one of those cases," he said distractedly, typing away quickly. "Then you can throw it around as much as you like."

"I don't do it on purpose."

"I'm sure you don't. Here you go. Does that work for you?"

I gave him a curious look as he handed the phone over. The heat was still in his eyes, as was the flush on his cheeks, but I caught a hint of...not vulnerability, not from Liam. Uncertainty?

I looked at the calendar.

He'd added an event on Saturday. It was blocked out for the whole day. And on Sunday. Monday. Tuesday. I swiped to the next month. And the next. And the next.

The next year.

The event said: Liam. He'd set it to recur every day. I didn't know if it was a cliche or the most romantic thing I'd ever come across in my life.

"Well?" he said.

"I think we can make it work."

28

We didn't get together on Saturday in the end, thanks to real life getting in the way in the form of Liam being snowed under at work. I didn't mind. As real life was what I actually wanted with Liam, not just convenient orgasms, I almost liked it.

Almost.

The day my second—and last—front-page article was published had been a hell of a rollercoaster. It had started off bad, crescendoed into the worst, taken a wild turn towards what the fuck, and ended with Liam kissing me on his doorstep, letting me go, pulling me back for one more, then standing and watching as I drove away.

Now here I was, two weeks later, and to my astonishment, I hadn't yet exploded from unsatisfied desire.

Probably because I'd satisfied myself a *lot*, on a daily basis. When I wasn't busy satisfying myself, I was working out like a fiend. That always helped to clear my mind. When I wasn't working out like a fiend, I was sitting cross-legged at my computer, my keyboard balanced on my lap, as I wrote like a man possessed.

My Liam Nash fanfic mojo was back with a vengeance.

One story I wrote was so filthy, I was half horrified at myself and my depraved imagination, and half aroused.

Okay, fully aroused, but still. The nerve of me.

What the hell would Liam think if he read this, I thought, merrily bashing away at the keyboard.

The caveman held my wrists locked together at my back and pushed me inexorably down to the pile of furs on the cold stone floor.

Firelight danced, warming the chill air of the cave where he'd taken me after accepting me as tribute from the rival tribe.

I thrashed beneath him but it was no good. Perhaps in the twenty-first century my fighting skills would have won my freedom but not here, and not now.

This powerful man had spent a lifetime wrestling sabre-toothed tigers, and mammoths and the like. What could a poor time traveller do?

I grunted and heaved against him. He straddled the back of my thighs and held me down without effort.

My struggles amused him. And aroused him—an enormous cock pressed against my quivering buttocks. He rumbled with amusement as he braced an arm beside my head and leaned over me to murmur something in my ear.

I couldn't understand a word of his mysterious language. His meaning, though, was clear as anything. He bit the back of my neck and gripped my nape with his teeth as he released my hands to slowly drag down my sweatpants—

I blinked and came back to myself.

If I'd tried writing this a few weeks ago, Liam would have probably stripped me, tied me to a stake and left me as a snack for the tigers. This was a big improvement.

I'd gone into the trash bin on my MacBook, restored all the deleted stories where Liam had rejected me over and over again, and put them in their own sub-folder inside my secret fanfic folder. It seemed a shame to destroy them. I'd worked hard on them, even though they all kept going sideways. Perhaps one day I'd reread them and rework a few.

What would Liam think if he read any of *those* ones, I thought, smiling to myself.

My smile faded.

Oh my god.

What would Liam think?

I sat back, hands held in fists in front of my chest, and stared wide-eyed at the computer.

He'd think I'd been writing porn about him for six years, that's what he'd think!

My breathing picked up.

And he wouldn't be wrong.

No. He would. He *would* be wrong.

I'd been writing *romance*.

My stories were the unfiltered, yearning, wild outpourings of my heart!

Yes, that took the form of Liam fucking me every possible way known to man. And alien. He'd been an alien a startling number of times. (Don't think about the tentacles. He'd definitely freak out about the tentacles.)

But it was *romance*.

And.

And.

Even if it was porn? So what? I wasn't putting it on the internet. No one would ever see it. No one even knew I did it.

It was personal. Fantasies. Everyone else got to fantasise while jerking off, why couldn't I? I liked words. Words got me hot. It wasn't a crime.

I could think what I want!

Liam would probably be fine with it. If he knew. Which he never would, unless I told him!

I jumped up from the desk chair, dropped to the ground, and started doing pushups.

The floor approached and receded like a soothing wave as I bent and straightened my arms. I switched to one-arm pushups. I switched to the other arm. Back to two. I stared at down the carpet. I needed to vacuum. When did I last vacuum?

Dropping flat, I groaned at the pressure on my half-erect cock, which hadn't deflated even a little bit from my panicked and scampering thoughts. I quickly flipped to my back.

V-sits. I busted out fifty.

Everything was fine.

The doorbell rang and I sprang to my feet.

I really, at this point, *really* should have expected it to be Liam when I opened the door. And yet, no.

"Hi," I said. My face burned.

"Hello," he said, smiling. He looked me over. "You're sweating."

"Yes," I said, and capped it with an inappropriately loud and nervous laugh. "Um. Just doing a quick conditioning stint between household chores. I was about to vacuum. It's important to warm up."

"Before vacuuming?"

"Yes."

"Ah." He stared at me. "Can I come in, or do you want me to come back after the vacuuming?"

"Sorry! Come in. Please." I stepped aside and waved him in like a butler. "Can I take your coat?"

His smile grew as he shut the door behind him with a

gentle click. "Thanks." He shrugged it off and handed it to me.

I hung it up next to mine on the coat pegs and went back to stand in front of him. He hadn't moved from the entrance.

"You seem nervous," he said.

"What? No, I don't. What do I have to be nervous about? *Nothing.*"

Liam's eyes half closed and he contemplated me.

"I haven't done anything wrong," I said.

"Okay." He reached out and laid a hand on my chest, leaning in to kiss me.

Before our lips met, he pulled back with a frown.

"Your heart's going pretty fast," he said.

"Is it? Oh."

Liam slid his hand up to my neck. He found my pulse. "Very fast. What kind of conditioning were you doing?"

"Pushups. V-sits. Don't worry. I've got a fast recovery period. I'm an athlete. I've got the resting heart rate of a lizard."

"Right," he said. "Only it's going faster now."

"No it isn't."

He shifted closer and stared deep into my eyes.

I held my breath, willing my pulse to slow down, but it was no good. I gasped.

"Jasper," Liam said, cupping my face. "Are you panicking?"

"No!" I'd been too loud; his eyes widened. I grasped his wrists and held on. "I'm...normal. This is normal. This is sexy anticipation, is what it is. I'm—"

"This is alarming, and I want you to come with me and sit down for a minute," he said.

I let him lead me into the sitting room and nudge me onto the sofa. He crouched in front of me. I immediately tried to slide down to my knees and join him, but he pushed me back.

"What's going on?" he said firmly. "What do you need?"

"Um. Forgiveness, probably?" Oh no. What was I saying?

"Why? What have you been up to? Out and about, committing crime?" he asked.

"Yes!"

Liam blinked.

"Oh, don't worry," I rushed to say. "Not crime against society in general. Just you."

For some reason, this made him start to smile again.

"Liam."

"Jasper."

I took in a deep breath. "I have to confess." I did, I realised. I couldn't start the rest of my life with this wrong-doing hanging over me. I had to tell him.

"Okay."

I folded at the waist and said to my knees, "You might hate me after. I'm thinking we should have sex first."

"I don't think that would be a good idea."

"Well, you're wrong. I think it's a great idea, and we should do it right now."

"No." His hand rested between my shoulder blades, a comforting weight. "Tell me in your own time."

I groaned. "Why aren't you freaking out? I could have done something awful. Historically, I have done awful things."

"Like what?" Amusement tinged his steady voice.

"How I behaved at your wedding," I muttered.

"You didn't commit any crimes."

"I'm pretty sure what I did to your car was vandalism."

"Vandalism, sure. Or a prank by a broken-hearted boy. I

didn't tell you that to make you feel bad, Jasper. Making you feel bad is the very last thing I want."

"See how you feel in a minute," I said.

The hand between my shoulder blades slid up to my neck and squeezed firmly. "Trust me," he said quietly.

I sighed, and mumbled, "I write stories."

"I know you do. Your last one caused quite the splash."

"About you."

Even though his hand was just resting there and holding me, I sensed him go still.

"Not published or anything," I said, sitting up sharply. "Oh my god, no."

Liam was watching me. It was his cool, assessing, professional cop face.

"No," I said again, "I would *never*. I would die first."

He continued to watch me.

"They are all on an encrypted hard drive, and I save them locally only. They don't sync to the cloud at all, not even for backups. The app is encrypted too, and they're all password protected."

"Those are robust security measures," he remarked.

I nodded enthusiastically.

"Which I find alarming. What kind of stories are you writing, Jasper?"

"Erotic."

Liam's face didn't change. He didn't say anything. He barely even breathed. Eventually, he said, "Not articles, then?"

"Oh. No, of course not. Was that why you looked worried? No. Fiction. Um. Do you know what fanfic is?"

"Yes, of course I know what fanfic is. Who...?" He trailed off.

"You. I write erotic Liam Nash fanfic. A lot. I've been doing it for years."

"Huh." He sat back.

I twisted to face him.

"That's your crime?" he said.

"Yes."

"And you haven't put it up online?"

"No! It's *personal*. You are the only one who even knows about it. Or ever will."

"Adam doesn't know?"

"Ew. No."

"That's comforting."

"Are you angry?"

"No."

"Because I can't tell what you're thinking."

"Mostly I'm thinking that the reality of being with me definitely won't be able to live up to years of erotic fan fiction. I'm going to give it a shot, obviously, but. Yeah."

I worried my lip. "They're just stories. I want the real you. Are you sure you're not angry?" I checked.

"Hmm. No. I'm processing."

I fidgeted. "You don't think it's a gross violation of you as a person?"

"People are allowed to think whatever the hell they want about whoever the hell they want. I'm not angry."

I sagged with relief.

"Was that all you were worrying about?" he said, curling me into his side.

I snuggled closer, slinging a leg over his thighs and an arm around his waist. "Yeah. I was in the middle of writing one when I suddenly thought, what if you found out? I panicked."

"In the middle of writing one, huh?"

"Mm-hmm." I was absently stroking a palm over his stomach. He sucked it in. I hid my smile. If I wanted to touch a six-pack, I had one of my own to play with. I adored his solid body. I glanced up. He was gazing at me thoughtfully.

"What was it about?" he asked

"You are a caveman and I'm the helpless captive time traveller offered to you as tribute. We're about to get busy."

"Tribute? It sounds like I'm an important caveman."

"The ruler of your tribe, and the overlord of ten smaller tribes."

"Not bad."

"You're the equivalent of the king back then. We're having communication problems, what with me being transported to a time before anyone spoke English, but don't worry." I patted his chest. "We'll get there in the end."

"Basically," he said, "you write down your sexy fantasies of me. And they come with a plot."

"Yeah."

"That sounds intriguing. Disastrous for my ego. But intriguing." He turned and pushed me to the cushions. When I realised where he was going with it, I helpfully rearranged myself so I was flat on my back and he was lying between my thighs. He curled his forearms around my head and gazed at me fondly.

"Do you...?" I couldn't believe I was going to ask this, but... "Do you want to read one?" It wasn't a bad idea. He'd at least see that I didn't, in fact, idealise him.

No, it was a terrible idea.

I'd die of embarrassment.

"Yeah," he said.

"Really?" My voice went up.

"Yeah." He rocked into me, letting me feel his erection.

Oh. He really did. "Okay," I said. "There are a lot. What are you into?"

"You."

"Yes, you are," I said, pecking a quick kiss on his lips. "Repeatedly, and in every single story."

He thrust against me lazily again.

"Apart from the dark timeline," I said.

He stopped. "What happens in the dark timeline?"

"You...are not interested in having sex with me?"

"So what happens if we're not having sex?"

Regretting this very much. "Don't worry, you have plenty of sex, it's fine."

"Who am I having sex with if not you?" he said indignantly.

This was not heading in the direction I wanted. "Random guys. And. Maybe Ray."

"You wrote stories about me having sex with Ray?"

"It's not like I was trying! Things got complicated back there for a while after we hooked up, and—"

"It wasn't a hook-up," he said fiercely, and kissed me. "I am such a dick for saying that and I'm sorry."

I kissed him back until I was breathless. "I know," I said. "I wasn't writing that stuff on purpose. Or the ones when you kept murdering me."

His eyes bugged out. "You wrote stories about me murdering you?"

"No! No, no." I clasped his face. "I mean, yes? But it's the same as with Ray and all your other concubines, I didn't plan to write—"

"*Concubines?*"

"And it wasn't murder for the sake of murder. Not all the time, anyway. Once, you shot me out the airlock to save humanity."

"I *shot* you out of an *airlock*?"

"I'm sorry! I didn't write it on purpose, I was trying to write a story where I got a happy ending with you at least in my imagination. It just kept going wrong."

"Jasper." He kissed me. "I would never shoot you out of an airlock. If it was necessary for the survival of humanity... somehow...that you were ejected into space, I'd go *with* you. Wow. I never thought that would be part of any big romantic declaration, but here we are." He pushed my hair back from my face. "I'm not going to hurt you again," he said.

I smiled up at him. "Of course you are. You're real, and real you is only human." I bit my lip.

Liam's eyes narrowed on mine. "Am I sometimes not human?"

Don't mention the tentacles.

"Jasper?"

Don't mention them.

"Eh. Sometimes you're a...you've been a vampire."

His lips curled in a sexy smirk. "Yeah?"

"And a werewolf."

"You're hiding something."

Tentacles.

"I am definitely not."

"Okay, let me read one." He pushed up and off me.

"Right now?" I said. I could think of better things to be doing.

"Yep."

I stood up, and took off my t-shirt. "Are you sure?"

"Yes."

I shucked my sweatpants. "How about now? Still sure you want to read about it rather than do it?"

His eyes darkened and he stepped quickly into my personal space. "Fuck, yeah," he said. He took hold of my cock in a possessive hand. "You've handed me the keys to the kingdom, do you realise that?" He stroked once, twice, then slid his hand down to cup my balls. He held my chin in one hand and his other hand continued to work between my legs as he stared into my eyes. Or he tried to. I couldn't quite meet his gaze. His hold on my chin gentled.

I panted and my forehead dropped to his shoulder.

Liam kissed the side of my head and whispered, "There's a lot I'll be able to do with those stories."

I shivered when he stroked behind my balls.

"I'll know what you want. All the way, deep, deep down. At the very core of you." His hand pushed further between my legs, and I went up on my toes as he stroked between my cheeks from below. "And I'm going to make sure I give it to you."

He stepped away, sat himself down in my desk chair, and hitched a thumb at the computer. "On here, is it?" he said.

I stood there in the middle of the room with a raging erection, naked apart from my white athletic socks, gaping at him.

He spun the chair to face me, leaned back, and hummed appreciatively as he took me in. "Jasper?"

"Yes. It's on there. But...ah! No, don't look. Wait." I rushed over and shoved him away from my MacBook. "Let me—oh." He put his hands on my hips and pulled me down to sit on his lap, my back to his chest.

"Good idea," he said, and set his teeth to the side of my neck. He nipped gently. "You can stay right there while I read it. Give me something to play with. Unless you want to read it out loud to me?"

I shuddered. "Never." That was my line, right there. I could write the words. I could read the words. I couldn't *say* them.

He made an interested noise.

"Let me—" I started to move.

"Ah-ah. Stay put. I like the feel of you on my cock."

Feeling like I'd made the biggest mistake of my life, I grabbed the mouse and wiggled it to wake up the screen. "Close your eyes while I type in the password," I said. "I'm trusting you not to peek."

"Closed."

I typed it in.

After the first fifteen keystrokes, Liam said, "You don't mess around with your passwords."

"Shh." I entered the last five, and hit enter.

His hands drifted up to my pecs and rubbed absently.

"Okay, so. This is my secret folder," I said. I maximised the window. I'd organised the files into sub-folders for the stories that were easily categorised, and left the outliers and current stories in the main folder.

"That's a lot of files," Liam said. "You've worked very hard on this. If I didn't know you, I'd be alarmed. Luckily, I know you. And I like weird."

"Am I weird?"

"Yeah. You're my kind of weird. I love it. I love you." A hand skated down my abs and cool fingers traced the damp tip of my cock. He paused, as if startled, then drew a slow, deliberate circle over the head.

My back arched involuntarily.

"Is this turning you on, Jasper?" he said.

"You touching me? Of course it is."

"I meant this." He tightened an arm around my waist. "Being held here. Helpless. Me clothed, you naked. Doing as you're told. Exposing yourself to me."

Oh my god, he hadn't even *read* any of them yet.

"It's okay." He pulled my head back and kissed the

corner of my mouth. "I know you like it. Now. Shall I pick one? Or do you want to pick one for me?" The fingers circling the head of my cock became a light grip, and he jacked me lazily. I whined and pushed my hips up, seeking more. He lifted his hand away until I sank back onto his lap. Only then did he touch me again.

"I think I'll choose," he said. "Hmm. What do we have here?" He scanned the titles of the folders—I assumed. I'd closed my eyes.

"There's a whole folder for warlords and barbarian conquerors," he said contemplatively. "I'm tempted by the caveman one here. You mentioned that earlier. Oh. What about this? *Alien Pirate Captain Liam Nash Plunders My Booty*. That sounds good."

"I'm terrible with titles! It's just a working title!"

He shook against me. "I think the warlord folder looks interesting."

I still had my eyes shut, but I heard the double click of the mouse.

"You should know," I told him, "you're not always the warlord." Eventually he was, but I didn't see any point going into details right now.

"I remember. Sometimes I'm your eager war prize and you mercilessly take me."

"You remember that?"

"Hard to forget," he said. "I'm interested to see how it would go. What about this one? Is this a good one?" The mouse clicked again. "*The Bastard Liam Nash Gets What's Coming: On His Face*."

It was one of the recently undeleted stories. "I suck at titles!"

"I don't know. That's compelling enough to make me want to read it."

I heard a few more clicks, then silence.

"Liam?" I said.

"Mhm." It was a rough noise at the back of his throat.

"Are you reading one?"

"Yeah."

"Which one?"

There was a beat of silence before I felt his chest press against my back as he shifted. Fingers brushed lightly over my closed eyes. "Sweetheart, why are your eyes closed?"

"I'm embarrassed."

His chest rose and fell beneath me, and he ran his hands up and down my thighs. I loved the way he couldn't seem to stop touching me. "Good embarrassed or bad embarrassed?" he said.

"I don't know."

"Can I finish reading?"

I nodded.

"Do you want to know which one it is?"

I shook my head and hunched a little against him. I was very conflicted. Excited, but conflicted.

He wrapped an arm around my chest and held me tight. "Do you want to go upstairs and wait for me while I finish?"

"God, yes," I said.

"You're leaving me with your computer unprotected, and I need to check you're okay with that as well, because you clearly take your privacy very seriously."

"I trust you."

He helped me up off his lap, turned me by the hips, and held me there between his legs for a moment, gazing up at me. His eyes were as dark as I'd ever seen them, the pupils so large only a sliver of the usual pale colour showed. He palmed the backs of my thighs. "I won't be long," he said gruffly. "Kiss me first."

Feeling shy, I bent down and pressed a chaste kiss to his lips.

Liam's hard face softened when I pulled away and he went to say something, but shook his head with a smile instead. "I'll be up in a minute."

29

Once again I found myself facedown on my bed, panting into the duvet as I waited for Liam to join me.

Last time, it had been a rush of frantic uncertainty, a desperate grasp to finally *feel* something with him, and nothing was on the table beyond the present moment.

This time, it was a beginning.

I pushed down into the mattress, enjoying the friction against my aching cock and the drag of crisp cotton over my sensitised pecs and nipples, but I held myself back. I was on the edge as it was.

My pulse had finally started to slow to normal levels when I heard his tread on the bottom stair.

I was still facedown. I quickly flipped over and spread myself over the dark blue duvet as invitingly as I knew how. Legs wide, arms too...no, that was stupid.

I tucked my arms behind my head, pulled my legs up and let them fall open to the sides...okay, a *hint* of subtlety, Jasper, come on.

I left my arms where they were, stretched my legs flat

and crossed my ankles. No, that was too relaxed. That said, *I'm enjoying the holiday sun on a week in Tenerife.* I was going for, *Please ravish me at once.*

I propped up on my elbows...nope.

This was awful.

I'd never been so awkwardly aware of my body.

Go with a classic, I thought. I flipped over and scrambled up onto all fours. Who doesn't like this one? I dipped my back low to really make my arse pop.

I twerked it experimentally. Eh. Hot stuff, I was sure, but it probably wasn't the way to kick off the long-awaited and romantic coming together that I was hoping for. I flumped down flat on my stomach again, and let out a muffled scream when cool fingers encircled my ankle.

"That was quite the show," Liam said, voice rough with amusement.

"Thanks," I said, cheeks heating. "Glad you liked it."

He let go of my ankle and trailed a light touch up the back of my calf, pausing to grip my thigh just above my knee. "I'm going to have you put on a real show for me one day," he said, "since you seem to like humping the bed. I think I'll put a chair right there by the window and get comfortable. You can writhe around for me as much as you like."

I choked. "What?"

"I'd lean back and admire this beautiful body from a distance. Watch all these muscles, working for me." His hand drifted up to cup my buttock. He *jiggled* it.

I snorted an embarrassed laugh into the duvet.

"You're not the only one with fantasies," he said.

"You fantasised about me?" I rolled over to my side and stretched out, watching as he stalked around the side of the bed.

"Fantasised. Stroked myself. Came saying your name."

My mouth dried out at the thought, baffling though it was. "Maybe I'll hump the bed for you if you do that for me." I tried for a sassy tone.

"Maybe." He reached out and held the side of my neck, gazing down at me. "You are without doubt the sweetest, most romantic boy I have ever met," he said.

I looked at him uncertainly. I wasn't sure about being called a boy to be honest, although I suppose to Liam, I was.

"I couldn't want you more," he said.

I beamed.

He smiled back instantly. Shifting so that he was cradling my head in both hands and holding me for it, he leaned down and murmured against my mouth, "I'd like to spend the rest of my life proving that."

There was an awkward beat of silence before I realised he was waiting for a reply. "Oh. Yes! Please, that sounds amazing. Sorry, I thought that was it. Big statement, not a question. I definitely want that, too."

Liam pressed a smiling kiss against my mouth, slid his tongue in a slow and dirty drag over mine, then pulled back.

"Now," he said. "On your knees, my helpless and trembling war prize. Yield to your conqueror."

I gaped at him. "Oh fuck, you read one of those ones."

"Of course I did. Now get over here and take my war breeches off."

I scrambled off the bed and my knees hit the carpet.

"Although I don't know what war breeches are," Liam continued as I went for his waistband.

"I don't either. I just thought it sounded sexier than trousers." I had him unbuttoned, unzipped, and everything down to mid-thigh in record time. I stopped and stared.

"While I do have a gigantic ego," Liam said conversationally, "even I can get nervous when the man of my dreams gets his first look at my dick and stops."

Ooops. I leaned in and pressed a cheerful kiss to the tip of his erection. "Sorry," I said. "Taking a mental snapshot."

"Of my dick."

"Yep." I gripped it at the base and gave the head a quick, hard suck.

Liam moaned. "Goddamn," he said.

I propped my chin on his abs and grinned up at him.

He stroked his hands up to frame my face. For a moment we stayed like that, gazing at each other. His thumbs traced my cheekbones. His chest rose and fell in a deep sigh. "Get on the bed, Jasper," he said softly. The humour and playfulness had faded, leaving nothing but need and focus on his face.

I helpfully shoved his trousers all the way down to his ankles, then threw myself back on the bed.

He let me see all of him. I don't think he was hiding deliberately before, at least not from a sense of awkwardness about his body. Probably it was a control thing. Holding himself back.

He wasn't holding anything back now.

He undressed without haste, watching me watch him as he did it.

He had a light furring of hair on his chest, sandy gold like his hair. Liam was built broad and solid. Back when he'd played rugby, he'd been one of the big guys who ploughed down the pitch with the ball, dragging ten grappling, swearing men behind him as he powered toward the goal. He had muscle—I'd felt his strength—but it wasn't as defined as mine.

His appearance spoke of strength. The stony face that I loved so much spoke of the will to use that strength to get his way. And yet no one had ever touched me as gently as Liam had.

No one had ever looked at me the way he was looking at me right now.

I pulled the pillow over my face.

Seconds later, he stretched over me and pulled it away, his gaze intense. He didn't say anything. He lifted my chin with two fingers and kissed me. Light and sweet and then, when I was chasing him for it, hard and wet.

His weight pushed me down into the mattress as he controlled the kiss, and by the time he pulled back enough to speak, I had both arms around him, trying to get closer.

"What do you want?" he said raggedly. "How do you want it?" He thrust against me and we both groaned at the electrifying sensation of our cocks sliding against each other.

"I don't know." He thrust again and my hands landed on his arse with a loud smack. I dug my fingers into the hard muscle and hauled him closer. "I don't care! I just want to be yours."

"Oh, you're mine," he said. "Don't ever doubt that." He rolled off me and strode over to where he'd left his clothes in a heap. He snagged his trousers, rustled around in the pocket, and came back with condoms and lubricant. His breathing was quick and harsh, his cheeks flushed. He ran his hot gaze over me and shivered.

I flexed. I couldn't help preening.

Liam's lips lifted at one side. "You're a bit of a showoff, aren't you?" he said, opening the lubricant.

"Seems that way. Only for you."

"Mhm." He settled back over me and used a knee to push my legs open. I felt his touch behind my balls then between my cheeks.

He watched me the whole time he prepared me, seeking out ways to make me catch my breath, to make my stomach tense or my legs twitch. One finger became two. At some point, it must have become three, but he was kissing me again and I lost all sense of reality. All I knew was Liam—on me, over me, his hand working between my legs, his lips playing over mine.

I had a horrible feeling I was making a stream of ridiculous noises, whimpering and gasping along with the constant restless motion as I slowly squirmed beneath him. I didn't try to censor myself, because he kept whispering things like, "Yes, that's it," and, "I love hearing you," and, "Does that feel good?"

I was dazed with the tender, thorough attention, feeling utterly spoiled and cherished by it. I barely had time to register the cool air as he moved away to put the condom on, and then he was back. He grasped my right leg around the knee and lifted it up and to the side, opening me.

I closed my eyes.

"Please look at me," he said. "Jasper."

I did. I had one hand loosely draped over his damp neck. He reached back and caught my wrist, then drew my arm down to lay it on the pillow above my head. He held me like that, pressing my wrist to the pillow as his cock eased deep, his body pressed against mine.

He went slow and steady until he was all the way in.

"Okay?" he said, kissing my parted lips.

It took some effort to focus on his face.

He waited, smiling, until I nodded and managed to say yes.

He started to move. For the first few strokes he kept it slow and easy, shifting his hips and adjusting his weight.

"Aahhhh," I cried out, my stomach tightening almost painfully as sensation lit up my pelvis. "Fuck."

"Yeah?" he said.

"Yeah. Yes. *Yes.* Oh, please. Do that again. It feels so good. Uhn. Uhn. Oh. Oh, Liam. Ohhhhh. F-f-fuuuuck. Yeah. Yeah. Right there."

He muffled my outpouring with a kiss as he worked his hips.

"Hhhhhn," I said into his mouth, and tore away to pant up at the ceiling.

He went for my neck instead, biting and kissing as he sped up.

"Ah," I said. "Ah. Ah. Ah. Uhn."

He was shaking against me and for a moment I thought he was coming already, but then it hit me: he was laughing.

"I know I'm loud. Oh! Oh! Oh my god. I know, I can't— oh, Liam. Please fuck me. Please, I need—"

He stopped kissing my neck to push up onto his forearms. He sped up again. The bed was creaking. The headboard started a fast, rapid bang against the wall.

My legs had been wrapped high around his waist. I let them drop, and pushed up into his thrusts. His eyes flared and his smile turned feral. I reached both arms over my head to brace against the headboard and push back hard against him.

"Yeah," he growled, and ducked down to quickly lick then bite at my mouth. "Fuck, you're strong. I love it."

I locked eyes with him and used my body to goad him on.

Liam's eyes were blazing. The tender, cherishing touches and smooth, rocking thrusts had given way to a fierce battle as we tussled our way toward orgasm.

Euphoria billowed inside me. I tipped my head back,

gasping, and moaned as he went for my exposed throat, sucking hard and scraping his teeth over my skin.

"Liam," I said, running a hand up his back, feeling the power in the rolling muscles of his shoulders. I gripped his hair. "*Liam.*"

"What? What do you want, what do you need? I'll give you—"

"Oh." I stuttered and my muscles locked as I started to come. I blinked up, startled, into his harsh face. "I love you."

He slowed his hips to a gentle pump and worked me through the orgasm, his body shaking with the effort of holding back. I relaxed into a shimmering heap of satisfaction beneath him, and smiled up at him.

He returned my smile, his expression wide open. "I love you," he said roughly, slid his knees wider, powered into me three more times, and came.

I held him through it, and I fell asleep even as he was gathering me in his arms and rolling us to the side.

30

I cracked my eyes open and stared blankly ahead. My room was softly lit by dim morning light. I had a fairly reliable body clock, and tended to wake up around six even without a phone alarm.

Which was a good thing, since my phone was downstairs in the kitchen where I'd left it before Liam had arrived. Nothing had existed for the last ten hours beyond my room, my bed, and my...boyfriend?

Liam.

He was spooning me.

The man had me in a full-body lock that I was going to have to do some serious work to squirm out of.

I was a cuddler, but Liam was next level. He was an octopus.

I got up once in the night to go to the loo. Within seconds of me staggering back to bed, he'd dragged me over the mattress, tucked me under him, grunted with satisfaction, and that was it.

I'd been quivering with excitement, more than ready for round two.

He, I'd realised when I prodded him after a good thirty seconds of nothing but heavy breathing ruffling my short hair, had been fast asleep.

Now, I was fizzing with energy. My joints felt spring-loaded. My blood was up, so was my dick, and Liam was snoring.

I pondered waking him for a quick good-morning blowjob before I headed out for my jog, but his body was lax with sleep. I didn't have the heart to disturb him.

A muscled arm was slung around my waist, and a thick thigh was shoved right between mine. I lifted the covers and peeked down.

I liked the view.

The juxtaposition of his hand, my cock, and his thigh, was giving me some interesting ideas. Still, I couldn't do anything without waking him up first, and he'd slept so hard he must have been exhausted.

I smiled slowly to myself in the dim room.

We had time. We had morning after morning after morning.

Okay.

I started with the arm. I carefully took hold of his wrist, lifted it, and slid it backwards until it was resting on my hip. Good start. I flexed my spine, bowing away from him, and clenched my teeth against the drag of my balls over his thigh. Throwing out a hand, I grabbed the edge of the mattress and started to haul myself over. As soon as I was clear, I'd—

Liam snatched me against him, rolled me to my stomach, and said grumpily in my ear, "What are you doing?"

"Trying not to disturb you," I said to the mattress.

"Fail." He grunted, and bit the side of my neck. "Try harder."

I rubbed back against him, checking out the situation.

"That's not helping," he said.

I pushed into the mattress and levered him up. He slid gracelessly off and onto his back. He groaned, throwing an arm over his eyes.

"Go to sleep," I said, leaning over and dropping a kiss on his nose. "I'm gonna go for a quick jog. I'll bring you a coffee in bed when I'm home."

He gave another half-hearted grunt, and I watched as he softened back into sleep.

I grabbed my running kit from the dresser and changed downstairs so I didn't disturb him. I bounded down the front steps and set off at an easy lope.

It didn't last long.

The reality of getting absolutely railed by Liam had me turning it around and walking gingerly home within ten minutes.

It had been a long time since I'd had anything up there, and nothing had been as substantial as Liam's cock. I'd been overoptimistic. It was fine.

Liam was up already when I got home.

I surprised him in the kitchen, staring into space with a dreamy smile on his pillow-creased face as he clutched a coffee mug to his chest and slumped against the counter. He'd made a pot of coffee, and had taken some eggs out of the fridge and set them beside a bowl.

Aw. He was making me breakfast.

I opened my mouth to say something just as he turned and saw me standing in the doorway. He flinched, but luckily didn't spill any coffee.

"That was a quick run," he accused.

"Were you making me a surprise breakfast?" I asked, crossing the kitchen to stand in front of him.

"Not much of a surprise now."

"I appreciate the thought," I said, and went to the fridge for another carton of eggs, setting it alongside the bowl. He raised his brows as I wandered back to him. "It takes a lot of protein to fuel this machine."

"Mm." He set a hand on my hip and tugged me close until he'd eased my weight against him. He buried his face in my neck and breathed deeply.

"Are you falling asleep?" I said, stroking his sides.

"Mm. Yeah. It takes a lot of coffee to fuel this machine. I'm a grump in the mornings. You should probably know. Don't let me get away with it."

"I won't." He was in his boxers and his undershirt. I slid a hand under the waistband and said, "I can think of a few ways to perk you up." I patted his cock then let it go in favour of holding him.

He set his coffee mug down and looped his arms around my waist. "Are you sore this morning?"

"A little. Hence the short run."

"I'm sorry," he said. "I'll make it up to you in the shower."

"Ooh. That sounds nice. But I have—oh, crap. I have spin class in a couple of hours." My seniors were in for a treat. No way could I handle an hour of energetic cycling. We were definitely taking the scenic route.

"Don't worry, I won't fuck you again today."

I made a disappointed noise.

He smiled. "I can think of plenty of other things to do. To start, I'll peel you out of all these tight things, get you naked and in the shower. Turn the heat up so it's all misty and warm in there."

I made an interested noise.

"And I'll wash you from head to toe."

I made a go-on noise.

"And then I'll turn you around and push you up against the tiles. I'll take hold of your cock, and let you fuck my fist while I get my cock between these spectacular cheeks, and—"

Someone made a gagging noise.

I looked at Liam, wide-eyed.

Liam's head had whipped to the side, and he was glaring at the doorway.

"No," Adam said. "Just, *no*. I don't want to hear that."

"Then leave," Liam said.

Adam ignored him and sauntered over to the coffee pot. He slapped my arse on the way. I jerked into Liam, who growled over my shoulder at Adam and laid a possessive hand on the slapped cheek.

"Adam has a key," I said, trying not to laugh.

"Which he will *not* be surrendering just because Jasper has lowered his standards enough to let you anywhere near him," Adam said. "Against all sensible counsel to the contrary, and in case you were about to suggest it."

"Adam, please." Liam sighed. "It's too early. You're too annoying. And this is Jasper's home. I don't have any say in who has a key."

Adam narrowed his eyes. "Too right."

"I'm sure you'll learn to call ahead after the third or fourth time you walk in on me with Jasper spread out—"

I clapped a hand over his mouth.

Liam kissed it and pulled it away, giving me a smouldering look. Then he said to Adam, "And if that doesn't teach you, walking in on *me* spread out should do it."

Adam went green, I burst out laughing, and Liam took his coffee cup with him as he headed upstairs.

I busied myself cracking eggs and whisking them industriously. "Breakfast?" I said.

"No, thanks. Ray's expecting me. I'm heading over to his in a minute. Thought I'd drop in after my night shift and see how you're doing. Ray says hi, by the way."

"Tell him hi back," I said over my shoulder, and turned the hob on. I set the pan on the heat.

I'd finally met Ray properly in the coffee shop last week. It had been one of the most awkward moments of my life, and that is saying something. We'd both ended up standing at the counter waiting for Charlie to make our drinks, studiously avoiding each other's eyes.

Ray was fidgeting, checking his Apple Watch every ten seconds. I was bouncing restlessly on the balls of my feet, trying not to bolt. It was Charlie who had broken the silence for us.

He marched up to the counter where we were standing shoulder to shoulder, a queue of two, and he set two cups down on one tray.

"Oh," Ray said. "I ordered mine to go?"

"Me too," I said.

"I don't care," Charlie said. "Look. There's a free table in the corner. Why don't you both go and drink your coffees over there?"

I slid a sideways glance at Ray. He looked up at me.

"In case either of you thought that was a suggestion," Charlie said, "it wasn't. Jasper. I am tired of watching you slink in here like a bad puppy and run away every time Ray comes in."

"I do *not*—" I started.

"Ray, you're a great customer, but Jasper consumes three times the amount of a normal human being, and if he stops coming in, it'll harm my bottom line."

"I never said he *couldn't*—" Ray began.

"Great. It's settled. Table's over there." Charlie walked off.

I looked at Ray. Ray looked at me.

"Stay there," I said. "I've got this."

I sidled to the corner of the counter, keeping my eye on Charlie at the other end. I was reaching for the to-go cups when Charlie said without turning around, "Jasper, if I see you on the wrong side of the counter again…"

I lunged back to the customer side, grabbed the tray, and said to Ray, "Come on."

After that, it was surprisingly easy. I apologised for the serial-killer-accusation thing. We had a long what-the-fuck conversation about the whole situation, once Ray had made me swear everything was off the record. I promised that my journalism days were over—unless he ever found another body, in which case all bets were off—and by the time Adam came in to meet Ray and did a double-take at the sight of us cosied up in the corner, we were on our second coffees, and Ray had sprung for a plate of brownies.

I briskly pushed the eggs around in the pan with a spatula. I sensed Adam come up behind me before he leaned himself against the counter. He stood with his hands in his pockets, ankles crossed negligently. A lock of his bright hair fell in his face as he looked at me.

"We did it," he said. "Hard to believe. But we finally did it." He sighed with satisfaction.

I cocked a brow and turned off the hob, setting the pan to one side. "Did what?"

"Got our men."

I turned and mirrored his pose. "Huh."

A couple of months ago, we were a pair of losers sitting

in the pub in the post-Christmas glum of early February. Now Adam had Ray. I had Liam.

"Took us long enough," Adam said, and a beautiful smile broke over his face, lighting up his hazel eyes.

"Hell of a fight to get here," I said. "Worth it, though."

"Yeah." Adam's smile settled to bone-deep happiness. I was pretty sure my face looked the same. Until he added, "Although what you see in Liam is *still* a mystery I will never be able to solve."

"Hey. I love that man," I said. "And so do you. Although in a very different way."

"Ugh. Yeah, but don't ever—"

"Oh, I heard," Liam said from where he was standing in the doorway.

"That's my cue to leave," Adam said. He knocked my shoulder affectionately with his. "See you at the gym later." He stalked past Liam, pausing to say, "Liam. I'm not going to waste my breath telling you not to hurt him or I will murder you, because Jasper can take care of himself. That said, if you hurt him?" His voice lowered menacingly. "I'll tell your mum."

"Okay. You do that." Liam reached out and ruffled Adam's hair as he passed.

Adam smacked his hand away without missing a beat. A few seconds later, the front door opened and shut.

Liam turned to me, smiling when he saw me balancing a plate of scrambled eggs in one hand and a fork in the other.

I swallowed a mouthful. "Sorry," I said, "this is rude, but I couldn't wait. I am starving. You might wake up cranky in the morning, but you should know, I wake up ravenous. Do you want some?"

He shook his head. "No, thanks. I usually eat later." He watched me shovel the rest of the food in my mouth.

He'd had a shower without me and was dressed. He wore yesterday's trousers, and had obviously raided my dresser because his socks were bright white athletic socks, and the t-shirt he was wearing said *SWEAT!!!* on it.

He looked *amazing*.

I set the empty plate down, poured myself a glass of water, and drank it self-consciously. He was still watching.

I finished the water and licked my lips.

Liam crossed the kitchen. He kept coming until he was pressed against me. One hand held the side of my neck; the other was at my hip.

He was more awake now, his blue-grey eyes alert.

"I," he said, "am going to make you a very happy man."

"What did you have in mind? Because I was liking the sound of the shower, although you went and had that without me."

He gave a small huff of amusement, then the humour drained away to leave nothing but a fierce, intense focus. "A very." He kissed me. "Happy." He kissed me again. "Man." Again. "For a lot longer than a romp in the shower."

"You're off to a great start," I told him sincerely.

"I'm off to a shit start. I messed you around. Made you think you weren't important. And you are, Jasper. You are. I don't know how I got lucky enough that you're willing to give me a chance to prove that I can be the best thing that ever happened to you, but so you know? That's my plan."

"You already are the best—"

"Not yet, but I will be." He leaned in and kissed me softly. "I will be. Let me prove it?"

"Okay."

"Yeah?"

I nodded enthusiastically.

He grinned at me. "All right. Now. Let's go. I've got three days off, and I have a lot of reading to do."

My stomach plunged with a mix of nerves and excitement.

"You didn't think I'd be satisfied with reading just one of your stories, did you?" he said.

"I hoped?"

"Yeah, no." He took my hand and led me out of the kitchen into the sitting room. "You can go to work, and the whole time you're at the gym, you can think of me here at your computer, prowling like a sexy panther shifter through your darkest erotic fantasies. Yes, I saw that title, *Liam Is A Sexy Panther Shifter: A/B/O version*. I'm not sure what A/B/O means, though. Guess I'll find out."

I moaned faintly with horror.

"I'll be taking notes," he said. "Making plans."

"Oh, god."

"Unless you don't want me to?"

"No. You can." I didn't hate the idea. "But maybe...okay, Liam?"

"Yes?"

"Maybe you don't read *all* the stories. Some of them are more out there than others."

Don't mention the tentacles.

He narrowed his eyes. "How out there are we talking? More out there than me being a panther shifter? Or a vampire or an alien?"

"I'll start you off easy. It's important to warm up."

END

ALSO BY ISABEL MURRAY

Romantic Comedy

Not That Complicated

Worth the Wait

Merman Romance

Catch and Release

Fantasy Romance

Gary of a Hundred Days

CATCH AND RELEASE EXCERPT

Chapter One

"The fuck is it?" Jerry said.

I shrugged. The mystery lump that had caught his attention lay two hundred feet from where we stood on the beach. A semi-solid curtain of driving rain hung between it and us. If he couldn't see what it was, how was I supposed to?

"Come on," he said, and bustled off.

Jerry Barnes was fifty-eight years old. He'd lived every single one of those years in a little harbour town tucked away in a fold of land between Scotland and England, and yet the man still got excited by every seaweed-wrapped heap of driftwood that was coughed up by the tide.

"Joe!" he said, prancing ahead in his bright yellow wellies. "Come on!"

Seriously. He had twenty years on me, and he moved like I had twenty on him.

I couldn't conjure that amount of energy and enthusiasm even five coffees into my morning.

Especially not for something that was bound to be either boring or disgusting, depending on how dead it was, and how long it had been that way.

I followed him, but only because Jerry was still carrying my tackle box.

Since I'd moved to Lynwick six years ago, I'd built myself quite the reputation. I was well-known around these parts for being the worst fisherman to cast a line on the east coast. For some unfathomable reason, Jerry took it as a personal challenge.

Jerry owned and operated a mid-size trawler, the *Mary Jane*, with his brothers. That morning, he'd spotted me on his way home from the harbour. As usual when I didn't see him first and have time for evasive manoeuvres, he came rushing over to impart the wisdom of his family's many, many generations of fishermen.

This morning's pearl had been, "Only thing you're gonna catch if you try casting in this wind is yourself, Joe."

I was well aware. It had already taken me half an hour of fumbling with numb fingers and rapidly vanishing patience to detach the hook from the seat of my trousers.

I wasn't a complete idiot. The weather had been *fine* when I started.

Jerry had helpfully collapsed my rod and packed it away for me, even though I hadn't actually agreed to stop fishing. He let me have the rod back and hefted up my tackle box before I could grab it. I had the sinking feeling that he was about to do something awkward, like offer me lessons again, when he was distracted.

Though the tide was high, it was on the turn. Sullen waves sucked back toward the horizon, hissing angrily under a dark metal sky. A distant liner slid ominously along the skyline, heading for Norway, or America, or maybe

Antarctica. I didn't see Jerry reach the tangled mass that had been abandoned by last night's storm but when I glanced over at him, he was motionless, frizzy ginger hair whipping about his head.

I hesitated at this un-Jerry-like lack of animation.

"Well?" I called. "What is it?"

Jerry flapped his arms in an oddly helpless gesture. If he gave any answer, it was lost to the wind.

"What?" I shouted.

He turned to face me. His stone-green eyes were wide and his bushy eyebrows were halfway up his craggy forehead. An expression of excited guilt sat queasily on his face. "It's a body!" he yelled after a brief pause.

"Of what? Not a dolphin?" It was big enough and then some. This close, I could see that the large mass had been all but cocooned in a knotted and tangled monofilament net.

"Noooo," Jerry said as I came to stand beside him.

I dropped my fishing rod alongside the tackle box. "Oh, shit."

It was a man.

A pale, pale man. His skin was the fairest I'd ever seen. Who knew how long he'd been in the water? Although, there was no obvious bloat. Nothing was sloughing off. Maybe he was naturally pale?

He was big, even prone and half curled. One leg lay straight; the other was hitched up protectively into his body. He lay on his side. A thickly muscled right arm covered his head and obscured his face. His left arm was tucked beneath him.

"His hair's blue," Jerry said, and flipped a lock of it with the toe of his boot, like he was turning shells. "Really blue."

I nudged him, hard.

"Ow," Jerry said.

"Don't be disrespectful."

"He's dead, mate. Think he cares?"

"I know *I* do."

Jerry sleeved scattered seawater and rain from his face. "Reckon he's one of them club kids, then?"

I frowned. "Club kids?"

"Yeah." Jerry flailed his hands in the air around his head and whooped.

I stared at him.

"Dancers," he said. "Dancey clubs. Raves. You ever been to one?"

"Have *you*?"

"Nah. I'd feel a right prat, going into one o' them places. Used to want to, though. Back in the day." He sighed wistfully. "Never did get around to it. Think I missed the boat on that one. So. You reckon? Club kid?"

"...because his hair is blue?"

Sometimes, I struggled to follow Jerry's train of thought. I hadn't decided if our communication misfires were a generational thing, a local thing, or a Jerry thing.

Jerry grunted.

Blue hair wasn't all that unusual, even around here. Neither was pink, purple, or green. I didn't know why it said alternative club lifestyle to Jerry. The sixtysomething librarian in the next town over, which was twice the size of Lynwick and had a permanent library rather than a retrofitted bus full of books that parked outside the pub once a week, had hair that she dyed an extraordinarily fake flat green. She wore it in a beehive. I thought it looked kind of amazing. Extra amazing when she shoved pencils in there.

The body's hair was also amazing, but nothing about it looked fake. It shone in a dark, wet snarl of indigo and cobalt, lying in long, thick ropes over his upper chest and face.

"Big 'un, isn't he?" Jerry said. "I'm thinking six four? Six five?"

"Yeah. Easy." He was closer to seven feet than six. I gazed down at him. "Who do you think he is?"

"He's not local, I can tell you that." Jerry squatted to pull at the net entangling the man. "There's no one around these parts the size of him." Jerry tipped his head to one side and paused thoughtfully. "Got a nice arse, though," he said.

I did a slow pan and gaped at him. So far as I knew, Jerry was straight.

So far as his *wife* knew, Jerry was straight.

He nodded at me encouragingly. "Right?"

I scanned the man without meaning to. A pale gleam of wet, white buttock peeked out through the holes in the net. Okay, yes. He had a nice arse.

For a corpse.

"Even I want to slap it." Jerry bent down.

I snagged him by the back of his collar and hauled him up. "Jerry, don't you dare get bi-curious and start slapping a dead man's arse."

Jerry batted my hands away. "Holy shit," he said. "Holy motherfucking shit."

"If you're having a gay crisis, I don't want to hear about it."

"Merman."

"I swear to God... Jerry. What the hell?"

"He's a...he's a..." Jerry bounced. "Merman!"

"Are you broken?" I dug around for my phone. I was going to call Marcy.

Jerry grabbed my face, angled it toward the body, and shouted, "Merman!"

"I don't see any tail."

"Okay, but what about that?"

"That's a penis."

Oh.

It sure was.

Large. Thick.

Hard.

...Wait.

When had he rolled over? He was now lying flat to the dark and sodden sand. Hadn't he been on his side? And his leg, had it moved? Wasn't it hitched up, covering his groin, and weren't his arms...?

"That's an erection," Jerry corrected me. "Probably rigor mortis."

I couldn't swear to it, but I didn't think an erection was part of the rigor mortis experience. Then again, my forensic knowledge had been acquired while squinting at the screen during the obligatory morgue scene in every crime show ever filmed, and waiting for it to pass. What did I know?

"Anyway, I'm talking about this." Jerry squatted down again, his hold on my face taking me with him. And, coincidentally, putting me eye level with the penis.

Jerry squeezed my jaw and redirected my gaze.

"Is it just me," he said, "or does the dead guy have gills?"

ABOUT THE AUTHOR

Isabel Murray is a writer, a reader, and a lover of love. She couldn't stick to a subgenre if her life depended on it, but MM romance is her jam. She lives in the UK, reads way too much, and cannot be trusted anywhere near chocolate.

You can find Isabel at her website, or on Goodreads, Amazon, and Bookbub.

www.isabelmurrayauthor.wordpress.com